"You're pretty sassy,"
he said in her ear.

She spun to face him. "I'm your cook, Tanner. We decided I'd make a better employee than a wife, remember?"

He shook his head. "No, I still haven't figured out the whys and wherefores."

"Changed your mind?" she asked breathlessly.

He was too close, his eyes were too knowing as they scanned her. Her heart missed a beat and fluttered. Pressing her lips together, she dared a glance at his face.

His jaw was taut, his nostrils flaring just a bit. And his eyes, those dark orbs that seemed to seek out her thoughts, were fastened on her face.

"No, I haven't changed my mind, honey," he whispered. "I want you to know what you're gettin' before I marry you."

"That's not part of our bargain," she countered.

"I'm not sure what kind of a bargain we struck," Tanner said softly....

Dear Reader,

Welcome to Harlequin Historicals, Harlequin/Silhouette's *only* historical romance line! We offer four unforgettable love stories each month, in a range of time periods, settings and sensuality. And they're written by some of the best writers in the field!

Carolyn Davidson is one of those writers. Her Americana stories are meaningful, morally rich and surprisingly sensuous—and they almost always feature tall, dark and handsome heroes. Continuing in that vein is *The Bachelor Tax,* an endearing marriage-of-convenience story about a least-likely-to-marry "bad boy" rancher who tries to avoid a local bachelor tax by proposing to the one woman he's *sure* will say no—the prim preacher's daughter....

My Lady Reluctant is a thrilling new medieval novel by Laurie Grant about a Norman lady who must travel to court to find a husband. En route, she is attacked by outlaws but rescued by a mysterious and handsome knight.... Rising talent Liz Ireland returns with a darling Western, *The Outlaw's Bride,* in which a reputed Texas outlaw and headstrong "nurse" fall in love—despite the odds against them!

And the ever-popular Deborah Simmons returns this month with *The Gentleman Thief,* a Regency tale about a beautiful bluestocking who stirs up trouble during a season at Bath when she investigates a jewel caper and finds herself scrutinizing—and falling for—an irresistible marquis.

Enjoy! And come back again next month for four more choices of the best in historical romance.

Sincerely,

Tracy Farrell
Senior Editor

Carolyn Davidson

THE Bachelor Tax

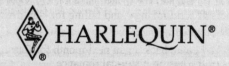

HARLEQUIN®

TORONTO • NEW YORK • LONDON
AMSTERDAM • PARIS • SYDNEY • HAMBURG
STOCKHOLM • ATHENS • TOKYO • MILAN • MADRID
PRAGUE • WARSAW • BUDAPEST • AUCKLAND

ISBN 0-373-29096-9

THE BACHELOR TAX

Copyright © 2000 by Carolyn Davidson

Visit us at www.romance.net

Printed in U.S.A.

Available from Harlequin Historicals and
CAROLYN DAVIDSON

Gerrity's Bride #298
Loving Katherine #325
The Forever Man #385
Runaway #416
The Wedding Promise #431
The Tender Stranger #456
The Midwife #475
The Bachelor Tax #496

Please address questions and book requests to:
Harlequin Reader Service
U.S.: 3010 Walden Ave., P.O. Box 1325, Buffalo, NY 14269
Canadian: P.O. Box 609, Fort Erie, Ont. L2A 5X3

To the women who share with me one Saturday afternoon a month, who attend my book signings, buy my books and then tell me how wonderful I am, this book is gratefully dedicated.... Without their support and affection, I would be lost! Thanks to all of you, members of the Lowcountry Romance Writers of America.

And as always, and especially for the trials and tribulations I put him through during the writing of this story, I dedicate this work to Mr. Ed, who loves me.

Chapter One

From the pages of the *Edgewood Gazette*...

July 6, 1882

Local legislature approved the use of the new Bachelor Tax for our town. Unless our male citizens who claim the status of bachelorhood can prove they have proposed to at least one eligible woman during the past year, they will be assessed a tax. This is for the purpose of promoting marriage among our citizens. All men of legal age are liable for taxation...

Edgewood, Texas, July 25, 1882

This could very likely be the most important day in her life. Rosemary Gibson appraised herself in the mirror hanging over her dresser, reaching to tug at a curl that hung in front of her left ear.

It was the only sign of feminine frippery she allowed herself, that and the matching ringlet on the other side of her face. Aside from those two small indulgences, she felt she was the perfect picture of a churchgoing, teetotalling, virtuous woman.

Hopefully, the image she presented would be enough to entice the man who was due to arrive on the morning train, just ten minutes from now. She lifted the gold watch from her bosom to check the time once more, and nodded decisively. A brisk walk would bring her to the train station just as the locomotive puffed its way into town.

She left the house by the front door, paced quickly down the path to the street, then made her way through the center of town. Her skirts swung just an inch from the instep of her shoes, and she frowned as she caught sight of the coating of dust covering them. And just when she needed so desperately to present a suitable image. Well, it couldn't be helped.

Her likeness was reflected from the window of the mercantile, and Rosemary tilted her head, admiring the subdued look of her black hat, then straightened her shoulders just a bit more firmly.

She passed the bank, nodding at Pace Frombert as he opened the double doors to the public, then stepped to the street. Crossing the alleyway that led to the row of houses comprising the poorer side of town, she glanced down its length.

Children played in the dusty road, their voices audible in the clear, summer air, and Rosemary smiled at their antics. She lifted her skirt, stepping up to the sidewalk once more. Then looked aside as she approached the bane of her existence, the Golden Slipper Saloon, only too aware of the tall figure positioned by its front door.

Gabe Tanner, he of the scornful glance and dark, piercing gaze. Only on occasion did she cross his path, and those times she was careful to remain aloof.

She dropped her eyes, observing only the scuffed toes of his boots as she passed, then stiffened as a low chuckle followed in her wake. She halted and turned back, unwilling to allow such an insult to go unnoticed.

His lips still curving in a sardonic grin, Tanner leaned back against the wall, hat tilted over his forehead. Dark eyes scanned her from stem to stern, and Rosemary felt a flush creep up her cheeks as she glared at him, then turned away, resuming her progress.

Men like Gabe Tanner should be outlawed from the human race, as far as she was concerned! Whether or not any of their sort appreciated her qualities was not a major issue this morning.

And yet, those same qualities were about to be judged, and very soon. For if the man who was scheduled to depart the train this morning did not deem her fit to be his wife, she might find herself in search of a roof over her head before nightfall. That thought was appalling, and Rosemary shuddered as it raced through her head. Finding a place to store her worldly possessions would be a distinct problem, one she refused to consider right now. Even though their letters had promised much, should Rosemary Gibson not fit the image of a parson's wife, Reverend Jorgenson had every right to deny her the title.

On the other hand, if he approved of what she had to offer, she might very well be a married woman this very day. Her steps quickened as that thought brought hope to her spinster's heart.

She'd not been offered for, ever, until the new minister had suggested in his letter that they might form an alliance of sorts. It seemed his bishop preferred married men in the pulpit, and Lars Jorgenson sounded willing to sacrifice his bachelorhood to the effort.

It was a stroke of luck she had not thought to encounter. Since the day her father had breathed his last, she had stayed on, the parishioners allowing her use of the parsonage, awaited the arrival of his replacement, keeping the parsonage in immaculate condition, praying for direction should she find herself without a home.

The final letter last week from the prospective minister had brought new hope to her heart. If he felt they suited, he would immediately notify his bishop. Until then, he felt his tentative plans must be held in abeyance.

Now, in just a few minutes, Lars Jorgenson would step from the train and search her out on the station platform. Rosemary scurried around the corner of the bank and picked her way through the weed-infested shortcut to the railroad tracks.

This might well be the most important day of her life.

Gabe Tanner's gaze scanned the wooden sidewalk again, the fifth time during the past ten minutes. His indolent posture was but a pose, his mission this morning more important than he was willing to admit, even to himself.

Ah, there she was. That mousy, dark-haired excuse for a woman, with her collar buttoned so tight it was a wonder she could breathe, her mincing little steps making her bosom rise and fall within her dress. She'd have a hissy fit if she knew how it caught his eye, and that thought brought a chuckle to his lips.

She turned back, her eyes widening in anger and insult, then resumed her marching gait, but not before he caught sight of the blush that rode her cheekbones. She ought to pinken them up regularly. It would make her look almost...

Naw, it'd take more than that to put some life into the old preacher's daughter, Tanner decided. He watched as she paraded on her way, her heels clicking on the wooden sidewalk.

And yet, he had decided, she might very well be the one to save him a bundle, not that the amount was likely to make him mortgage his spread. Rather, he couldn't abide the thought of the new law, passed less than a year ago and soon to catch him in its web.

Bachelor Tax. The phrase alone was enough to make his mouth pucker in distaste. The thought that a man would be subject to a tax burden such as this was loathsome.

If asking Miss High-and-Mighty to accept his hand in marriage would alleviate the burden for another whole year, he'd give it a shot. The knowledge that she would shudder and step back from his imposing presence was insurance enough to allow his consideration.

He tilted his hat back and stood erect, casting one last glance at the shuttered windows of the Golden Slipper Saloon. Too early for business yet, although the sound of Herbie's broom sweeping the perpetually dusty floor could be heard beyond the swinging doors. Jason Stillwell was no doubt in bed, owing to the late hours he kept running the place.

Tanner's footsteps were heavy on the boardwalk as he followed his prey. She was heading for the train station, just as he had suspected.

The new preacher was supposed to be coming in today. Word had it that Rosemary Gibson was holding out hopes the bachelor minister would marry her and allow her to stay on in the parsonage, where she'd already spent the past ten years of her life.

He moved more quickly, noting the puffs of dust that rose as Miss Gibson made her way across the vacant lot. Her hips swayed quite nicely, he thought. Tanner doubted if the new preacher would appreciate the view as much as a rancher with a long dry spell behind him might.

When it got so a spinster looked good at ten o'clock in the morning, a man was in pretty bad shape, Tanner decided.

The train slowed, its whistle announcing its arrival with three short blasts as it shuddered to a stop. The conductor stepped briskly onto the platform and turned to assist the passengers from the metal steps.

There was more than one this morning, Rosemary

saw with some surprise. All she had anticipated was the man who had been chosen to fill her father's shoes. Those shoes she had polished for the final time just last month. Her tears fought to escape and she blinked furiously, lest she meet Lars Jorgenson with damp cheeks.

A woman stepped to the platform, a small boy right behind her. Next, a tall man with a tiny girl clutched against his shoulder eased past the conductor. They stood there, looking around as if they expected to be met, and Rosemary glanced over her shoulder at the empty platform. Surely they were someone's relatives, or perhaps simply a new family moving to Edgewood, Texas, and in need of a conveyance.

The sight of Gabe Tanner rounding the corner of the station platform caught Rosemary's eye and she turned quickly from the cocky grin he shot in her direction.

Another passenger stepped from the train and Rosemary held her breath. Surely this was Lars, this fine-looking, youthful gentleman whose gaze searched the length of the wooden platform. She lifted her head, settling a pleasant smile on her lips as she allowed her eyes to rest on his handsome face.

Behind her, a hand touched her shoulder and she spun about, a muffled shriek passing her lips.

"Ma'am?"

"I beg your pardon." Her words might have been cast in stone, so firmly did they fall from her lips.

Gabe Tanner swept his hat from his head and his grin showed an abundance of white teeth, marred only by the slight chip gracing the one directly beneath his left nostril.

"May I have your attention for just a moment?" he asked politely.

She glanced back distractedly at the gentleman who watched her from the side of the train. "What is it?" she muttered, her gaze cutting to Tanner's sun-warmed face.

"I'd like to ask you to be my wife," he said simply. "Will you marry me, Miss Gibson?"

She felt her eyes widen, even as her mouth dropped open in total amazement. "You...surely you..." The words would not come. She dampened her lips with the tip of her tongue and blinked at the man facing her, his dark hair ruffling against his collar.

"I take it that was a yes?" he asked, his grin widening.

Her mouth opened and closed, as if she were struck speechless. And then she uttered one word.

"Why?"

"Why?" he parroted.

"Yes, why? Whatever would make you ask me such a thing?"

"I need a wife, ma'am. And you seem a likely candidate."

She shook her head again. "Do not molest me further, sir. I am here to welcome the new minister to my father's church."

"Yeah, I know," Tanner said, with glee spilling from his dark eyes. "I take it that was a firm refusal then, ma'am?"

"I cannot believe this!" Rosemary spun from him

and tugged at her black bombazine jacket, relieved as she heard his boots strike the platform in retreat.

The young man still watched her and she smiled, just a bit. He approached her, sweeping his hat from his head, exposing a lush head of golden hair. Of course, she thought, with a name like Lars Jorgenson, he would be fair-haired, and blue-eyed, too, she noted.

"Pardon me, miss. Do you know where I could find the owner of the Golden Slipper at this time of day?" He ducked his head a bit. "I'm sure you would have no direct knowledge of the man, but perhaps..."

Rosemary gulped, choking on the very air she breathed. "The Golden Slipper?"

He nodded. "I'm to be the new piano player there, and he was to meet the train this morning." His eyes appraised her carefully. "You wouldn't know, would you?" he asked, a trace of regret in his voice.

"No, certainly not. In fact, I assumed..." And at that fallacy, she shook her head. "Well, never mind that. I just thought you were someone else, sir." With her breath still fluttering in her chest, she watched him as he walked away. It was unbelievable, truly unbelievable. He had fit the description her heart had supplied, and disappointment filled her to the brim.

Rosemary turned, her attention caught by the flurry of activity behind her. The family of four had gathered their belongings from the baggage car, and the gentleman approached her as she hesitated. Her eyes still searching the Pullman car windows for another passenger about to disembark, she welcomed him with a distracted air.

"Was there another gentleman leaving the train behind you, sir?"

"Why, no. I don't believe so." He paused, then swept his hat from his head. "Are you by chance Rosemary Gibson?"

The momentary silence was pierced by the shrill cry of a hawk, swooping midair to catch his prey. Rosemary looked up, then back at the gentleman facing her.

"Yes, I am, sir."

He extended his hand and grasped the one she offered in an automatic gesture. "I'm the new minister for your father's church," he said, just a bit of pride coloring his words.

"But...I expected..."

He nodded, his eyes darkening as he considered her for a moment. "The bishop changed his mind at the last minute," he said quietly. "He decided that young Jorgenson was not the man for this church, not being married and all. He thought a family man with responsibilities would be a better choice."

"Oh!" Rosemary knew the meaning of despair as his words washed over her and engulfed her in that most hideous of emotions.

"Ma'am? Can you direct us to the parsonage perhaps? My wife is bone weary from the train ride, and I fear my son is becoming downright testy."

Rosemary nodded. "Yes, of course. I'll ask the stationmaster to watch your things until we can arrange for them to be transported." Her steps were rapid as she approached the open window and bent to speak to the old man within.

"Mr. Pagan…"

"Yup, I heard what you said to the gentleman, missy." Homer Pagan nodded his head. "I'll have my Joey run to the livery stable and ask for a wagon."

"Thank you," Rosemary said, her thoughts muddled as she turned back to the man who awaited her.

"Is it close by? Can we walk there?" he asked. Behind him, his wife waited, an uncertain smile on her lips. "This is Beatrice, my wife, and our children."

Rosemary nodded. "I'm pleased to meet all of you, I'm sure." And if that wasn't the biggest lie she'd ever told, she'd be forced to eat her hat. Even though she'd much rather cast it to the ground and stomp on it with both feet.

"We surely didn't mean to impose on you, Miss Gibson. I know the parsonage was your home for a long time, and the bishop should have given you warning that you would be expected to vacate it for our benefit." James Worth was obviously distressed by his position as he faced Rosemary in the small parlor.

"I have nowhere to store my belongings," she admitted. "Perhaps you can allow me to stay here until I find a house."

His smile was brilliant, a hint of relief visible as he nodded his head. "Certainly, certainly. We'll be happy to give you a week or so to find your way. It will take that long for our own furnishings to arrive."

He leaned toward her, his look filled with concern.

"Perhaps you have family somewhere who will be happy for your company."

She shook her head. "I have no one, sir. My mother died six years ago, and I kept house for my father until last month when he passed away."

"It was sudden, I understand."

Rosemary nodded. "He simply didn't wake up one morning. The doctor said he had grieved himself to death over the past years, since my mother…"

"What a shame. But then, God works in mysterious ways. We know that."

And how that bit of comfort was supposed to help her, Rosemary found it difficult to fathom. Right now it seemed that God had totally forsaken her.

"It worked! By damn, it worked! I asked the little puritan to marry me and she turned me down flat." Tanner raised his glass high. "I'm free of the Bachelor Tax for another year."

"Stupidest blame thing I ever heard of," Jason Stillwell grumbled from behind the burnished walnut bar. His towel brushed away a speck of dust, and he cast a look of pride at the gleaming length.

"Well, I beat it, sure enough," Tanner bragged, downing the remains of his glass of whiskey with one swallow. "Caught her on the station platform just as she was about to meet the new preacher."

The memory was fresh and he basked in it. "She's not too bad lookin', up close," he reminisced. "Just too prim and proper for any man to get excited over. Although that head full of dark hair looks to be…" He shook his head, grinning at his own thoughts.

"I heard tell you were out and about early today," Jason said. "Sounds like you were up close and right on top of the lady. Sure you wouldn't like to take her home with you? Your place could use a woman's touch, if I remember right."

Tanner shook his head. "Not a chance. Mama Pearl comes in and does for us once a week. Other than that, we do just fine."

Jason grinned. "That's not what your ranch hands say. I hear that the only decent meal they get all week is when that old woman cooks for them on Wednesdays."

Tanner's brow drew down. "Women are nothing but a pain in the neck."

"That's not what I heard you say last year when you were seeing the Widow Courtland."

Tanner shrugged. "She was a nice lady. Too bad she took Hale Carpenter up on his offer."

"I'd say you were lucky Rosemary Gibson refused you, Tanner. That was taking a mighty big chance, with her daddy leaving her on her own, and all."

"Yeah, I thought about that all day, how I'd risked my neck. Made me crave a touch of the hard stuff." Tanner considered his empty glass. One drink was all he ever allowed himself, the perils of overindulgence being brought home to him by the memory of his own father. He turned the tumbler upside down and sighed his aggravation at his own good sense.

With a whisk of his towel and a quick hand on the heavy glass, Jason cleaned away the evidence of Tanner's single drink for the night. "Gonna stay around to hear my new piano player?'' he asked idly, his gaze on the big upright at the end of the bar.

Tanner shook his head. "Naw. I need to head on back.''

"You're gonna miss a real treat. I brought him in from St. Louis. Just got here this morning. A friend back there told me about him, said the young man was wantin' to try his fortune in the West, and I thought I'd give him a chance.''

"Just got here this morning? I saw everyone who got off the train, Jason. Didn't know you'd taken to hiring family men for your place.''

Jason's brow puckered. "He's as much a bachelor as you, Tanner. Take a look—here he comes now.''

Down the stairway, a golden-haired Adonis approached, a wide smile on his lips. He lifted a hand in greeting to the man behind the bar and headed for the piano. His hands lifted the lid over the keyboard in a reverent gesture, and he seated himself on the stool.

"Damn, that thing never sounded so good before,'' Jason said in a subdued tone, as music spilled from the fingers of the talented young man who bent low over the black-and-white keys.

"*That's* your new piano player?'' Tanner leaned back, both elbows resting on the walnut surface behind him.

"Yup! What do you think?'' Jason's words were filled with pride as he considered his new employee.

"I think he looks more like a preacher. In fact, that's what I thought he was,'' Tanner muttered.

"And I'll warrant that's what Miss High-and-Mighty thought he was, too."

"Miss High-and-Mighty? Are we talking about Miss Gibson? Has she met my new piano player?"

"She met the train this morning," Tanner said, his gaze resting on the man who was filling the saloon with music.

"She thought Dex Sawyer was the new preacher?" Jason Stillwell wore an astonished look as his towel moved faster across the surface of his bar. "Holy cats, Tanner. She turned you down because she thought…"

"Yeah." Gabe faced the bar. "I wonder what happened to the man she was expecting to see this morning."

"If we're still talkin' about the new preacher, I can answer that. He's all settled in at the parsonage already, him and his wife and two children." Jason's mouth turned down in an expression of gloom. "Probably already plottin' how he can put a dent in my business. These preachers can't leave well enough alone, always have to be convertin' my crowd, instead of stickin' to their own."

"I heard tell the new fella was single, and Miss Gibson thought she stood a chance of sharing the parsonage with him," Tanner said casually.

Jason shook his head. "Who knows? Must be somebody changed their mind."

"Well, if a whole new family's coming in, I wonder where the spinster's going to live?" Tanner asked.

Jason shrugged. "Who's to know. Probably have to find herself a house, or rent a room somewhere. I imagine she'll get a job. If she stays around town, that is. Maybe she's got family back East she can go live with.''

"Maybe." Tanner eyed the bottles on the shelf behind the bar. A dark, lethal-looking liquid appealed to him, and he wet his lips as he considered the jolt it would bring.

"Thought you were goin' home," Jason said, following the path of Tanner's interested gaze. "Never knew you to take a second drink, Tanner. Is thinking about that Gibson woman drivin' you to—"

Tanner backed away. "There's no woman alive capable of doing that, Jason. Certainly not that one."

Tanner pushed through the doors of the saloon and headed for the livery stable. Just outside the wide double doors, his wagon awaited him, his load of supplies for the ranch neatly in place.

He climbed atop the wagon seat, and with a wave, turned his team toward the ranch. It was a decent ride, almost an hour driving the wagon. Maybe with the moonlight on the road, he could take the team at a faster clip.

Either way, it was time to reflect on his blessings. He'd managed to save himself a tidy sum today.

Chapter Two

"Rosemary, much as I'd like to take you on, the store just doesn't need another helping hand."

Rosemary sighed deeply, as if she were sorely disappointed. And so she was, having just been refused work in the Edgewood Mercantile. Not that she felt equipped for the position. It was just that she wasn't well equipped for much of anything outside a home. Keeping a parsonage neat and clean and ironing white shirts at the rate of seven a week for her father had not served to prepare her for the indignity of looking for a position.

"Maybe you can stay on and be a nursemaid to the new preacher's little ones," Phillipa Boone suggested. She sat atop her high stool in a rare moment of relaxation, eyeing the woebegone expression on Rosemary Gibson's face.

Rosemary looked around the mercantile and sighed. At least there was no one else in the store to share in this moment of shame. To be turned down for her first job application was grating on her pride.

Thank goodness Pip was a friend, else the embarrassment would have been unbearable.

"I doubt the new minister can afford to hire me. He looks about as penniless as the rest of his kind. And I ought to know, having lived in a parsonage all of my life."

Glumly, she eyed the colorful display of fabrics on the counter before her. "And I can't, in all good conscience, buy myself anything but dark colors for the next year. Papa wasn't much one for mourning clothes, but my own self-respect is going to limit me." She ran her fingers over a particularly bright floral print. "Not that I can afford anything new anyway."

Pip Boone slid from her perch and leaned across the width of the counter. "You could always marry Gabe Tanner. He did ask, after all." The challenge was whispered, as if the thought were too scandalous to be uttered aloud.

Rosemary's lips pinched tightly together and she turned away. Ramrod straight, she headed for the doorway.

"Rosemary! Don't leave. I was only funning you." Phillipa scooted around the counter, her words calling a halt to Rosemary's departure.

"I couldn't. I couldn't possibly marry that man. Even if he were serious, it would be..." Rosemary turned, her cheeks crimson, her breathing rapid. "It would be a sacrilege of the worst sort."

Phillips's brow furrowed, her eyes narrowing. "Now, how do you figure that?"

"He's rowdy, for one thing." The tip of her tongue

delivered moisture to lips suddenly gone dry as Rosemary thought of the teasing grin she'd encountered only yesterday.

"Rowdy doesn't seem too great a sin to me," Phillipa said with a grin of her own.

"You know what I mean," Rosemary told her. "Papa would turn over in his grave if I married a man who frequented the Golden Slipper. I let him know in no uncertain terms that I wasn't interested." Her chin tilted as she considered the unexpected proposal she had received. "Mr. Tanner was only putting me on, anyway."

Phillipa reached to lay a comforting hand on Rosemary's shoulder. "But, you didn't refuse him flat out, did you? You know, Rosemary, your papa would be pleased if you married a man who would treat you well, no matter if he did take a drink once in a while. And from what I hear, Gabe Tanner is far from a drinking man."

Her eyes wrinkled in delight, as if she considered some pleasant thought. "He strikes me as the sort of man who might treat you even better than you know, Rosemary. And he's very handsome."

Rosemary's mouth fell open in surprise. "Pip Boone! What a thing to say. The man uses vile language and partakes of hard liquor. Besides, I'd be willing to bet my bottom dollar that he was only offering marriage so that he wouldn't have to pay the new Bachelor Tax."

"Pooh! No man would propose marriage unless he was prepared to back it up, honey. Even Gabe Tanner wouldn't take a chance like that, unless..." She glanced away.

"He was sure I'd say no, wasn't he?" Rosemary's eyes dampened with hasty tears, and she blinked them away. "He thought he wasn't taking any kind of a chance at all, coming at me that way. He figured I'd turn him down flat."

As if she'd been kicked by a recalcitrant mule, she clutched her stomach. "I think I've been insulted, Pip. I wish now I'd had the sense to make my position totally clear. I should have said no in a hundred ways, just to be sure he got the message."

"Well, I think maybe you're jumping to the wrong conclusion about him. The man probably decided his place needs a woman's touch, and thought that a fine, upstanding preacher's daughter would be the perfect choice."

Phillipa's staunch reply sounded a bit hollow, but Rosemary smiled anyway. "He looked at me as if I were a drudge all right. I didn't see one speck of interest in his eyes, just that hateful way he has of looking at me sometimes, as if he can see beneath my clothes and doesn't like what's there."

Phillipa's eyes rounded and her lips twitched, then widened into a grin. "Why, Rosemary Gibson! You've peeked at Gabe Tanner before, haven't you?"

Rosemary shook her head. "Peeked? I don't peek. And I certainly—" She spun from Phillipa and looked out the wide front window of the emporium. "This is all a waste of time, anyway. I need to find a place to work and somewhere to stay, Pip. I can't impose on Reverend Worth and his family much longer.''

"How long before their furniture comes?" Pip asked.

"He said it would be here in a week. That doesn't give me much time.''

"You can move in with my folks," Pip offered. "We always have room for one more.''

Rosemary shook her head. "You barely squeeze into that house as it is, Pip. I couldn't do that.''

"How about a job at the newspaper office? Or maybe the hotel?''

Rosemary nodded. "I thought about working at the hotel, but I'm not sure I could earn enough to live on my own.''

"There's only one way to find out. Just march on down there and see what Mr. Westcott has to say.''

"I'd surely like to lend a helping hand, Miss Gibson, but the only thing I could put you to work at is emptying slop jars and keeping the floors clean. And that's stretching it. I'd only need you for about three hours a day. I doubt you could do much more than pay for your food and a bed at the boarding house down the street." Samuel Westcott looked uncomfortable, standing before his desk, his hands clasped behind him.

"I'd surely like to do something to help you out, seeing as how your father was such a good influence on the town, and all.''

"Thank you, sir. I understand your position," Rosemary told him, forcing a smile.

"Too bad you're not a gentleman looking for work. I heard tell that Jason Stillwell is thinking about hiring an accountant."

Rosemary felt a fine film of perspiration on her forehead as she listened to Samuel Westcott. "Yes, well, it seems that men have the upper hand all the way around, don't they, sir?"

If she hadn't been looking through a veil of hot tears, Rosemary would never have missed the ball rolling down the sidewalk. And if the man riding his horse had been looking the other way, he wouldn't have caught sight of her slender legs as her dress flew up in a billowing flurry.

"Oh, my word!" One foot stepping directly on the leather-encased ball, Rosemary lost her balance. Her arms flapped uselessly, her hat slid over one eye, and her skirts settled around her knees as she landed on the wooden walkway.

"Oh, my," she repeated, one hand pushing at her hat brim, the other pressing against her chest as she fought to gain her breath.

"Ma'am? Let me help you up." Directly before her eyes a long-fingered, gloved hand offered assistance.

Rosemary lifted her gaze to find that Gabe Tanner's was focused on the long length of her lower limbs, properly garbed in black, ribbed lisle hosiery. She shoved at her rumpled skirts, gaining a small amount of dignity as she managed to cover her knees and a good portion of her calves.

"Miss Gibson?" His eyes sparkled with humor as

he wiggled his fingers in her direction. "I'd be happy to help you up." He gripped her hand firmly and tugged, lifting her to stand before him. "Don't know when I've had a young lady throw herself at my feet so nicely before."

Rosemary's cheeks burned with shame. "I tripped over something," she said hastily, shaking her skirts and brushing her hands together. Her palms stung and her bottom felt bruised, but none of that bothered her nearly so much as the painful humiliation of this morning's series of failures.

Tanner's voice lowered. "I was only joshin' you, Miss Gibson. I didn't mean to embarrass you." He released her hand and she staggered at the absence of his touch.

"Ma'am? Can you walk? Are you all right?" He bent to look at her face, one gloved finger beneath her chin.

Rosemary ground her teeth together and glared at him. "I'm fine, thank you. Just a little…" There was no way in heaven she would reveal the particulars of her injury. It was enough that her ankle had twisted as she fell. Admitting to this man that she could not sustain her full weight on her right foot was beyond—

"Miss Gibson, I don't believe you can walk, can you?"

"Of course, I can. Just be on your way. I'll be fine, as soon as I catch my breath for a few moments."

She lowered her right foot to the sidewalk again, gingerly testing it, then balanced precariously on the toe of her boot. Measuring the distance to the emporium, across the street and down past the bank, she drew a deep breath and bit at her lip.

Gabe Tanner backed away, his eyes skeptical, as if he gauged her ability to walk. "You know, ma'am, I can sling you over my horse and take you home, quick as a wink."

"That won't be necessary." She moved gingerly, turning from him and taking two painful steps, only to find herself caught up in strong arms and pressed against a firm chest.

The smell of leather and horseflesh, tinged with a more intangible scent, filled her nostrils. Like fresh hay in the fields, she decided, not at all what she would have expected, and then shook her head at the fanciful thought.

He shifted her in his arms, gripping more firmly beneath her thighs. "You're just being foolish, ma'am, tryin' to walk when something is hurtin' you. What'd you do? Twist your ankle?"

"Yes, I suppose I did," she blurted, her embarrassment made complete by her position, as he strode across the dusty street.

"I'll just…" He stopped, halfway across the wide expanse and looked down at her, frowning. "Where am I takin' you, ma'am? Where are you stayin' these days? Maybe I'd do better to load you on my horse to get you there?"

Rosemary closed her eyes against the utter humiliation of this day. "Just let me down, sir. I'll make my way alone."

He sighed in an exaggerated fashion. "Can't do that, Miss Gibson. You'd fall on your face, and my mama would roll over if she knew I'd treated a lady so badly.''

"So far, you've proposed to me under false pretenses and made a public spectacle of me, carrying me down the middle of the street. How much worse could it get?" she asked, stiffening her body within his hold.

He tightened his grip. "If you don't stop wiggling, sweetheart, I'll drop you. And then you *will* be in a fix.'' His eyes darkened, and he glowered at her as if he wished he'd never sullied his hands with her.

She closed her eyes. "Just across the street, please. I'll walk from there." Her hands seemed useless appendages, and she folded her arms firmly across her breasts, making fists of her fingers, lest she be tempted to push them against him in a bid for release.

He bounced her in his arms again, as if to get a better grip, and her breath escaped in an audible puff of air. The brim of Rosemary's hat tilted precariously over her forehead and she was sure that her lower limbs were on view to whoever might be observing from the sidewalk.

The urge to weep was almost irresistible, and she drove her fingernails into her palms, gritting her teeth against the impulse. In moments, Tanner stepped up onto the wooden sidewalk and deftly lowered her to her feet.

"There you go, ma'am. I hope I've been of some service to you."

She cast him a sidelong look, her hands busy with brushing her skirts into place. "Yes, I'm sure you have, Mr. Tanner. You've been a real blessing."

He clucked his tongue disapprovingly. "Was that a note of sarcasm I heard? And after all I've done?"

He was drawing a crowd, Rosemary realized, suddenly aware of the ladies who had stepped from the bank. A handful of old gentlemen lingered nearby, their trip to the emporium for their usual game of cribbage interrupted by her misfortune.

"Just go away, sir," she managed to whisper, the appearance of tears becoming a real possibility.

He was silent for a moment, unmoving before her, and Rosemary drew in a quavering breath, wishing she might just vanish from this place and from his presence.

Tanner's fingers gripped her chin and he tilted her face upward, peering down into her eyes. "Are you gonna cry, sweetheart?"

"No! I never cry," she lied, even as a tear escaped from each eye.

Damn, he was in a spot. Half the town was within hearing distance and he was in over his head, trying to make amends for being a gentleman for once in his life. Even as he mulled over his options, a tear dropped to the front of her dingy dress and soaked into the dark fabric.

She was about the most pitiful sight he'd seen in a month of Sundays, with most all of her hair twisted up somewhere beneath that drooping hat she wore, only bits and pieces of it peeking out. It wasn't the dark brown he'd thought, but a pretty color, sort of brown and red put together. And somehow she'd managed to hide it under the ugliest piece of black straw he'd ever laid eyes on.

"Ma'am?" His fingers tightened their grip, and he saw her wince. With a grunt of regret, he released her chin, aware of the soft texture of the skin he'd probably bruised with his clumsy touch. Her mouth quivered, and he watched even, white teeth clamp down on her lower lip.

"Ma'am, I didn't mean to make you cry," he murmured, aware that the ladies who had stepped closer were probably being eaten alive with curiosity. He'd almost put his head in the noose once with this female. Now he'd managed to get himself in a hullabaloo with folks looking on.

"I'm fine, Mr. Tanner. You may go on your way." She looked to be balanced pretty well on both feet, and Gabe stepped back, sweeping his hat from his head.

"I'm glad I was able to be of service, ma'am," he mumbled for the benefit of the onlookers. "You'd better get that ankle looked at." His gaze dropped to where her foot was barely grazing the wood beneath it, only the toe of her boot brushing the sidewalk.

Maybe he should… Hell, no! He wasn't about to make any offers. He could just see himself pulling off her boot and running his hands over her foot and the bones of her ankle. Then he *would* be in hot water with the fine female citizenry of Edgewood. They'd have him at the altar in no time flat.

Yet, Rosemary's legs had been most appealing, he admitted to himself, almost grinning at the memory. Curving up from the top of her low boots, they'd been a tempting sight. He'd warrant her feet were narrow and well formed, her ankles slender.

"Rosemary, are you all right?" From out of nowhere, Phillipa Boone arrived, breathless and concerned.

"She tripped on a ball in front of the hotel," Tanner offered. "I helped her across the street, but she says she can walk now."

Phillipa nodded. "I saw you carrying her from my front window." Her lips curled into a knowing grin. "I'm sure you were a big help, sir."

Tanner replaced his hat, tugging the brim down sharply over his brow. "I'll be on my way. Hope your foot's all right, Miss Gibson."

He turned from the gathering, aware of Phillipa Boone's words of commiseration and the answering murmur of Rosemary's voice. *What a mess.* Twice now, he'd been in close proximity with the woman. He'd better keep his distance before the creature thought he really *was* interested in her.

His steps quickened as he headed for his horse, and with a final glance at the ladies who were intent on tending to the preacher's daughter, he rode toward the livery stable. Bates Comstock greeted him with a grin. "What's this I hear about you offering for Gibson's girl, Tanner? You plannin' on bein' domesticated like the rest of us?"

Gabe felt a shudder of dread down the length of his spine. "It got me out of payin' the Bachelor Tax, and that's a fact. Damn tax is ridiculous anyway. Why the town thinks it has to meddle is beyond me."

"They're tryin' to raise money for the new schoolhouse they want to build."

"Hell, if they count on the new tax to pay the bill,

it'll be a long time till the first wall goes up. There's not that many bachelors around these parts.''

''What are you doin' in town, Tanner?'' Bates asked.

''Fact is, I was on my way to see you when Miss Gibson took a fall out in front of the hotel. I carted her across the street and let Pip Boone take over with her.''

''You're gettin' in deep, boy. You'd do well to steer clear of that gal, or she'll be takin' you up on your offer.''

Tanner kicked at a stone, venting his irritation, one hand propped on his hip. ''Forget it, Bates. She's not about to take me on, and that's that. Now, I need to know how many horses you want from my place. I'm givin' you first pick.''

Bates slid his hands in his pockets and rocked back on his heels. ''I need three or four. Town's growin' and I get calls most every week for a carriage or somebody lookin' to buy a horse. Your animals broke to harness?''

Gabe shrugged. ''Whatever you're lookin' for, I've probably got. I'm cullin' out some of the three-year-olds, those that are saddle-broke and a couple I've been working with, pulling my buggy.''

''Let me come out tomorrow and take a look,'' Bates said. ''How are the prices?''

Tanner grinned. ''High. I've got the best horses in east Texas, and you know that as well as I do.''

''What are you gonna do with the rest of them?''

''There's a dealer in Shreveport ready to take anything I've got to sell.''

Bates nodded. "I'd best beat him to it then, hadn't I? I'll be out in the morning."

"If I were a man I could have a job doing the accounts for Mr. Stillwell at the Golden Slipper," Rosemary said, propping her chin on her fist, one foot stretched before her with a cool cloth covering her ankle.

"Don't even think it," Pip said sharply. "Even if you were a man, you wouldn't want to work for a saloon keeper."

"Not much chance anyway," Rosemary said with a defeated shrug. "He'd never hire any kin of my father. They were on opposite sides of the fence till the day papa died."

Pip bent over the injured foot and lifted the towel, swinging it in the air to cool it. "I'll bet you're going to be laid up for a couple of days," she pronounced grimly. "You've really done it, Rosemary. I'll tell you what. As soon as I lock up here, I'll give you a shoulder to lean on and walk you home."

The thought of stepping with her full weight on the swollen ankle made Rosemary wince, but there was no getting around it. The parsonage was over two hundred feet from the back door of the store, and she needed help.

The sun was heading for the horizon when the two young women turned the corner and the humble home Rosemary had shared with her father came into view. Before it, a large wagon was backed to the gate, and several men were unloading pieces of furniture.

"I thought it wouldn't be arriving for three more

days," Rosemary said quietly, too upset by this turn of events to hold back the tears that filled her eyes.

"Where is your furniture?" Pip asked, as a large sofa was turned on end to fit through the doorway.

Rosemary was beyond speech and only shook her head.

"Miss Gibson!" The tall figure of James Worth hastened to where the two women stood. "I'm so sorry I didn't come and get you when the wagon arrived. We've been busy unloading, as you can see. I fear we had to put your things out on the grass, and these gentlemen will load them on the wagon and take them to the livery stable until you can decide what to do with them."

"All right," Rosemary answered stoutly, blinking her eyes, determined not to show the sorrow that filled her to brimming. She'd known for three days that a decision must be made, and now she was out in the cold. No miracle had occurred. No angels had appeared to wave their wings on her behalf.

If only Lars Jorgenson had not been set aside for another, she might even now be fixing the evening meal for her husband.

And at that thought, she burst into tears.

Chapter Three

The back door to the saloon was tightly shut, only a crack of light appearing below the heavy pine portal. Rosemary stood in the darkness and listened to the sounds from within. A woman's laughter rippled past her hearing, then the lower tones of a man's voice, accompanied by a thumping beat as music from the front of the saloon filtered through the crowd.

Her dark clothing hid her from those who might be passing by the alleyway, a narrow lane running between the town's business community and a row of houses behind it. Rosemary lifted her hand and formed a fist, rapping hesitantly on the wooden panel.

From within, there was no cessation of sound, only an additional voice added to the others. "I don't care if you just rinse them out. Get those glasses back to the bar. Ain't there any warm water on the stove?"

The female answered with assurance. "I'm neither cook nor dishwasher, Jason. You're just lucky I'm good-natured, or I wouldn't be helpin' out."

"And you're lucky I'm payin' you good money for sashayin' your fanny across that stage, Laura Lee. Most places, you'd be workin' for tips from your gentlemen friends out front."

"Go take care of your customers, sweetie. I'll bring your glasses out in a minute," the woman's voice replied.

Rosemary lifted her hand to rap again.

"You'll have to pound harder, miss. They can't hear above the noise, lessen you bang good and loud." The voice from behind her spun Rosemary in place. She staggered as her injured ankle gave way, and her hand grasped for purchase on the shoulder of the young boy facing her.

"You startled me," she croaked. "I thought I was alone here."

He grinned widely, tugging his cap from his head. "I don't make no noise, ma'am. I been watchin' you, and I figured you needed some advice."

Before Rosemary could utter a word of protest, his fist made contact with the door three times, each thump hard enough to rattle the hinges. She looked around, anxious lest anyone should see her in such a place, and was about to make her escape when the door creaked open.

"See, what'd I tell you?" the boy asked, his grin visible in the light streaming from the open doorway.

"Ma'am?" The golden-haired woman inside the building appeared to take Rosemary's measure. Her lips curled in a smile of amusement and she swept her hand in welcome. "Come on in, why don't you?

No sense in standin' around outside. You come to see old Jason? Or maybe to convert the customers?''

Rosemary stepped within the doorway, casting a glance behind her for the youth who had hastened this moment. He was gone, not even a shadow betraying his presence.

"You're the preacher's girl, aren't you?" the woman asked.

Rosemary nodded, assailed by the scent of hard drink and heavy perfume. "I wanted to talk to the owner, Mr. Stillwell, if he's available."

"He's at the bar," the blond woman told her. "I'm Laura Lee, his…" She smiled, then waved her hand in Rosemary's direction. "I work here, honey. What do you need with Jason?"

The door across the room swung open and a dark-haired man strode in, the noise from behind him assailing Rosemary's ears with a harsh symphony of sound. "Where in hell's those glasses, Laura Lee? I need them now."

He halted abruptly when he saw Rosemary, and his brows rose in question. "Didn't know we had company," he said slowly.

"I'll get the glasses," Laura Lee told him, turning to the sink. "The young lady wants to see you, Jason."

Jason moved closer to Rosemary. "Last time I saw you, you was walkin' behind your daddy's coffin on the way to the cemetery. You're a long way from the parsonage, ma'am."

"I wanted to see you, Mr. Stillwell, and I thought

this might be the best time. I hesitated to come to your business establishment during the day.''

He nodded, and then, as if he had just remembered his manners, he pulled a chair from the table and offered her a seat. Rosemary settled herself on the edge of the chair, aware of the sidelong looks she was receiving from Laura Lee, who splashed water from the stove into a dishpan.

Rosemary leaned forward, hoping she would not sound too much like a beggar asking for alms. ''I need a job, Mr. Stillwell, and I heard that you were looking for an accountant to do your books. I'm very good with figures, sir, and I desperately need work. I thought I might be able to—''

Jason held up a hand, halting her effectively. ''You want to work for *me*, ma'am? I don't think so.'' He grinned widely. ''I'd have every woman in town after my head if I were to take you on in any way, shape or form. Surely a lady like you can find respectable work without having to knock on my back door.''

''You'd think so, wouldn't you,'' Rosemary said glumly. ''But, I've been everywhere in town that might need help, and no one has a position open.''

''Your daddy didn't leave you too well fixed, did he?''

''No. He truly thought he had years ahead of him to see to my future. There was only a little money in the bank, and the funeral took a good share of that. I need to find work and a place to live.'' She cast him a look of chagrin. ''Believe me, I looked everywhere else first. I still can't believe I had the nerve to come here. You were my last resort.''

Laura Lee sashayed past with the tray of wet glasses, and leaned down to whisper loudly in Jason's ear. "You could always use a new singer, Jason. Bet she has a repertoire that'd set your customers on their ear."

"Don't give the lady a hard time, Laura Lee," he said with a chuckle, one wide palm swatting the blond's ruffled skirt as she passed the table and went on through the swinging door.

"I need a bookkeeper, sure enough, Miss Gibson, but it's a job for a man. Besides, you know I wouldn't dare hire you. I only stay in business by the skin of my teeth as it is, what with half the women in town wantin' to close me down."

"They do?"

Jason leaned closer. "They don't approve of their husbands coming in for a drink or a hand of cards, let alone climbin' the stairs to visit—" He frowned. "I don't think you need to hear that, ma'am."

Rosemary felt a flush creep up her throat and splash color on her cheeks. "I understand, sir." She rose and clutched her reticule before her. "It was sort of a last chance, coming here."

"I wish I could help, ma'am. If I hear of anything, I'll get a message to you."

Rosemary groped for the doorknob behind her and twisted it, tugging the door open quickly. "Thank you, Mr. Stillwell. I'm sorry to have bothered you."

"No bother, ma'am. You be careful going home, you hear?" He watched her, stepping out into the alley as she made her way from sight.

"You get a job, ma'am?" From the shadows behind the hotel, a slight figure stepped forth. In the moonlight, he exhibited a cheerful smile, sweeping his cap from his head politely.

Things were going poorly when a grimy scallywag possessed the friendliest face in town, Rosemary decided. At least, the most welcoming smile she'd been offered today. The rejection she'd received from Samuel Westcott was no easier to accept because it had been delivered with a tight-lipped smile. And the grim refusal of Duncan Blackstone at the newspaper office had left her with nothing but a sense of failure.

Even Pip had found it hard to smile when she turned down Rosemary for a position. The banker, Pace Frombert, had only shaken his head disapprovingly, as if a woman inside his establishment was not to be considered, unless she was a customer.

At least Jason Stillwell had been kindly in his refusal.

"Well, at least you're still smilin'," the boy before her said cheerfully. "I was afraid you'd need me close by, ma'am. That's why I hung around till you came out."

Rosemary looked down at him gravely. "I do appreciate your thoughtfulness, young man. You're the Pender boy, aren't you? Your name's Scat, if I remember correctly." She glanced over his shoulder at the houses that lined the back street of town. "Won't your father be concerned about your whereabouts? It's been dark for a long time."

He shook his head. "No, ma'am. My pa's got a ·bottle, and he don't care where I am." He stepped back and motioned to the footpath. "I'll walk you home, if you want me to."

Rosemary nodded. There wasn't anywhere else to go, and James Worth and his family would probably be wondering where she had gotten to, leaving the way she had.

"All right. Thank you," Rosemary said, stepping ahead of the lad.

Hopelessness surrounded her as she trudged the path, turning in at the gate to the parsonage and lifting a hand to wave at Scat. She could not, in all good conscience, stay any longer with the Worth family. They had been kind and generous, but the parsonage was crowded.

"Don't you have family, Miss Gibson?" James Worth had asked only this evening at the supper table.

"No. I have no one."

"Well, you are welcome here," he'd answered *staunchly, even as his wife had lifted her brows as if to doubt his offer.*

Rosemary stepped onto the porch, crossed to the door and opened the screen, smiling as the tight spring announced her arrival with a twang. She stepped into the parlor, nodding at Mr. and Mrs. Worth.

"I'll be going to bed now. Thank you again for the lovely meal, Mrs. Worth," she said quietly.

She made her way to the bedroom she had once called her own. Now a small girl lay sprawled in the double bed and Rosemary carefully edged her past the middle, making room for herself.

Tomorrow. It was the last day she would look for

work in Edgewood. She slipped from her dress and draped it over a chair, bending to roll her stockings down her legs. After tomorrow, she'd have to look beyond the boundaries of town. Maybe she could cook for a rancher or keep house for a farm family. And at that thought, she slid her nightgown over her head and stripped from her petticoat and drawers beneath its billowing folds.

Tomorrow, she'd decide what to do.

"Have you heard if anyone needs a live-in?" Rosemary's hopeful query brought consternation to Phillipa's round face.

"A live-in what?"

Rosemary glanced around the general store, where only two other customers browsed at this early hour. She faced Pip across the wide counter. "Maybe as a housekeeper or..." Her hands gripped each other at her waist as she groped for another position she might be capable of filling.

Pip shook her head. "Nobody hereabouts can really afford to hire in help. Maybe some of the ranchers, but most all of them have wives." She halted, her eyes widening.

"Rosemary..." Pip leaned over the counter, whispering her thoughts aloud. "Maybe you ought to reconsider Gabe Tanner's proposal."

"No!" Her single word of denial exploded, and both browsers turned her way, openmouthed. Rosemary bent her head and spoke in a low tone. "I couldn't possibly, Pip. I just couldn't."

Bernice Comstock stepped up to the counter.

"Hello there, Rosemary. I understand you've been looking for work," she said. "It's a pity your daddy didn't provide a little better for you, isn't it? Though I'd think you're equipped for something."

Rosemary attempted to smile, cringing within at the faint praise the other woman offered. "Well, if I am, I'm sure I don't know what it is," she answered. "Whatever my talents are, there doesn't seem to be a place for them here. I've tried at the hotel, the newspaper and even pestered poor Phillipa here."

From her left, Geraldine Frombert cut in abruptly. "You need to marry and have a family, child. A young woman with your upbringing would make a fine wife for any man. Matter of fact, I'm surprised you haven't been snatched up before this."

Pip opened her mouth, then snapped it shut after a quick look in Rosemary's direction.

"The Bachelor Tax will send some of these men scurrying for a wife, I'll warrant, now that the year's almost up," Bernice Comstock said briskly.

Rosemary's heartbeat sped up, pounding in her ears. She felt cornered, as if she were a project being taken on by this pair of ladies. "I'd really rather seek employment," she announced firmly.

The door opened and all eyes swept in that direction. A hush fell among the women as Dex Sawyer entered the store, removing his hat in deference to their presence as he approached the counter.

"Ladies." He nodded at each one in turn, receiving only a frosty glare from Bernice and Geraldine. Pip grinned invitingly.

"Mr. Sawyer, what can I do for you?"

For a moment, he looked uncomfortable, then waved at the supply of linens Pip's father had arranged on the highest shelves. "I've found a furnished place to rent. I need to have a set of sheets and a couple of towels, Miss Boone."

Pip's gaze followed his pointing finger and she turned aside, hastening to scoot her ladder into place.

"May I climb up there for you?" Dex asked politely.

Pip stood back, allowing him space, and watched as he made his way up several steps until he could reach his goal. "Are these arranged by size?" His hand hesitated, as he glanced down at the woman below.

She shook her head. "They're all the same. If your bed is smaller than regular size, you just have to tuck them in farther. The pillowcases are to the right, next to the towels."

With an adept twist of his wrist, Dex tugged what he needed from the stack and handed them down to Phillipa. He climbed down, facing her behind the counter. "I'll need foodstuffs, along with these linens."

"I'm sure my mother has an extra quilt she can let you use," Pip said, her cheeks pink, her eyes shining as she spoke.

From either side of her, Rosemary noted the departure of the two women. Probably didn't want to associate with a man who made his living at the saloon, she thought. He turned to Rosemary, and his eyes were kind. "I don't mean to infringe on your privacy, Miss Gibson, but I wondered if you had found employment yet, or a place to live.''

Pip turned away, Dex's list in her hand, gathering items from the shelves. Rosemary shook her head.

''No, not yet. I can't pay rent for a room until I have some income. I fear it's a vicious circle, Mr. Sawyer.''

He leaned closer, lowering his voice as he glanced aside at Phillipa, as if assuring himself she was not within hearing distance. ''I have to admit I've been thinking about you. If you have nowhere else to go, I can offer you a haven, ma'am. I have room and to spare.''

Rosemary's cheeks burned with a rush of heat. ''I couldn't even consider such a thing,'' she said hastily.

''It would be better than nothing,'' he said quietly.

Rosemary was stunned for a moment at his words. ''Are you offering me a room, sir? Or a position?''

''Perhaps I should not have put such a suggestion to you. However...''

''You want me to be your...'' She could not utter the word aloud. The insult was too great to be considered, and Rosemary turned away, her injured ankle not allowing as dignifed an exit as she would have liked.

He was behind her, his hand grasping her elbow. ''Wait. I didn't mean to give offense, although I'm sure it must seem that way to you. I'm offering room and board in exchange for your services in my home.''

Rosemary shuddered, her perception of Dex Sawyer shattered. At first glance, on the train platform, she had thought him the picture of elegance, a perfect choice for the new preacher and certainly for a husband.

Now, he had proved himself to be a blackguard of the worst kind. She jerked from his grasp. "I cannot tell you how outraged I am at your suggestion," she said between gritted teeth.

He rolled his eyes, shaking his head. "I'm sure there is a misconception here, Miss Gibson. I am simply offering you shelter. I beg your pardon for infringing on your dignity, but I only meant that you could cook my meals and keep my house in order until you find a better position."

"The only offer I will ever accept from a man will be an honorable proposal of marriage," she said firmly.

"Have you had one?" His tone was dubious.

Her chin tilted and her mouth was primly set as she spoke her reply. "Yes, as a matter of fact, I have."

A flush rose to color his cheeks, and Dex ducked his head. "I beg your pardon, Miss Rosemary. I spoke in haste, and I fear I have offended you greatly. I can only offer my deepest apologies."

"They are not acceptable, I fear," Rosemary whispered, her only thought that of escape from his presence. With steps that limped ever so slightly, she left the store. Glancing back, she hesitated for just a moment as Pip mouthed words she could not hear, her arms full of foodstuffs.

From the other side of the glass, Dex watched her departure, his mouth twisted in a half smile that hinted of regret, even as he lifted two fingers to his brow in a salute.

It was impossible that the man would think she'd even consider such a thing. Rosemary's feet scuffed up clouds of dust as she crossed the street. How could he think she would keep house for a single gentleman? She could only imagine the gossip such an arrangement would cause. The wooden sidewalk beneath her feet now, she barely felt the pain in her injured foot, so great was her distress.

How he could even imagine that she would take him up on the idea was beyond her comprehension. And yet, what had anyone else offered her? she asked herself in a burst of honesty. At least the man had been aboveboard with his proposal. And quick with his apology.

Proposal. She'd thrown the word in his face. She'd said in no uncertain terms that a *proposal* had been offered. And so it had. An ambiguous proposition, to be sure. And yet...

She stopped suddenly, coming to a halt in front of the newspaper office. Inside, Duncan Blackstone glanced at her, then quickly away.

She ignored his back as he turned away, her mind on the conversation with Gabe Tanner when he had offered his hand so casually and with such a lack of dignity. Had she turned him down flat? She didn't think so.

The scene filled her mind. She'd told him not to molest her. She'd sputtered words she could not even recall. Yet...she hadn't refused him outright.

Not once had she said the single word he'd apparently expected to hear.

He was not off the hook.

As first choice, he rated below a rattlesnake, she decided. And yet, what were her other options? To be housekeeper to the piano player from the saloon? To beg on the street corner? To degrade herself further by going from ranch to ranch, seeking employment?

Maybe she could make a deal with him. Perhaps she could earn her way without having to... The thought of what being Gabe Tanner's wife entailed was almost too much for her to consider.

At any rate, she'd reached the bottom of the barrel. Staying at the parsonage was not an option any longer, and living with Phillipa's family would be an imposition.

She turned on her heel and marched haltingly toward the livery stable. If passersby spoke, she was not aware of their greetings, her mind set on the goal she must attain before she lost her nerve.

Bates Comstock, leading a bay mare, stepped from inside the big barn. He tipped his hat politely. "Miss Gibson, what can I do for you? You wanting to go for a ride?"

"How much would it cost to rent a buggy from you for a couple of hours?" she asked.

"Whereabouts you heading?" He tied the mare to a hitching post and slid his hands into his pockets.

She felt the flush climb her cheeks. She'd done more blushing lately than in the whole past year, and it seemed she had no control over it. "I need to ride out to Gabe Tanner's place."

Bates hesitated for a moment, then grinned, his eyes crinkling with what appeared to be an inordinate amount of delight, Rosemary thought. Why her destination should inspire such interest on his part was rather odd.

"Well, it happens I'm on my way there myself," Bates said jovially. "He's sellin' me three horses and I'm gonna pick them up this afternoon. Why don't I just take the buggy instead of my mare, and I'll give you a lift. Won't cost you a thing."

Rosemary cast him a doubtful look, then considered the paltry sum she had in her reticule. "That sounds fine," she said politely. "I'm ready to go whenever you are."

Chapter Four

Gabe Tanner squinted his eyes against the afternoon sun, peering at the conveyance that was approaching his house. If he didn't know better, he'd swear Bates Comstock was hauling that Gibson woman around in his buggy. With a muffled curse, he left the barn.

If it wasn't Rosemary Gibson, it was her twin. And whatever her reason for coming, it probably didn't bode well for him, he decided glumly.

The buggy halted with a flourish, the mare tossing her head, her hooves pawing at the ground. Bates snapped on a lead line and tied it to the hitching rail, then turned back to assist his passenger from the buggy.

"You come for your horses, Bates?" Gabe asked, hat tilted back, arms akimbo.

Bate's grin was wide as Rosemary's feet touched the ground amid a flurry of skirts. "Yeah. I was about to ride out on my mare when Miss Gibson here walked up and asked for a buggy to hire. Thought we'd kill two birds with one stone and take the trip together.''

"You were coming to see me?'' Tanner turned his gaze upon Rosemary. "You're wantin' to buy some horses, too?''

"Don't make sport of me, Mr. Tanner,'' Rosemary told him. "I'm sure you're more than aware that I have no use for your livestock.'' She glanced around, her eyes flitting from house to barn, to the chicken coop and back again.

"Lookin' things over, Miss Gibson?'' Tanner drawled.

She met his look squarely, her nostrils flaring, her mouth fixed. "You know why I'm here, Mr. Tanner.''

One big hand over his mouth, Bates muffled his laughter as best he could, attempting to turn the snorting noise into a coughing spell.

"Do I, now?'' Tanner stepped forward, his callused palm reaching to tilt Rosemary's face upward. Defiant blue eyes met his, and a shiver snaked its way down his back.

"No,'' he said in a harsh whisper, "I don't know why you're here. Why don't you tell me?'' His fingertips moved ever so slightly, brushing the delicate texture of her skin and his gaze shifted, as if drawn to the movement.

"May we speak privately?'' she asked, her eyes darting to the side, where Bates watched, wide-eyed.

"Bates, go check with Cotton about your horses,'' Tanner said through clenched teeth, his gaze intent on the woman his fingers held captive.

Bates shuffled away, obviously disgruntled by this

turn of events. Probably the best fun he'd had all week, Tanner thought.

But if the female before him was enjoying the event, she took great pains to hide the fact. Her skin had lost its color, her eyelids fluttered, and she had her teeth clenched firmly into her lower lip, just inches from where his fingers touched her skin.

"You're gonna be bleedin' in a minute if you don't quit chewin' on your mouth like that," Tanner warned her, then winced as her teeth clenched and a tiny speck of blood formed on her lip.

"Ah, hell, cut that out!" Tanner's whisper rose to a growl and Rosemary's eyes flew open.

His grip tightened. "Just spit it out, Miss Gibson. I've got work to do. Tell me what you're doin' on my place, and I won't be gettin' riled up."

She jerked from his touch, and he watched with dismay as four small red marks appeared where his fingertips had pressed her skin. The word he muttered beneath his breath opened her eyes wider still, and she looked around as if seeking a way out of the predicament she'd managed to create.

"I think I've changed my mind." She backed from him until her skirts touched the wheel of the buggy.

He followed, his anger appeased by the confusion she could not hide. She was breathless, her lush bosom almost vibrating with her effort to fill her lungs, and he found it impossible to keep his eyes from the sight.

"Please let me get back in the buggy, Mr. Tanner. I shouldn't have come here."

He shook his head. "You're the one who came

visitin', sweetheart. Now, tell me why.'' He'd never enjoyed pestering a woman so much, and for a moment he was ashamed. She was no match for him, this big-eyed little fugitive from the parsonage.

Amusement won out over shame and he leaned closer.

It was a mistake. Her mouth was trembling, her eyes frantic in their appeal, and her hands lifted to spread against his chest. The movement carried with it a faint scent of flowers and he bent his head, inhaling the hint of fragrance. Dowdy be damned. She smelled good enough to eat, and for a moment he felt starved for sustenance.

Those fingers clenched into fists and her chin lifted defiantly. ''I think you're trying to intimidate me, Mr. Tanner.''

He grinned. ''No, I'm tryin' to figure out what you smell like.'' His nose dipped into the curve of her neck, just beneath her ear, and she swallowed a shriek, its sound muffled in her throat.

Her whisper was thready. ''Whatever do you mean?''

''You smell good, sweetheart. I noticed it the other day when I carried you across the street in town.''

''It's apple blossom cologne,'' Rosemary said hastily. ''Pip sells it at the emporium.''

His thighs leaned into her, and he nudged her face with his own, tilting it upward. Her lips were pink, almost matching the flush that bloomed from her throat to her forehead, and he watched as they parted.

The movement of her mouth caught his attention,

and with a muffled sound he kissed her, planting his lips directly on hers.

She had nothing to compare it with, this hot, damp capturing of her mouth. No other man had ever claimed her lips in this manner. Granted, her experience was sorely limited, only a chaste brush against her cheek one afternoon in the churchyard, years ago.

Rosemary sagged against him, her fists captured between their bodies, her eyes crossing as she fought for breath. She uttered muffled imprecations, only to find his tongue whispering along the seam between her lips, as if he would beg admittance. Her head was captured by a large hand that had somehow scooped beneath her hat to fit long fingers through her carefully twisted and pinned locks.

Not only had he taken her breath, but now the ribbon of her bonnet was cutting into her throat as his hand wedged between the black straw and her head. And then, as if he had discovered her plight, he eased the fingers of his other hand beneath her chin, and with a quick movement, the bonnet was released and tossed to the ground.

Tanner's mouth eased from hers, brushing back and forth, each tingling increment sending shivers down her spine.

Her hands clenched, fingers gripping fabric warmed by the flesh beneath it, and she leaned against him, her legs seemingly useless beneath her.

If Tanner had thought to frighten her half to death, he was well on the way to success, Rosemary thought frantically. His big body was wedging her against the buggy wheel and his mouth had taken unforgivable

liberties. His grin had vanished, and now he was looking at her as if he were angry as sin.

His dark eyes were mere slits, his skin was pulled
tight over his cheek and jaw, and his mouth was only
inches from her own. Rosemary opened her lips,
whether to speak or call for help, she couldn't decide,
and then closed her eyes against the sight of his
frightening visage.

"Now, sweetheart," he whispered harshly. "Tell
me why you came to visit."

Her lashes flew open, and he shook his head. "No,
just shut those blue eyes and answer me."

"I can't," she wailed.

His voice was a purr. "Sure you can."

She inhaled sharply and the words spurted forth, as
if shot by rifle fire. "I came to take you up on your
offer, but I've changed my mind."

"Changed your mind? Why?"

"I can't do this. I thought I could, but I can't."

"Did you get a better offer?" His eyes glittered,
his head lifting a bit as he scanned her face.

"No!" She shrank from him, the buggy wheel un-
forgiving against her back.

"I thought you didn't want to marry me. You
turned me down, Miss Gibson."

How he could call her by such a formal address
when his tongue had been almost touching her teeth
just moments ago was beyond her comprehension. "I
didn't, actually," Rosemary muttered.

"Sure sounded like it to me."

Rosemary shook her head. "As I recall, I only

asked you why you wanted to marry me. I didn't turn you down flat."

He leaned back, his eyes flashing, his jaw jutting forward. The lips that had touched hers were still damp and he barely opened them as he spoke. "You didn't?"

"No, I didn't."

"Now you've decided to take me up on the offer?"

"I don't think so. Well, maybe."

His hands moved, long fingers tugging at the pins that held her hair in place. The heavy bone pins fell to the ground, and she was aware of the weight of her long hair falling around her shoulders.

"What are you doing?"

"If you're gonna marry me, I have a right to look at what I'm gettin', don't I?"

"Now?"

His grin was quick and lethal, taking her breath. "I can't think of a better time." He lifted the weight of her hair and allowed it to cling to his long fingers, running his hands through the tresses, watching intently as the waves flowed across her shoulders to rest against her bosom.

"Please, Mr. Tanner," she managed to squeak. "I think you're taking liberties with me."

His fingers clenched for a moment, and then he released her with an oath muttered beneath his breath. She cringed from the sound.

"I haven't hurt you, Miss Gibson. You've no reason to flinch from me." He stepped back from her, and his wide palms and long fingers formed fists.

Her gaze sought the whereabouts of those formidable weapons and she shivered, even as hot sunshine poured from above. "You look ready to do battle, Mr. Tanner."

He followed her gaze and slowly unclenched his hands, wiping them distractedly against the sides of his denim pants. "I might use them on a deserving sidewinder on occasion, but I don't hit ladies. Ever."

"That's most reassuring, sir." She hated the slight tremor in her voice, despised the weakness in her knees, and abhorred the fate that had sent her to this man. And yet, there was no help for it. She'd had to come. Her mind grasped at words Bates Comstock had spoken during the hour long ride.

Perhaps she might have the answer to the problem. She took a deep breath and squared her shoulders.

"Maybe marriage is not the answer for us. I understand you need a cook," Rosemary said, calling forth her reserves of courage. Whether or not she could bear the sight of this man on a daily basis was not a question to be considered right now. Nor was his ability to send icy fingers of alarm down her backbone.

He frowned, looking puzzled. "A cook?"

Rosemary smirked at him. Tanner decided there was no other word to describe the look that possessed her features as her gaze slid over his face. "Yes, you know. One of those women who stand in front of a stove and serve up food for hungry menfolk."

He shoved his palms into the back pockets of his pants and rocked on his heels. "Oh, yes. I'm very aware of the duties of a cook, Miss Gibson...but I didn't know that you were."

"Really? You might be surprised. Perhaps you would like to hire me. I bake wonderful pies." Rosemary's eyes were defiant, her jaw set.

"Mama Pearl does for us. What makes you think I'm in the market for someone else?" he asked. "Besides, I thought you were hell-bent on being my wife."

Her lashes drifted to rest against her cheek for a moment, then rose, and he was struck by the brilliance of her eyes, as blue as the birds that nested in his fenceposts on the far side of the pasture.

"Put that aside for the moment. I have to wonder what you eat the other six days of the week when Mama Pearl isn't here," she murmured, those smart-aleck words sliding artlessly from between rosy lips.

"We make do." And that was the truth. "Make do" was about the best he and his men had done. They'd gotten sick of meat tossed into a frying pan and cooked to shoe leather. They'd eaten eggs every which way but edible, and choked them down because not one man Jack of them knew how to make them taste any better than the last.

"Make do?" She eyed him dubiously. "Just what does that mean?"

Tanner's chin jutted, and he felt the heat rise from his throat. Now she had him defending the food his ranch hands ate. And how the conversation had taken this tack he surely didn't know.

"It won't matter once I marry you, will it? And who told you I needed a cook here, anyway?"

"Mr. Comstock mentioned it on the way out from town."

"I'll just bet he did," Gabe muttered, his frustrated glare aimed at the barn. "So which position are you applying for, Miss Gibson? Or are you just tryin' to get my goat?"

"Maybe."

"Maybe? Maybe, what?"

"I've been looking for a job in town, without much success. Perhaps working for you might be the answer. To tell you the truth, cooking for you beats accepting your marriage proposal."

"I think I just took it back, anyway," Tanner said bluntly. "I'm not sure you'd be the sort of wife I need."

Gabe watched as her jaw clenched, and her skin lost its color. Then his gaze traveled her length and he bit at his tongue, almost ashamed of the scornful words he'd aimed in her direction.

He'd be willing to bet his best filly that she was shaking in her boots. But, damn! He had to give her credit. She was toe-to-toe with him and not backing down one little bit.

"I'm not sure a marriage proposal is retractable," she told him primly. "Not if you plan on dodging the new tax on bachelors, anyway."

"Make up your mind, sweetheart. Either you want to be my cook or my wife. Which is it?" And then he waited for a long moment as she hesitated. It'd be just like the woman to call his bluff, and if there was anything Gabe Tanner didn't need, it was a female nagging at his heels every blessed day of his life.

At least not one that had any rights over him.

"I'd just as soon try the job as a cook, if it's all the same to you," she said.

He dragged his gaze from her mouth and his thoughts from the memory of how sweet those lips had tasted. His mind registered the words she had just spoken.

A cook. He'd just hired himself a cook, and for the life of him, he couldn't figure out how that piece of business had come to pass.

"You got your duds with you?" He peered into the buggy, then stepped back. "Must be you're plannin' on walkin' back and forth to town every day. Or else buyin' a rig to travel in. You sure don't want to live on a ranch with a bunch of rowdy cowhands and a bachelor."

Rosemary shook her head. "I don't believe I could be here in time to cook breakfast, Mr. Tanner. And as for living in your house, I wouldn't mind. You could always join your men wherever they sleep, I suppose."

"I hardly think so, ma'am." He tilted his head, nodding at the long, low building at the far side of the barn. "That there's the bunkhouse." He turned, aiming one long finger at the dwelling he'd helped to construct. "That's my house. I sleep in it, every night of my life."

Her gaze followed the line his pointing finger indicated, and he watched as her throat moved, grinning as he recognized the swallow she could not conceal. "I suppose the house is large enough for me to find a space for my belongings, Mr. Tanner.

"I have several pieces of furniture that I would

need to store, sir. Perhaps there might be an extra room I could use.'' She swung her head to face him and her eyes were bleak, the brilliant blue fading, as if sadness had drawn a shade, making her gaze colorless and dull.

"Furniture?"

She nodded. "Some things of my mother's. Things I can't...well, just family..." She halted, her hands moving helplessly against her dress.

Suddenly the baiting ceased to be enjoyable, and he spoke soberly. "There are a couple of empty rooms, Rosemary." How he'd managed to acquire a cook was a moot question. Now that he had, the particulars of the situation were the issue to be faced.

"You know you'll be the talk of the town, don't you?"

Her shrug was eloquent. "I haven't found employment there. I shouldn't think it would be anyone's business. Besides—" she looked up at him and hesitated. "I need a place to stay."

The woman was in desperate straits. He released the breath he'd been holding, and the sound was audible between them. "We'll see how it works. Maybe something else will turn up that'll suit you better."

She scanned the house, her eyes measuring the height and breadth of the structure, and he turned, wondering what she saw that held her interest. It was just a house, with four bedrooms up and four rooms down, one a big, bright kitchen, another the formal parlor his father had ceased using once his mother left. The dining room was useless these days—never had been much call for formal dining in this house.

And then there was the study where his father had done his drinking. Gabe seldom went past the wide doorway. A ghost lived there, and a passing glance could almost persuade him that the grizzled man who had sired him still sat behind that desk some nights.

"You want to go inside?" he asked abruptly, the vision in his mind making his voice harsh.

"No, that isn't necessary. I'll just have Mr. Comstock take me back to town so I can arrange to have my things brought here."

"All right. He won't be long."

As if he had a vested interest in her well-being, Bates Comstock went about the moving of Rosemary Gibson. Driving a heavily laden wagon up to the parsonage the next day, he brought his team of dray horses to a halt and ordered the two sturdy young men to work.

Rosemary stood on the porch, watching their approach and motioned to her meager belongings. A satchel and three boxes comprised her personal effects, and they were quickly added to the furniture that filled the rear of the big wagon.

"Hop on up here, ma'am," Bates said cheerfully, offering her his hand. "We'll have you all settled right quick."

The two young men climbed into the back of the wagon and Rosemary caught her breath. This was really happening. Of all the circumstances in which she might have thought to find herself, this was the least likely.

And yet it had come to pass, more rapidly than she'd have thought possible.

From the house, Reverend Worth watched. Then, stepping onto the porch he raised his hand. "Don't forget what I told you, Miss Gibson."

Rosemary nodded, deciding that no answer was required.

"What'd he tell you, ma'am?" Bates asked.

Rosemary tugged at the strings of her bonnet and fussed with her gloves. "I suspect you already know, sir." She looked straight ahead as the wagon made its way down the main street of Edgewood. "He's going to pray for my safety."

Bates slapped the reins across the broad backs of his team. "Nuthin' wrong with that, I guess. But I'll tell you one thing, ma'am. Gabe Tanner won't let any harm come to you out there on his place."

"Well, that's encouraging," she said, turning her head aside as Dex Sawyer stepped onto the broad sidewalk from the swinging doors of the Golden Slipper Saloon.

From the corner of her eye, she caught sight of his uplifted hand, and her chin tilted higher.

"I think the new piano player's taken a shine to you, Miss Gibson," Bates said cheerfully.

"I doubt that."

Bates shrugged and grinned. "You're a good-lookin' woman. I'm just surprised you haven't been snatched up before now. 'Course, with your daddy needin' you in the parsonage, some of the men were kinda put off. Facin' the preacher and askin' for his daughter's hand might'a seemed a bit much to most young fellas.''

''I didn't notice any of them lining up on the porch,'' Rosemary said, holding her handkerchief to her nose and mouth as the dust billowed up from the horse's hooves.

''We sure do need a good rain,'' Bates announced, pulling his own kerchief in place from around his neck. The wind had picked up, and a swirling dust devil scampered across the road in front of them, dying out as it reached the grassy verge.

''The sky was red this morning,'' Rosemary said. ''That usually means wet weather ahead.''

Bates nodded and urged his team into a faster gait.

The furniture was duly deposited in an empty upstairs room, and the two husky young men breathed deeply as they made their last trip into the house with Rosemary's boxes and satchel.

''Where will I be staying?'' she asked Tanner, who had supervised the move from the top of the stairs.

''Either in the dining room or one of the other rooms up here, ma'am,'' he announced, his words not giving a hint as to his druthers.

''The dining room?'' Rosemary stepped to the wide doorway that led into that dimly lit area, the furniture shrouded as if mourning were the order of the day.

''There is no door for privacy,'' she said quietly, her eyes seeking him as he watched her from the head of the stairs.

"Your choice, ma'am. There are two other rooms up here, and both of 'em have doors...and locks."

The two young men dropped her belongings to the floor and looked at each other, one with a sly grin that bespoke his thoughts.

It was too much. To start out with such an attitude was unforgivable. "How about the study, Mr. Tanner?"

His eyes narrowed and his lips tightened. "You were in my father's study?"

Rosemary scented anger. She'd hit a sore spot, sure enough. "I took the liberty of looking into all the rooms, Mr. Tanner. I didn't know that any of them were out of bounds to me."

"It's full of my father's things." His words were abrupt.

"Your father?" If the man was here, Rosemary surely hadn't seen any sign of him.

"I had a father, Miss Gibson. Like yours, he is no longer with us."

She flinched from his words, recognizing his intention to cause pain. The man had a cruel streak. "Then he will no longer be needing the room, will he?" she asked quietly.

Tanner's mouth twisted and his nostrils flared briefly, as his boots clattered against the stairs. Reaching the bottom, he halted before her.

"Now that you mention it, I don't suppose he will." His chest rose and fell as he hesitated.

"If it's too much trouble, I can..." she began, wishing she had not begun this battle.

"You'll have to put up with one of the rooms upstairs, until I can sort his things out. Shouldn't take me more than a couple of evenings.''

She cast a look at the dim interior of the dining room. ''Why not use...''

''I'll take care of it.'' His tone ended the discussion and Rosemary pinched her lips together as Tanner looked at the duet of husky men, jerking his thumb up the stairs in the direction of the bedrooms there. In less than a minute, her belongings had been carried up and deposited in the first bedroom, Tanner directing the move.

Bates spoke from the porch, his voice carrying through the kitchen. ''You boys about ready? Supper's gonna be late, and your ma don't like keepin' food hot, Sonny.''

''All right, Pa,'' the largest of the two young men answered, grinning quickly at Rosemary as he passed.

They were gone. Just that quickly, they climbed aboard the big wagon and Bates disappeared from view.

Rosemary walked into the kitchen, halting in front of the big bureau that held an assortment of crocks and utensils.

From behind her, Tanner's footsteps crossed the floor. ''I'll expect supper on the table in two hours, Miss Gibson. There'll be six hands and myself.''

''Do I get to eat, too?'' She couldn't resist. His words begged for rebuttal, and to her dismay, her sharp tongue offered it without pause.

''You'd better make plenty, or there might not be any left for you, ma'am. You're cookin' for hungry men.''

That was an understatement, Rosemary decided later, watching as the seven men devoured her efforts. In less than ten minutes they had plowed through two platters of beef steak she'd breaded and fried, then placed in the oven to bake. A big bowl of pale gravy was poured without prejudice over their plates, covering potatoes, biscuits and meat, the spoon she had provided even now staining the tablecloth she'd used.

Two quart jars of green beans had disappeared, and the dried apples she'd made up into a dessert, with sugar and cinnamon and sweet dough on top, were but a memory.

It was as if a horde of locusts had descended and devoured every scrap of available food, she decided, watching with wide eyes as one of the men wiped the gravy bowl clean with a piece of biscuit, then stuffed the dripping bite into his mouth.

"Sure is good grub, ma'am," he announced, shoving his chair back from the table as he gained his feet. "Pert near as good as Mama Pearl's."

The glow ignited by his offhand compliment faded as Rosemary registered his final words. "What does Mama Pearl cook for you?" she asked hastily as the men clustered at the doorway, filing out onto the porch.

Tanner sat at the other end of the long table and leaned back in his chair. "You'll get a chance to ask her tomorrow. It's her day to show up here."

He eyed the empty bowls and his grin was unrepentant. "Doesn't look like they left you much, Miss Gibson. You can't say I didn't warn you."

She nodded. "That's true."

Tanner rose from his chair, nodding at her as he pushed it beneath the table's edge. His fingers raised in a half salute as he strolled from the kitchen. "I might as well start on the study, ma'am. There may be part of a loaf of bread left in the pantry if you're hungry."

"I took you at your word, Mr. Tanner," she said beneath her breath.

He paused at the doorway. "Oh? How's that?"

She turned, opening the oven and, with a heavy pot holder, drew forth a plate upon which she had placed a generous portion of the meal she had prepared.

"I got mine first. Just in case." With a flourish, she sat down at the table, spreading a dish towel across her lap. Folding her hands before her, she closed her eyes, her mind searching for words of thanksgiving.

For the first time in her life, she met a blank wall. The presence of the Almighty seemed not to occupy this room, and the simple prayer she was accustomed to speaking before her meals was somehow gone from her mind.

She compromised, closing her eyes, whispering a few words of thanks for her food, and asking only for safe refuge in this place. The image of Gabe Tanner's face flashed before her closed eyes, his lips curved in a smug grin, his gaze flashing a challenge.

Her eyes opened and she gritted her teeth. The man was determined to be an aggravation. With fingers that trembled, she picked up her knife and fork and sawed at a piece of steak, reconsidering her quick petition to the Almighty.

Perhaps, she thought, she should have asked instead for patience.

Chapter Five

The rain began during the night, blowing through the window, sending a fresh breeze into Rosemary's bedroom. She awoke with a start, only a sheet covering her, the residue of a dream fogging her mind. Rising quickly, she moved toward the window, where filmy curtains billowed in the wind, the fabric soaking up the dampness. Beneath her feet raindrops spattered the floor, and she shivered as chills vibrated through her body.

Arms circling like those of a windmill, her legs wobbling beneath her, she slid in an awkward dance across the wet, bare wooden floor. With a loud thump, her left hand banged against the wall, and she cried aloud as she fell, her bottom landing with bruising force. The fabric of her nightgown soaked up the puddle she sat in, and between the throbbing of her hand and the chill of the soggy material wrapped around her, she was beyond discomfort.

Outside the open window the rain increased, and she winced as the lightning flashed, a loud clap of thunder following on its heels, battering her eardrums. It was not, she decided, an auspicious beginning for this, her first night in this house.

"Miss Gibson? Rosemary?" From the doorway, Tanner's booming voice filled the room. He stepped quickly to the bed as if he sought her there, and then moved around it to where she sprawled inelegantly on the floor in front of the open window.

"If you want to take a bath, there's easier ways to go about it, ma'am." He reached past her to close the window, before squatting beside her. Bathed in another flash of light, he leaned toward her, bare chested, his smile raffish. It was too much to bear— this man with his sarcasm, the rain drenching her, a wet curtain draped across her head, and the knowledge that she wore her only clean nightgown.

She drew up her legs, her arms circling her knees, and then lowered her forehead to rest there. If only Tanner would go away she could get up and find something to wear.

And so her words were grumpier than she'd have liked as she responded to his jest. "Why don't you just go back to bed, Mr. Tanner? I'm fine, really."

"Are you?" His voice had changed, become softer, as if he rued the mocking words he'd tossed at her so glibly just moments past. Against her chilled skin, the warmth of his hands on her shoulders penetrated the wet fabric of her nightgown, and she lifted her head to meet his gaze in the dim light. His frown was evident as he brushed the wet curtain from her head.

"You're really cold, aren't you?" With ease, he rose and stepped to the bed, retrieving a quilt and opening it between his outstretched arms. "Let's wrap you in this. You need to get warmed up."

She nodded, attempting to rise. He was there, one hand gripping hers, then moving to encircle her waist as he helped her stand. The quilt was withheld for a moment as he scanned her pale form in the shadows.

"You need to take off that nightgown first, I think. There's no sense in wrapping you up in a dry quilt, when you're soaked through." He glanced at the corner of the room where a four-part screen allowed privacy for washing and use of the chamber pot.

The lightning flashed again and Rosemary's head turned quickly toward the window, her long braid whipping through the air. As if she were caught in the light of a lantern, she covered her eyes with one hand.

"Go strip off that wet thing. I'll hand you the quilt." His breath was warm against her cheek, his voice ragged, as if he fought to force the words between his lips.

"I don't think so, Mr. Tanner. Why don't you just go back to your room, and I'll find some clothes to put on instead."

"Whatever you say." His movement was abrupt as he turned from her, tossing the quilt to the bed as he made his way to the doorway. Before she could phrase a reply, the door closed and he was gone. And yet his presence remained, his lingering scent that reminded her of hay and horses and fresh air. She tested it again, her nostrils flaring.

For the first time in her life, she had been alone in her bedroom with a man. Gabe Tanner had viewed her in her nightgown. In near darkness, to be sure. But even as she considered the idea, another flash of lightning exposed her for a moment, and she was aghast as she looked down at the sight of her feminine form with the garment plastered to every curve and hollow.

Rosemary staggered to the dresser where she'd stored her pitiful supply of underwear and found a pair of drawers and a camisole. The petticoat could wait until morning, she decided. Right now, she needed to be warm and decently covered.

Draping the gown over the back of a chair, she dried off quickly with a towel, then slid into her underwear. With haste she made her way into bed, pulling the quilt up over her shoulder, rolling within its folds.

"Rosemary?" From outside her door, Tanner's voice was firm, as if he would not be denied a reply.

"I'm fine," she said quickly, sitting up in the middle of the bed. "I'm getting warm."

She heard his footsteps moving down the hallway and she flopped back on the pillow. Her left hand hurt like the very dickens. She peered at it, holding it before her eyes, as if she could discern the degree of injury. It felt swollen, and she shook her head at the thought of putting together breakfast with one hand.

Mama Pearl would be here, Tanner had said. At least for one day she would have help.

Outside her bedroom door, Tanner stood listening to her movements inside. The scrape of wood on wood announced the opening of her dresser drawer, and in a few moments the creaking of the bedstead told him she had crawled between the sheets.

"Rosemary?" He wanted to open the door. In the very worst way he wanted to see for himself that she was dry and warm, and his hand hovered over the doorknob.

"I'm fine," she announced. "I'm getting warm."

His eyes closed as he envisioned the glimpses he'd had of her, her nightgown clinging like the paper on the wall. She was slender, but nicely rounded, and he almost groaned aloud as he recalled the curving lines the wet gown had so neatly exposed.

There was no excuse to linger. She'd as much as told him to be on his way. He trudged to his bedroom and rolled across the wide mattress, pulling the quilt over him. He'd pulled some boners in his life, but getting talked into taking Rosemary Gibson on as a cook was about the dumbest thing he'd ever done.

He'd thought her a drab little thing, all done up in her black straw hat and dowdy dress. But once she opened that sassy mouth and flashed those blue eyes in his direction, he'd seen her in a new light.

Damn, if he was anywhere near interested in getting hitched, she'd be a likely candidate.

He'd wager she could hold her own in an argument. That stubborn chin came with a guarantee. The preacher's daughter wasn't nearly the brown wren he'd thought her to be. In fact, the form he'd seen in the flashes of lightning just minutes past held enough clout to keep him awake for a while.

The woman was big, her smile wide, white teeth gleaming as she greeted Rosemary. Mama Pearl turned from the stove with a large spoon in one hand. Over a high forehead, curly black hair peeked from beneath a scarf. Her body was encased in a sparkling white apron that almost totally covered the brightly printed dress beneath it.

"You're Mama Pearl?"

"And who else would I be, child?" The spoon bore bits of sausage and gravy, and the woman turned back to the stove to rest it in the huge skillet she'd been tending. "Heard tell Tanner had himself a new cook. Sure hope you don't mind me takin' over your kitchen this way, but these fellas look for my biscuits and gravy once a week. I hate to disappoint 'em, honey."

"Certainly not," Rosemary said with relief. "I didn't realize it was so late until Mr. Tanner knocked on my door a few minutes ago."

"Well, you might want to throw some plates on the table, honey. Those men are 'bout done with the early chores, and they'll be plowin' in the door any minute now, all hungry and ready for a plateful." Mama Pearl opened the big oven door and pulled out two pans of biscuits. With deft movements they were dumped into a huge crockery bowl and placed in the middle of the long table.

"Better get hoppin', missy," Mama Pearl said, nudging Rosemary into action.

Opening the door of the buffet, Rosemary counted out seven plates and carried them to the table. Her left hand was of more use than she had expected, the fingers loosening as she flexed them carefully. The plates were in place, the silverware nudging them from either side, and heavy, thick china mugs were filled with coffee as the men entered from the porch.

"Good mornin'," Mama Pearl sang out. "Sit down and get your share, boys." Placing a ladle in the bowl of gravy, she settled it at one end of the table and stepped back. Another bowl containing scrambled eggs sat in the warming oven, and accompanying it was a black skillet mounded with fried potatoes.

"Y'all better save some for Tanner," Mama Pearl warned quickly as the sixth man scooped his share from the skillet.

"You ought to take lessons from the new cook," Tanner said from the kitchen doorway. "She puts hers aside first." His grin teased Rosemary and then his gaze washed over her, as if he searched for damage.

"You all right?" he asked, his words spoken softly as he halted before her.

She nodded and met his gaze. "I appreciate your concern, Mr. Tanner. I don't believe I even thanked you for coming to my rescue."

"You better get your grub, boss," Mama Pearl said with a laugh. "These men are puttin' it away like they been starvin' for a week."

"Well, they didn't suffer any at suppertime last night," Tanner said.

Rosemary felt a flush climb her cheeks at the faint praise he doled out so readily, watching as he seated himself at the table. He scraped the remaining eggs and potatoes onto his plate, then broke open two biscuits and covered them with the gravy. He peered into the bowl, fishing for bits of sausage, then glared at the men who watched him.

"You could have saved me a little meat," he said, picking up his fork and plunging it into the pile of potatoes.

"I put some aside. I knew these fellas'd be like vultures on fresh kill come six in the morning." Mama Pearl laughed at Rosemary's look of distaste, scooping two sausage patties from a small plate on the back of the stove. She deposited the meat on Tanner's biscuits and received his grin of thanks.

"You just be sure to always take good care of the boss, Miss Rosemary." The coffeepot made the rounds again, then Mama Pearl lowered it onto the stove with a bang before she set the skillets to soak in the sink.

"Anybody got washing for me to do better have it up here in an hour," she announced to the men. "I'm gonna set up the scrub board, and I don't plan on workin' past noon on your dirty duds. You're just lucky the rain blew over this mornin'. I'll be able to hang 'em out for you."

The men nodded hastily, swallowing their coffee and scooting their chairs from the table as Mama Pearl spoke.

Rosemary's eyes widened in disbelief. That they could have put away all that food in so short a time was beyond her comprehension. Yet they had. By dint of shoveling it in without pause, they had finished their meal in not much more than five minutes.

They had a lot to learn about manners, it seemed. Table talk was an unknown here, as was the common courtesy of thanking the woman who had prepared their meal.

Tanner leaned back in his chair. "Any more coffee in that pot?" He held up his mug and Rosemary hastened to bring the big coffeepot to the table, holding the lid in place with her left hand as she poured.

"Whoa. Let me see that hand." His tone of voice left her no leeway, and she rested the pot on the wooden table as he inspected her injury.

Rosemary looked down at the purpling bruise she had acquired during the night and slipped her hand from his grip, sweeping the evidence behind her back. "I'm fine. It hit the wall when I fell, but it hardly hurts now."

His eyes narrowed as he wiggled his fingers in her direction. "Your hand, Rosemary."

With a sigh, she placed it in his, watching as he turned it one way, then the other. "Why didn't you tell me last night you'd hurt it? I could have gotten a cold cloth, or put some witch hazel on it."

"It felt cold enough already," she said with a laugh, pulling at his grip. Her gaze fluttered to where Mama Pearl walked across the floor, hands full of plates and silverware.

"Don't abuse it today," he said. "You'll have the place to yourself tomorrow. Time enough then to find out how badly you've damaged it."

"Let me see, child." Mama Pearl scooped Rosemary's hand into her own and clucked her tongue. "How'd you manage to do that, girl?"

"She fell getting up to close her window during the night," Tanner supplied.

"And where were you while all this was goin'
on?" Mama Pearl asked, her eyes sharp on Tanner's
face. "You got no business in this girl's bedroom."

"I heard her fall, and I went to see if she was all
right. I didn't do one damn thing to damage her vir-
tue." His face was hard, his jaw tight, as he spoke
his piece and Rosemary shivered, remembering the
sight of herself in the flare of lightning.

Tanner's eyes were dark as he met her gaze, his
mouth taut. "You want to assure Mama Pearl that I
didn't assault you, Miss Gibson?"

"He didn't. Truly, he was a gentleman," she said
quickly, feeling a flush rise to color her cheeks as she
sang his praises.

Mama Pearl nodded, apparently accepting Rosemary's word. "Well, I guess we both know that floor
needs a rug 'longside of the bed. I'll see to it today."

Rosemary tugged her hand free from the other
woman's grip. "It hardly hurts any more. And if
you'll direct me, I wouldn't mind locating a rug to
keep my feet dry."

Tanner nodded. "There's a whole pile of stuff in
the attic. I'll warrant you can find what you need right
at the top of the stairs. Everything's pretty much covered up with sheets, but you can poke around and find
somethin' that'll do."

He'd noticeably relaxed, his frown replaced with a
grin as he left the kitchen. "Good breakfast," he
called back, the screen door slamming behind him.

"Well, we got rid of all the menfolk. Now to set
some water heatin' for the wash," Pearl told Rosemary.

"You do the laundry for all those men?"

"Sure enough. Just scrub 'em out and hang 'em over the line. They come and pick out their own at supper time. I don't iron or fold, exceptin' for Tanner's things. And they just mostly get a lick and a promise."

She poured a cup of coffee for herself and lifted an eyebrow in Rosemary's direction. "You want some? It's pretty strong, but you can add some hot water to thin it down if you like."

Rosemary nodded. "I'll just make it half and half with cream, instead." She sat at the table, the events of the morning overwhelming her, as she considered the job she had taken on.

"Mr. Tanner hired me to be his cook, but I think he'll probably expect me to do more than that, don't you?"

Mama Pearl nodded. "You got that right. There'll be sweepin' and dustin' and the like. And if you want the eggs from the chicken coop, you'd do well to gather 'em up yourself. Otherwise, they're liable to be a hodgepodge of fresh and old, all together. Those men don't do but a halfway job sometimes when it comes to the chores."

"Who milks the cow?" Rosemary asked, pouring a dab more of the rich, yellow cream into her coffee.

"Whoever gets out there first, I reckon. They cart the pail to the milk house and Tanner lets the cream rise till night, then pours it off and brings it in."

"Do you make butter?" Rosemary asked.

"Some weeks I get a chance to. Others, I don't. Tanner does it sometimes himself." Mama Pearl lifted a full boiler of water to the top of the stove. She settled herself at the table and lifted her big mug of coffee, her look pensive as she scrutinized Rosemary.

"It's hard gettin' a woman to work a place like this, and Tanner's had his share up and quit when they found out what a job it is, tendin' to all the cookin' and keepin' up with the house." She eyed Rosemary with curiosity. "Sure you don't want to marry him? You'd be better off thataway. He'd probably get you somebody to help out with the heavy work. You're just a little bit of a thing, Miss Rosemary. I don't see how you can handle this big house."

Mama Pearl sipped at her coffee and leaned back in her chair. Her eyes were so dark a brown they were almost black, Rosemary noted. And her skin was like sleek mahogany, not a wrinkle marring its surface.

"I don't know why I can't," Rosemary said. "It needs catching up with the sweeping and dusting, but I can do that."

"Well, folks are not gonna cotton to you bein' here with Tanner, and no chaperon person to look after you, child."

Rosemary felt a flush stain her cheeks. It seemed to be a perpetual condition this morning. "I don't think I'm in any danger from Mr. Tanner."

"Well, you didn't notice the way he was lookin' at you, then."

Rosemary looked up to meet Mama Pearl's wide grin. "What are you talking about?"

"I think he's taken a shine to you, honey. I heard

that he asked you to marry him last week. Why didn't you snap him up?''

"How did you know that?" Rosemary asked. "I certainly didn't spread the word."

"He was braggin' that he'd saved himself payin' the Bachelor Tax.'' Her dark eyes gleamed. "I was sure enough hopin' you'd take him up on it. That man could use some civilizin'."

"He's treated me quite nicely," Rosemary said quickly. Except for sniffing her neck and plastering himself all over her front, out there in the yard.

"He's a man," Mama Pearl announced. "And puttin' it bluntly, child, he's rarin' to go. He needs himself a woman of his own."

"Well, he took his proposal back the day he hired me."

"I don't think he can do that." Mama Pearl's brow furrowed as she considered the idea.

"That's what I told him. But then, I'd just about decided it wasn't a good idea anyway." Rosemary swallowed the last of her coffee and pushed away from the table, her mind filled with the memory of Tanner's lips touching hers. "I think I'd better find something to cook for dinner," she said hastily, carrying her dishes to the sink.

"There's a ham hangin' in the pantry," Mama Pearl told her, nodding agreement. "Brought it in from the smokehouse last week, but it doesn't look like anybody had a mind to stick it in the oven. You'll want to wash it off good first, maybe cut off some of the fat, and then put it in that big roaster that's on the pantry shelf. It'll take a good five hours or maybe more to bake up nice and tender.''

Rosemary nodded. She'd never cooked a whole ham before, and the prospect was a bit daunting. ''Tanner has a smokehouse?''

''Out beyond the barn. There's slabs of bacon and hams out there, and sausage, too. You won't find anything lackin' in this house. I helped can up the garden last fall, and there's still some of that left. If it wasn't for the Bachelor Tax, Tanner'd still have the last housekeeper he hired. Fella in town asked Lulu Cox to marry him, and she figured it was easier to tend one man than seven.''

Mama Pearl hoisted her bulk from the chair and stretched her back. ''I reckon I'd better set up my washtubs out in the yard. My water's gettin' hot, and I'll bet you there's a porch full of dirty duds.''

''I thought you asked Miss Gibson to marry you,'' Cotton said, peering back over his shoulder at the tall figure of his boss.

''Changed my mind.'' Tanner shot him a glare and reached for a pitchfork. Some good hard work ought to erase the memory of Rosemary with that white nightgown plastered over her in the middle of the night.

''Can you do that?'' Cotton asked dubiously, then jumped to one side as a forkful of manure-caked straw landed on his feet.

''I reckon.'' Another load of smelly stuff sent Cotton into the next stall.

''You want me to do that, boss?'' he asked, looking

over the partition as Tanner sent the contents of the standing stall flying into the aisle.

"Go work those yearlings," Tanner said, the words erupting between grunts of exertion as he completed the stall he'd begun only moments past.

He moved on to the next, eyeing the mess with a jaundiced glare. He'd worked up half a sweat already, and the picture of Rosemary Gibson was still there, her breasts outlined faithfully by the clinging gown, her belly button indented and a hint of... Damn! He should have stayed in the hallway and let her get her fanny off the floor by herself.

He surely didn't need a woman in the room next to his, certainly not one with a sweet shape that invited his hands to measure her waist and...

Cotton trudged down the aisle, looking back at the furiously working man. "I'll send someone in to clean up the aisle, boss."

Tanner's only reply was a muttered curse as he stepped up his pace.

He finished up the row of stalls quickly, reaching the last one as Bootie trundled in the wide doors, shoving a wheelbarrow before him.

"You sure are makin' a mess, boss," he called out cheerfully. His shovel made short work of the residue from the first stall, and he headed for the back of the barn with his load.

Tanner followed him, hanging the pitchfork on a handy nail. His gloves tucked into his back pocket, he wiped his forehead with the red bandanna that he'd tied around his neck first thing upon arising. It came in handy throughout the day, and by nightfall it would be ripe with sweat.

He'd managed to work off the horny mood he'd been nursing all morning. Ever since the middle of the night, to tell the truth, he admitted glumly. Having Rosemary around might not work out as well as he'd thought. Not if he kept getting in a state every time he thought about her.

He'd give a nickel to see that wad of hair all untwisted from the back of her head. The dark braid hung all the way down her back, heavy and thick. His fingers itched to tug at the assortment of pins she'd probably anchored it in place with this morning, and he ground his teeth.

Maybe he should have just married her and had it over with. Then that white nightgown would lay beside *his* bed every night.

Chapter Six

By Saturday, Rosemary felt she'd cooked enough food to supply a small army. Mama Pearl was right. They were a hungry bunch. Every bit of food deposited on the table disappeared within minutes. Somehow it seemed a shame that all her hard work vanished so quickly.

Sunday morning set a slower pace. Tanner had said the men got up a little later, probably because they'd gone to town the night before, she suspected.

By the time she arrived in the kitchen, the sun was shining brightly and Tanner had made coffee. He sat at the kitchen table, a pencil stub in his hand, painstakingly writing figures in a ledger.

His slow glance swept her from top to bottom and she looked down at herself, wondering if she'd left a button undone or her hair unkempt. One hand brushed back a wisp from her forehead, the other surreptitiously counted her buttons in a quick survey.

"Morning, Miss Gibson." His eyes lingered on her hair, and she patted the twisted bun self-consciously.

"Is something wrong? Do I have pins sticking out?"

He shook his head slowly, his grin appearing. "No, ma'am." One hand motioned to the stove. "Coffee's made. Pour yourself a cup, why don't you, Rosie."

"Rosie?" Her voice escalated as she repeated the word. "I don't answer to such an abbreviated version of my name, Mr. Tanner. I've never been one for nicknames, I'm afraid."

"I kinda like it," he answered softly. "It suits you, I think."

Ire rose to envelop her as she considered the man at the table. He was determined to get under her skin this morning, it seemed, with his teasing and that way of examining her, as if he would expose all her flaws to his view.

She turned to the stove, determined that he not sense her exasperation. "I'm late starting breakfast as it is," she said firmly.

"Take your time. The boys'll be another half hour or so. Couple of 'em drank a little too much last night."

At least he hadn't called her *Rosie* again. Her lips firmed, and she looked back at him. "Did you go to town?"

It had been quiet once the horses set off before dark, and she hadn't been quick enough to see how many riders made up the group.

Tanner shook his head. "I don't usually. Didn't want to leave you here alone anyway."

"I'd have been all right. I'm used to being alone."

"Not on a ranch, a mile from the nearest neighbor,

you aren't," he countered. He leaned back in his chair, the pencil stub stuck behind his ear. "I had things to do in the barn most of the evening. Your room was dark when I came in."

Somehow the thought of Gabe Tanner passing her room after dark and entering his own right next door sent a shiver up her spine. "I read my Bible for a while," she told him. "But the candle didn't give a lot of light."

"Take a lantern up next time." He closed his ledger and rose from the table. "I wouldn't want you to miss a minute of your psalm singin'."

"You're not a religious man, are you, Mr. Tanner?"

"Nope."

And that seemed to be that. One more reason why his marriage proposal had been made to the wrong woman.

She turned from the stove, her hands greasy from the bacon she'd arranged in the skillet. A dish towel lay on the sink board and she snatched it up, dampening it in the pan of water there. "I want to talk to you for a minute, please."

He halted in the doorway. "I'm listening, Miss Gibson."

"I need a ride to church this morning. Could I use your buggy?"

"I'll have one of the boys take you," he offered.

"Do any of them go to church?"

His grin curved one side of his mouth. "Not often."

Probably never, she thought privately. Oh well, at

least one of them would this morning. And then she smiled sweetly. "Perhaps you'd like to take me, Mr. Tanner?"

"Not likely."

Rosemary turned back to the stove, long-handled fork in hand as the bacon sizzled in the pan. From the yard a shout caught her ear, another answering from near the barn. The men were up, after all. And she hadn't even begun biscuits.

Seven uncovered heads showed evidence of Rosemary's newest edict. Headwear would not be worn at the table, she'd announced on Saturday morning. Three wide-brimmed hats had been deposited on appropriate hooks near the door as soon as she delivered the rule, and this morning, the headgear had been left in the bunkhouse or barn, she was pleased to note.

Six pair of eyes watched her eagerly as she delivered twin platters heaped with bacon and fried eggs onto the table. A basket of biscuits followed, and a crock of gravy was lifted from her grasp by eager hands.

"Stop!" The seventh pair of eyes surveyed her lazily, and Tanner allowed his lips to form a slow grin as she spoke the single word.

The six ranch hands halted, one with his fork upraised, another half out of his seat, the better to reach the platter of eggs. They eyed her and settled down in their chairs.

"I've watched you gobble your food for five days now," Rosemary said, a slight tremor betraying her firm stance. "I don't know where you were raised, but I'll guarantee more than one of you learned how to say grace before you ate at your mother's table.''

Six pair of eyes focused on her, their owners frowning, and casting long looks at Tanner, who appeared blissfully unaware of the hassle his new cook was creating this morning. ''From now on, you will fold your hands until thanks is given for the food,'' Rosemary said, her words breathless as she made her stand. She knew her cheeks were crimson, and her eyelids fluttered as she clenched her jaw.

''Who's gonna say the words?'' Cotton asked.

''You can take turns if you like,'' she suggested. ''Or I will, if none of you is capable.''

Tanner rose, shoving his chair back, and her eyes flew to his tall, imposing figure. Perhaps she'd gone too far. First inquiring as to his religious leanings, then asking for a ride to church. And now, demanding that grace be spoken over the meals from now on.

She met the dark eyes with trepidation, but tilted her chin. ''Mr. Tanner?''

''This is my house. I'll do the honors.'' His glance at the men on either side of the long table sent a message they understood, and six heads bowed as Gabe Tanner spoke a brief prayer. His chair scraped the floor as he sat down, and then he met Rosemary's gaze once more.

''You find any jam in that pantry, ma'am? I'm partial to strawberry on my biscuits.''

She inhaled deeply. At least he hadn't called her Rosie. It was going to be all right. He'd backed her up. She couldn't have lasted one more meal with these heathens gobbling their food without even being grateful for it.

Her plate was in the warming oven, and she pulled out the empty chair at the end of the table opposite Tanner, sliding onto the seat gracefully.

The men all stopped eating to gape at her. For the first time, their cook was joining them for a meal.

"Now," Rosemary said cheerfully. "I'd like to hear all your names, first and last, please. Tell me where you came from and about your families while we eat a nice meal together."

"I never saw so many dropped jaws in one place in my life," Cotton told his boss. "Tipper pret' near swallowed his tongue when that pretty little gal nodded at him. He's so damn shy around women, we never even been able to get him upstairs at the Golden Slipper, no matter how drunk he gets."

"He'll find his way up those stairs when he's good and ready," Tanner said harshly. "Leave him be."

"Well, I figured he'd be the best one to take Miss Rosemary to town this morning," Cotton said with a nod. "She's pretty safe with him, anyway."

"She'd better be safe with every one of you," Tanner warned bluntly. "Pass the word. If anybody says so much as a word out of line, I'll beat the livin' daylights out of him. And that's a fact."

"She sure looks different than she did the first day she got here, don't she?" Cotton asked. "She quit wearin' that ugly black dress anyway. Seems to me that awful hat oughta be burned though."

"If she'd left it here, I'd have considered it," Tanner told him. "But she wore it to church. I think it's the only one she has."

Rosemary had apparently decided that her mourning clothes weren't suitable for the heat of the kitchen. She must have dug deep in that valise of hers and found other dresses to wear. Although far from stylish, they were at least lighter in color and fabric, and halfway fitted to her narrow waist, he'd noticed.

He'd watched the buggy leave the yard, Tipper holding the reins, his smile eager as he spoke to his passenger.

"I can drive the buggy," she'd assured Tanner, emerging from the house. "I truly don't need an escort, Mr. Tanner."

"I say you do," he'd said firmly, offering his hand to help her atop the seat.

She'd mumbled something he ignored as he stepped back to watch her arrange her skirts, then fold her hands in her lap. That abominable black straw hat perched squarely on her head, and he shook his head at the sight.

Now, he wished for just a moment that he'd taken her himself. That he'd made conversation with her during the ride to town, escorted her into the church where a pew bore the Tanner name on a small brass plate.

He'd ignored the church and the pew since the day his father died. The old man had been a hypocrite of the very worst sort, sitting beneath the roof of that sacred place on Sunday and living like a demon the rest of the week.

Damn. He hadn't thought of Walt Tanner in the

better part of a week. Not since the evening of the day Rosemary Gibson had driven down the lane and announced that she was ready to be his cook, rather than his bride.

The Reverend Worth clasped Rosemary's hand in his and shook it with vigor. "I'm so happy to see you in church, Miss Gibson. And who is this fine young man?"

Beside her, Tipper Henderson removed the hat he'd just deposited on his head. "I'm one of the hands at Gabe Tanner's place, sir."

"Miss Gibson? This is a permanent situation?" James Worth asked with a frown marring the fine line of his forehead.

"I'm the cook there."

"She does pret' near everything, but the washing," Tipper volunteered. "Mama Pearl comes on Wednesdays and does that and helps out in the kitchen. Course, now that Miss Rosemary's there, we don't hardly need no one else."

"Do you have a proper chaperon?" the preacher asked.

Rosemary had known it was coming. As sure as the sun rose in the east, it was guaranteed that someone would bring up her status as the only woman on the ranch.

"I'm quite safe, sir," she said primly. "I am treated like a lady, and Mr. Tanner has been more than kind to me."

She turned to the buggy, Tipper hot on her heels, his hand eager to assist her to the seat. The eyes of half the population of Edgewood bore into her back. Some of them were probably wondering what she did at the ranch. The rest were no doubt speculating how long it would be before she married Gabe Tanner.

The story of his proposal was all over town, according to Pip. Once Bates Comstock told his wife, Bernice had made it her bounden duty to spread the word.

This morning folks had discovered that Rosemary was the cook, not a prospective bride, and she sighed as she recognized that tongues would surely wag in great style.

"Let's go, Tipper," she said, her spine erect, her hat perched squarely on her head, and her best gloves in place.

Reins in hand, he nodded, lifting a hand to wave at the congregation as he urged the mare into motion. "Those folks think well of you, Miss Rosemary," he offered. "I'm sure enough surprised you haven't been snatched up by one of the fellas in town before this."

"Having a minister for your father discourages young men who might think about courting," she said. "And I'm really beyond the age of marriage anyway. Most men want a younger woman."

Tipper was silent for a moment, then slanted a sidelong glance at her. "I don't see that you're too old, ma'am. I suspect the boss doesn't, either. I mean he asked you to marry him and all."

"Well, he didn't squawk when I offered to be his cook instead," Rosemary answered.

Tipper looked back over his shoulder to where the church was fading into the distance. "You suppose that preacher will give you a hard time about living on the ranch, without a chaperon?''

''I think he has better things to worry about.''

Tipper looked doubtful.

It did Rosemary's heart good to see the look on Mama Pearl's face when the men entered the kitchen on Wednesday morning. Clean and bareheaded, they assembled around the table and waited quietly as the food was put before them.

Mama Pearl stepped back, anticipating the usual rush, only to watch, openmouthed, as Tanner bowed his head and spoke several words of grace.

''What's this?'' she whispered against Rosemary's ear as she snatched up the coffee pot from the stove.

''Coffee?'' Rosemary's chuckle was low as she responded, widening her eyes innocently.

Mama Pearl's snort spoke volumes as she approached the table, pouring coffee with a steady hand.

''Will you join us for breakfast?'' Rosemary asked her, drawing two plates from the warming oven.

Her response was a penetrating stare. *Not enough that these men were behaving like a bunch of boys at Sunday school,* her expression seemed to say. *Now we're going to eat with them?*

Rosemary nodded at Tipper, who obligingly made room on the long bench for one more, then joined him there, leaving the big chair at the end of the table for the other woman.

Tanner took advantage of the silence to begin issuing orders for the day, pointing his fork at one man, then another as he assigned duties.

"I told Miss Rosemary I'd carry in the bushels of tomatoes first, boss," Tipper said glibly. "They're pretty heavy, and she needs all the canning jars down from the pantry."

"Mama Pearl will help me," Rosemary interjected, noting Tanner's frown. "We can manage."

"I'll give you a hand." Tanner's voice left no room to maneuver, and Tipper nodded, his disappointment visible.

"If you're in the mood to be totin' stuff, you can carry out the boiler, Tanner. The wash water's almost hot. Thought I'd get an early start." Mama Pearl made her announcement between bites, her eyes twinkling as she looked from Tanner to Rosemary and back.

"Tipper can do that," Tanner allowed, nodding at Pearl, his gaze acknowledging her gibe.

Rosemary ate in silence, not initiating a conversation this morning. Wednesday was a busy day, with Mama Pearl in and out of the kitchen, and now it seemed Tanner would be helping her ready the tomatoes for canning. The thought of sharing the kitchen with him made the walls shrink.

Within a half hour Mama Pearl's low melodic voice formed a background to the sounds within the house. She scrubbed with long motions, her sleeves rolled above her elbows, her strong arms muscular. She wrung out the heavy trousers with so little effort, Rosemary thought, almost envious of the strength the woman possessed.

"Where do you want these jars?" Tanner asked from behind her, his arms filled with a covered box.

"Here," Rosemary answered, motioning at the sink. "I have to scrub all of them first, before I scald them in the big kettle."

"You know what you're doin'?" he asked dubiously. "I'll warrant Mama Pearl would come an extra day to help with this if you want her to."

Rosemary's eyebrow rose, as if she had been insulted. "I'm quite capable, Tanner. I've run the parsonage for several years, and that included all the canning that was done."

"We're talkin' about three bushels of tomatoes, honey," he said with a grin. "And more of them by the day after tomorrow."

"I'll manage." Rosemary lifted the teakettle of hot water from the stove and poured it into the dishpan. "I'm strong and I'm healthy, and I took this job in good faith."

"Nobody's askin' you to kill yourself, Rosie. If you need help, just call out and you'll have some."

"If you want to be helpful, carry out that big bucket of hot water to the yard and see where Mama Pearl wants it, then fill it back up at the pump and put it on the stove."

"I feel like the chore boy here," Tanner muttered.

"You offered," she reminded him.

He walked across the kitchen to where she sorted out jars from the box, placing the quart-size ones in the soapy water.

"And you're pretty sassy," he said in her ear.

She spun to face him. "I'm your cook, Tanner. We decided I'd make a better employee than a wife, remember?"

He shook his head. "No, I don't, to tell the truth. I still haven't figured out the whys and wherefores."

"Changed your mind?" she asked breathlessly.

He was too close, his eyes were too knowing as they scanned her, as if he saw something in her that was better not revealed to his gaze. Her heart missed a beat and fluttered as it caught up to its usual rhythm. Pressing her lips together, she dared a glance at his face.

His jaw was taut, his nostrils flaring just a bit, as if he caught a scent in the air. And his eyes, those dark orbs that seemed to seek out her thoughts, were fastened on her face.

"No, I haven't changed my mind, honey," he whispered. "I want you to know what you're gettin' before I marry you."

"That's not part of our bargain," she countered.

"I'm not sure what kind of a bargain we struck," Tanner said softly. "But I know I like what you've done to my house. I like knowin' you're here every night when I go to bed and when I hear you movin' around in your bedroom every morning."

He bent closer to her as she opened her mouth to speak, and touched the soft flesh with his index finger.

"Tanner?" Her mouth trembled as his finger brushed across the small bow of her upper lip.

"Yeah." His head dipped lower and his fingertip was replaced by the brush of his mouth, his lips softening as they made contact with hers.

She'd forgotten the potency of his kiss, the power of his touch. That one fingertip that touched her chin, and those two lips that made her think of dark and forbidden things.

Rosemary sagged where she stood. Her fingers clenched tightly into small fists and she closed her eyes. She should draw back, perhaps scold him roundly for taking advantage of her. Maybe even let him have the side of her tongue and offer an indignant protest. That's what she should do, she thought, aware only of the man who held her immobile with just the pressure of his mouth against hers.

And then Tanner's hands touched her waistline, his fingertips meeting in the center of her back. He drew her closer, until her breasts were pressed indecently against his broad chest, until her feet were stumbling to find purchase between his boots.

Rosemary whimpered, a soft sound that was caught by the parting of his lips, and heard his answering chuckle as if he interpreted the wordless protest, and considered it but naught.

His mouth eased from hers. If he'd meant to soothe her with tenderness, he'd missed the boat. And yet it was almost a comforting gesture, perhaps asking her pardon, she thought hopefully.

"I shouldn't have come here," she blurted out. "I didn't bargain for this."

His laugh was low, and she felt the vibration beneath her hands. "You came here to accept my marriage proposal, Rosie. Didn't you think there'd be kissin' involved?"

"I changed my mind almost as soon as I got here," she said breathlessly.

"Did you? Why?"

"I knew I couldn't do it. I really meant to, but then…"

"I doubt you got a better offer," he said glibly.

She shook her head. "No, I didn't. But…"

"But, what?" he prompted.

She shook her head. "Nothing. I'm happy to be your cook, Tanner. I just don't want you kissing me. It's not proper. I have a reputation to uphold."

"Honey, your reputation is worth diddly unless I miss my guess. Tipper said the preacher called you on the issue."

Her hands trembled as she eased from his hold, and he stepped back, awaiting her reply. She reached for another jar and placed it in the soapy water.

"I knew what I was getting into, Tanner. I'll be just fine."

He was dismissed. There was no other way to put it, and he shrugged, ambling toward the door, snatching his hat off a nail as he went.

Rosemary waited until the screen door slammed, then turned to look over her shoulder at the tall man who stepped down from the porch. He was more than she'd bargained for, more than she'd envisioned when she considered his proposal on the buggy ride to this place.

She watched as he heeded a call from Mama Pearl, approaching her as she bent over the scrub board. The older woman looked up at him and spoke a few words. Rosemary slipped to stand beside the door, her curiosity aroused. But to no avail.

Only the deep rumble of Tanner's voice reached her, the terse sound of his reply muffled.

"I'm tellin' you straight, Tanner." Mama Pearl's warning words vibrated in the still air, and Rosemary drew in a breath.

Whatever they were talking about, they were apparently on opposite sides of the issue.

And she'd be willing to bet a week's wages that Rosemary Gibson was the topic under discussion.

Chapter Seven

"Ma'am?" Cotton spun from the horse he was tending. His eyes widened as he considered the woman who'd entered the fringes of his domain, standing in the sunshine just outside the wide barn door. "You lost, Miss Rosemary?"

She waved a hand, dismissing his question as foolish. "I know perfectly well where I am, Mr. Cotton."

"Just Cotton, if you don't mind," he muttered as he slid his hands into the front pockets of his denim trousers. "You lookin' for the boss?"

She stepped inside, still wrapped in the golden rays of sunshine that penetrated several feet inside the barn, her shadow preceding her. "No, I'm just looking," she said, tilting her head back as she gazed upward.

"Nothin' up there but a haymow," Cotton told her.

She scanned the long aisle that ran the length of the barn, one side divided into stalls, some narrow and open-ended, several square, with sturdy doors attached. An inquisitive nose poked over the nearest gate, and a soft nicker met Rosemary's ear.

"My, what a beauty," she murmured, her gaze caught by the gentle eyes of the animal. Her hand lifted as if she would reach to touch the elegant head; then, as though she thought better of it, she tucked her fingers inside the pocket of her apron.

Rosemary was silent, intent on her surroundings, peering beyond the stalls to where an open doorway led to the corral, and then returned her survey to the opposite wall.

Tools hung in place, pitchforks and shovels, between a series of shelves laden with scattered implements she did not recognize. Open doorways led off into other rooms and she caught a glimpse of a saddle balanced on a sawhorse, one stirrup flung upward.

"I just wanted to see—" Rosemary looked around again and shrugged her shoulders. "I guess I was curious, really. I've been here over two weeks, and I needed to see something other than the inside of the house and the chicken coop. I've done my share of gathering eggs, but I've not spent much time in a barn before."

"Where have you been all your life?"

"I was raised in a parsonage, Cotton. In town. We had chickens in the backyard, but our milk came from a neighbor."

"Well, let me give you a grand tour," he said, grinning widely. "Ain't nobody around here knows more about barns than Cotton Weatherby."

"Unless it's Gabe Tanner." A long shadow joined

Rosemary's in the doorway as Tanner stepped across the threshold.

From the shaded aisle, Cotton tossed his boss a look of chagrin. "Shoot, here I thought I was gonna get a chance to do the honors."

"You've got enough to do without playing escort to Miss Rosemary," Tanner told him, his eyes taking a possessive survey of the woman beside him. "I'll show her around."

"I don't want to take anyone from their work," she said quickly, the breath leaving her body, and her heart stuttering in her chest. It was downright frustrating, the way Gabe Tanner could affect her with no effort at all on his part. She opened her mouth, her breath catching in her throat, and one hand crept up to fist against her left breast.

"You all right, Rosie?" He leaned toward her, his brow lowering as he bent to peer directly into her face.

"Yes," she managed to whisper. "Of course. I just swallowed wrong."

He straightened, shooting her another look, one that doubted her words. "Well, we'll take it slow. Maybe it's all the hay up top that's givin' you trouble. We had one fella I hired on who couldn't be in the barn for five minutes at a time. Said the haymow had a bad effect on him. Never did figure out how he planned to work on a ranch."

Rosemary sniffed the air, relieved that her heart had ceased its rapid pumping, slowing to its usual pace. "No, I don't think the hay will give me a problem. I like the smell." She looked up at Tanner. "Did you keep him around? The man who couldn't stand the hay?''

He laughed. ''For about as long as it took him to pack his gear and head out. Last I heard he was workin' for the sheriff.''

Rosemary smiled, moving to stand before the large stall where the inquisitive horse still bobbed its head. One hand lifted tentatively and her fingers touched the velvet nose.

With a snort, the creature tossed its head, mane flying wildly. Rosemary stepped back abruptly, only to find Tanner directly behind her, his body a solid wall.

She muffled a shriek, shivering from the contact. He was stock-still, and as she turned her head, her cheek brushed against dark fabric. The scent of Mama Pearl's lye soap mixed with another aroma, that of sunshine and leather. She inhaled the mix, her nose nearly touching his shirt.

His fingers grasped her shoulders. ''You all right?'' Her senses fairly reeling, she stiffened, moving from the shelter of his big body, and then was left yearning for the warmth he exuded.

''I'm fine,'' she replied. ''Just startled, I think.'' Her hand extended again to the horse's nose. A soft whinny greeted her touch, and Rosemary's palm moved to the side of the creature's face, where her fingers lingered, widespread against the dark, smooth surface.

''She's so silky,'' she whispered.

Behind her, Tanner bent his head, his mouth barely

brushing her ear, emphasizing each word he spoke. "She's a he."

Amusement laced his whisper, and Rosemary found a foolish smile curving her lips. There was gentleness in Tanner today, at least in her direction. He'd been a bit abrupt with Cotton she remembered, but now his touch, his words, his whole demeanor were that of a man toward a woman he cares about.

Not that she had any illusions about Tanner's feelings in her direction. He had scented her out more than once, like a creature of the wild seeking its prey, and that alone had made her wary. This, today, had served to warn her that his approach now might be a direct opposite to that of other days and times, but the end result would be what Tanner willed.

Rosemary leaned forward as the horse allowed her touch, and bent to peer within the box stall. "He's awfully big, isn't he?" She stood on tiptoe, feeling brave with Tanner at her back, her fingers untangling the heavy mane as she inhaled the smell of horse and hay.

"He must have clean bedding. It smells fresh."

"You'd know if it wasn't," Tanner said with a chuckle, stepping to stand beside her. His long arm eased into place at her waist; she was aware of the heat of his palm as it rested there, fingers outspread and reaching, as if he sought the texture of her skin beneath the layers of clothing.

Skin that burned beneath that exquisite pressure, almost as though each fingertip sought a spot upon which to leave a brand, that would surely appear tomorrow as a reminder of her lingering here with him.

"Yes, Miss Gibson?" A chuckle rumbled in his chest and she felt its vibration against her shoulder, there where his powerful body touched her.

"I ask you not to mock me, sir. I beg you to take your hands from me."

"So sweetly you put me in my place," he murmured.

She darted a look at him, turning her head to catch a glimpse of his face as his laughter erupted. He stepped back, his hand leaving the curve of her waist, instead tucking itself into the taut crease of his pocket, as though he must contain it.

She turned, allowing the stall door to support her, since her lower limbs seemed incapable of doing so with any degree of stability. The horse's muzzle nudged at her shoulder, and she scented again the clean animal smell of him.

"I believe you've lost your fear of my stud," Tanner said, his eyes twinkling with some barely contained emotion.

"Are you laughing at me, sir?"

"No, only enjoying your blushes, Rosie. I'm not familiar with women who find themselves flustered when I appear." His eyes flickered to the proud head of his stallion, then back to meet hers. "It does seem you've lost your fear of my horse. The lesser of two evils?"

"I don't fear you, Mr. Tanner. You are my employer. I owe you respect, but unless you cease touching me, I will be hard-pressed to give you your due."

"You mean you don't want me kissin' you, honey?"

The lazy drawl mocked her firm declaration and she tilted her chin, her jaw firming. "You know exactly what I mean, sir."

From the yard beyond the wide doors, voices meshed with her words, and Tanner's gaze left her, his attention caught by the interruption.

"Where's that Tanner?" Mama Pearl's distinctive accents reached where they stood, and Tanner strode quickly to the doorway.

"What brings you here?" he asked as he made his way toward her.

Her posture was regal as she perched atop the dilapidated wagon that bore her. A turban wound tightly around her head, a brilliant purple-and-orange print that only served to emphasize the proud lines of her face. She looked down at him, narrowed eyes intent on his.

"I come to stay." There was no hesitation in her announcement, only a firm declaration of intent.

"You come to stay," he repeated, his brow furrowing, his mouth pursing over the words.

Mama Pearl nodded emphatically. "My girl found herself a man, and there ain't no room in that house for a mama hangin' around. I figure you got room here for me to park my carcass, and plenty of reason for havin' me in your house, Gabe Tanner. You can just slip me some spendin' money once in a while and we'll call it good."

He was silent, digesting her words, examining the stoic expression she wore. And then he nodded, a barely noticeable incline of his head, but one she accepted with a like motion of the brilliant turban.

"I'll be taking my belongings inside." She lifted the reins and hesitated, glancing toward the house, then back at the man who watched her. "Where's that young'un?"

"You mean Miss Gibson?" Tanner asked smoothly. He tilted his head to one side, his voice carrying easily to where Rosemary waited, inside the barn. "Come on out, young'un."

Mama Pearl watched in silence as Rosemary stepped from the shadowed interior, blinking as the brilliant sunlight narrowed her eyes.

"Climb up here, girl. I'll give you a lift back to the house, and then you can help me tote my parcels inside."

Rosemary stepped to the wagon, holding her skirt to the side as she reached with the other hand for a grip on the wooden seat. Before her foot could seek purchase, two big hands clasped her waist and she was lifted into the air and placed beside Mama Pearl. Below her, Tanner grinned as she turned a startled look in his direction.

"Guess you got your orders, ma'am," he announced.

The wagon lumbered toward the back door of his house and he watched it go. The two women spoke, their heads tilting together, and he wondered for a moment at the way in which women formed alliances so easily.

He'd missed such a bond in his life, had never really sought the friendship of another man. Mentally he dismissed the everyday words he exchanged with Cotton and the men who helped him run his ranch.

That sort of give-and-take was easy to come by. He found it simple to speak with the men in town, the barkeep, even one or another of Laura Lee's girls, who occasionally sidled up to him in hopes of adding him to their clientele. With them he could laugh and talk of everyday things with ease, even as he resisted their charms.

But deep inside, he felt a greater need, mostly in the long hours of darkness. He'd almost found such a bond with the Widow Courtland. There'd been times she'd drawn from him emotions he'd hidden, even from himself. Fears he'd conquered over the years, memories he'd tucked away lest they weaken him.

She'd been a good friend. Not a woman to arouse any but the most natural of his urges, and yet he'd missed her, once she'd sought security in the proposal of Hale Carpenter.

He watched as Rosemary slid easily from the wagon seat, noted with acute interest as her rising hemline exposed neat ankles and just a hint of rounded calves. Mama Pearl maneuvered the descent more slowly, and then the two women gathered bundles from the wagon bed, carrying them to the porch and into the house.

Tanner heard a peal of laughter from the older woman, caught her eye as she turned in the doorway to cast him a glance that spoke of warning, and noted that her good humor was not aimed in his direction.

He shrugged. He wouldn't argue with her. She probably knew him inside and out, if the truth be known. At least she'd had a long-term acquaintance with the leanings of the male species. That her presence would be a deterrent to his pursuit of Rosemary Gibson was a fact.

And the truth was that Rosemary was becoming more and more of a temptation with each day she resided in his home, with each night she slept just beyond his bedroom wall. Who would have thought that the prim-and-proper preacher's daughter held such a wealth of untapped passion within her small, rounded body?

For he'd felt it, felt the humming tension that sang between them, had sensed the unawakened yearnings she fought to subdue each time he touched her. And so, as if he could not resist the unwrapping of her latent layers of feminine need, he found himself hovering like a bee who has found a particularly sweet source of nectar and must sate himself in its depths.

Tanner shook his head, aware that he stared in rapt attention at an empty porch and a closed screen door. One hand tilted his hat lower over his eyes as he turned back to the barn, empty now, save for the big stallion that watched him over the door of his box stall.

Tanner strolled toward the animal, and his fingers tangled in the creature's forelock. He tugged gently, then allowed his hand to brush the same pathway as had Rosemary's only moments before. The stud nudged him, nose snuffling against his shirtfront, and Tanner laughed aloud.

"Got a problem, old fella?" He scratched beneath the stallion's jaw, and his words were soft, spoken almost in a caressing tone. "I reckon that makes two of us."

"Where will you stay?" Rosemary asked, her hands busily molding freshly chopped beef for a meat loaf. She'd added two large onions, blinking teary eyes as she turned the handle on the gadget that ground up the meat. Next, she'd torn up a whole loaf of bread left from the last baking day plus a double handful of oatmeal to add to the mixture. Two quarts of stewed tomatoes, and half a dozen eggs had filled the largest mixing bowl almost to the brim until she was hard put to keep the ingredients within their boundaries.

Mama Pearl peeled potatoes with slashing movements of her knife, barely watching what she did. "Right acrost the hall from your room, honey." She put aside the potato she held, glancing to inspect it briefly, and took another in hand.

"I been watchin' how Tanner looks at you, girl. He's got urges like any man, and even if he thinks he's a gentleman from the word go, he's not above seein' just how far he can push you." She looked up at Rosemary and grinned.

"I saw how he came outta that barn, like he'd like to throttle whoever was causin' an interruption to what was goin' on out there."

"Nothing was going on," Rosemary said emphatically, squeezing the mixture between her fingers. It was about ready for the pan and she gave the loaf that was forming within her grasp a final pat. "We were talking, and I was looking at his horse."

Mama Pearl nodded knowingly. "I'll bet he was lookin' at more than that big stallion of his. I know a man set on stealin' more than a kiss from a woman."

Rosemary slid the mixing bowl toward the big baking pan, then turned out the meat loaf with a practiced move. It settled squarely in the center of the pan, and she gave it a satisfied pat. "He's my employer, and I've reminded him of that fact."

"Well, I'm here to see that he remembers it."

Mama Pearl snatched up another potato and glanced out the window to where the sun's rays cast a short shadow from the house against the ground. "We better be gettin' that meat in the oven. Those men'll be headin' this way before it gets done if we're not careful."

Rosemary opened the big oven door and slid the meat inside, then closed the door quickly. She lifted a stove lid on top of the range and selected two pieces of wood, adding them to the fire that glowed within. "I'll get the beans I cleaned yesterday. There's time for them to cook."

"Go get a piece of side pork to flavor 'em up good," Mama Pearl said. She tightened her lips as she considered the younger woman. "Here I am, tellin' you how to cook, and you been doin' all right on your own."

Rosemary halted halfway to the pantry. "I still have to remind myself how many men come storming through that door three times a day. This is a far cry from fixing meals for my father."

"Well, I'm here now. And I'll warrant that between us, we can keep these hungry men fed and get this house redd up like it oughta be.''

Rosemary cast her a grateful look. "It's more work than I thought, and I'll admit I've fallen behind. But then, it's just bedrooms I have to keep up. Nobody has time to lollygag around in the parlor anyway. We don't even use the dining room, and Tanner's been trying to set his father's office to rights most every evening after supper.''

"Well, we'll find you some time to lollygag," Mama Pearl promised. "You've been workin' yourself to a frazzle, now that Tanner's left it all up to you.''

"I don't mind. I like it here," Rosemary said, looking around the cheerful kitchen. "It's beginning to feel like home.''

Mama Pearl's head nodded, and her mouth curved in a smile, as if she were well pleased with the turn of events.

"...coffee, flour and a pail of lard. You got all that written down, girl?'' From the pantry, Mama Pearl's voice boomed the words, and Rosemary's pencil scribbled rapidly on her scrap of paper.

"I think I'll splurge on a box of tea," she murmured, adding that item to her list. Working in tandem was becoming a habit after only a week of having Mama Pearl living in. Tea time was becoming a ritual, one she savored.

"I ought to have you to knock on the back door of the saloon and get me a new supply for my...''

Mama Pearl's musing words were interrupted by Tanner's booming voice.

"You're not sendin' the preacher's daughter to the Golden Slipper. She probably couldn't find the back door anyway. You need a nip once in a while, old Cotton's got a stash hid away."

Rosemary stiffened, remembering all too well her sole venture into the back room of the saloon. The weeks spent on Gabe Tanner's ranch had removed her far from those few days of fearful existence. "I suspect I could find most any door in town if I had to," she said quietly. "It's just that I…"

"Never you mind, girl," Mama Pearl said quickly. "I know a whiskey man. I just like a little nip once in a while. Keeps my rheumatiz from actin' up."

"You going to town, Rosemary?" Tanner wanted to know.

She nodded. "I asked Tipper to get the buggy ready for me."

"I'll take you."

She shook her head, meeting his gaze forthrightly. "I don't want you carting me around town, Tanner. It makes folks think we're together, like a couple. I heard remarks at church again on Sunday as it is."

Tanner stepped from the doorway and halted beside her chair. The dratted man made her feel like a silly goose, all shaky inside, and her fingers trembled, allowing her pencil to slip from her grasp. It rolled to the table's edge and Tanner's hand snatched it as it fell.

He unrolled her clenched fist and placed the pencil in her palm, curling her fingers around it to hold it in place. His hand was warm, his fingers firm and agile, and she watched the movement of their hands, felt the abrasion of his callused palm against her flesh.

"Your fingers are cold, Rosie," he murmured, bending to whisper against her ear. "You scared of me?"

Her head snapped up, eyes wide as she denied his suggestion. "Certainly not! I'm not cold. You're just..."

His eyes narrowed and his lips curved. "Yeah, I am."

"You 'am' what, Tanner?" Mama Pearl asked sharply, arms akimbo as she stood before the pantry door.

"Am sendin' my hired help to town," Tanner said smoothly, patting Rosemary's hand a final time.

From the back porch, Tipper's voice rang out. "Got the buggy all set, Miss Rosemary. It's tied to the rail. Sure you don't need somebody to go along and help?" His words were wistful as he peered through the screen.

"She turned me down, boy. What makes you think she'll take you?" Tanner's query was softly spoken, but it gained the expected result. Tipper backed from the door, stumbling from the porch and muttering beneath his breath.

"You're mean to that boy," Rosemary said quietly.

"That *boy* has eyes for you," he told her.

Mama Pearl's snort of laughter rang out as she slid a bucket of water onto the surface of the stove. "Ain't you the one to talk!"

Rosemary felt squeezed between two adversaries as

Tanner shot a forbidding look at the other woman. His dark eyes held hidden messages she sometimes feared to decipher, but this morning he made no secret of his meaning.

Mama Pearl had stepped on his toes.

A firm hand gripped her elbow, and Rosemary was assisted from her chair. "Come on. I'll walk you out."

With a final glance at Mama Pearl, she headed for the door. It opened before her, Tanner's hand holding it ajar, and she hurried across the porch, aware of the pressure he exerted on her arm.

"You can let go of me," she said sharply. "I know how—"

"I'm very aware of what you know and what you can do, Rosemary." His steps were long and she scampered to keep up. "If I thought it was important for me to go along with you this morning, the townsfolk and their opinions couldn't keep me home. They can consider us a couple if they want to. That's fine with me." He lifted her to the buggy seat, her skirts flying, then handed her the reins.

"Being a couple involves marriage, Tanner," she said, gripping the leather straps tightly, unwilling to meet his gaze.

"I know exactly what it means. I've changed my mind about that, Rosemary. I know you turned me down, and that was all right with me, then. But, things are different now."

"Different?" She focused on the mare in front of her.

"You know what I'm talkin' about. I don't know

how many more nights I can hear you movin' around in the next room and not want to be in there with you, and see you in that white nightgown of yours again.''

Rosemary closed her eyes, clenching her fists abruptly. The mare backed up a step and the buggy jolted. Tanner reached to cover her hands with one of his. ''Undo those fists, honey. You know I'm not fool enough to do such a thing. Not with your watchdog in there.'' His head nodded toward the house.

Her fists clenched even tighter, and his wide palm curved to clasp them in its grip. A small embrace, it brought to life a mixture of urges with which she struggled to cope. The need to be held raged uppermost, and yet not by just any person. Only Tanner. And another, a dreadful compulsion to explore the lure of this masculine being, enveloped her with frightful yearnings.

''I like being your cook and keeping up your house, Tanner,'' she said, aware of the blush that colored her cheeks, the breathless sound of her voice. So easily, he confused her. So thoroughly, he managed to make her feel witless and unsure.

Her words were so softly spoken, they were but a whisper as she denied the longing of her heart. ''I don't know that I really want to be married.''

His big hand scooped behind her head, crushing the back of her black straw hat. With a force she could not deny, he pulled her toward him, his mouth covering hers in a kiss that held but a vestige of tenderness. It was hot and brief, a claiming gesture that only in the final swift second of its existence allowed their lips to soften and brush gently.

Tanner's grip softened and he released her, stepping back. His narrowed gaze was all encompassing as he nodded his head. "We'll see."

Chapter Eight

Pip's embrace was welcome, her arms strong as she clutched Rosemary. "I'm so glad to see you," she whispered.

Rosemary leaned back, her eyes searching Pip's face. Tears hovered, Pip's eyes glittering with their presence, and her smile was wistful. "You have no idea how much I've missed having you drop by most every day."

"I was here just…" Rosemary halted, her mind spinning back to the last trip she'd made to town. "Well, now that I think about it, it's been over two weeks, hasn't it?"

"Yes, it has. And I didn't get to church the past two Sundays, what with spelling Ma in the sickroom. My little brothers both had the mumps, one at a time, and my pa right in the midst of them. He was sicker than anybody ever ought to be, and we all had to pitch in. It was a rest to come back to the store on Monday morning."

"I hadn't even heard," Rosemary said ruefully,

"But I'm here now." Truth to tell, she'd scooted out of church early on Sunday, lest she find herself within a clutch of women, all bent on advising her.

Rosemary dug into her pocket, drawing forth three scraps of paper, each covered with her bold writing. "I've got things written down all over, enough to choke a horse." She frowned, holding one piece sideways, then turning it over.

"I'm not sure where to begin. Every time I thought of something we needed, I just scratched it on my list, and then I ran out of room and found another piece of paper to write on. By the time I got finished, I'd scribbled on both sides and all along the edges."

Pip grinned, scooping the assortment from Rosemary's hand. "I learned how to read your writing a long time ago. If you feel like jabbering at me, go ahead. I'll just gather up as I go along."

Rosemary pulled a keg close to the counter, glancing around to see who might be within listening distance. She leaned forward a bit and watched as Pip delivered a pail of lard and two boxes of tea to the counter.

"I don't hear you talkin'. And I'll just bet you've got a tale to tell." Pip leaned on the lard pail, her eyes twinkling. "What's it like, living with Tanner?"

Rosemary frowned and then the memory of Tanner's kiss assaulted her mind. "It's downright confusing is what it is."

Pip leaned closer. "Confusing?"

"He makes me feel things, and he watches me sometimes."

''What things do you feel?'' Pip's eyes were round, shiny with anticipation.

Rosemary took inventory of the list. ''Afraid...''

Pip gasped. ''Surely not!''

''Oh, not of him. Never that.'' Except for when he'd trapped her between his long, hard body and the wagon wheel that first day, she thought.

''Confused, mostly,'' she said finally. ''I'm not sure I should be there, but there wasn't any choice, was there?''

Pip's head swung from side to side. ''No, of course not.''

''I really like him,'' Rosemary confided quietly.

''I'm sure. What woman wouldn't?''

Rosemary's hand flew up, denying the unspoken meaning Pip had defined with her smile. ''Not that way. It's just that he...''

What he did defied description, she realized. It was beyond her experience, and she could not explain the clutch of excitement when his hand touched her, or when his mouth fit itself against her lips.

Pip watched her for a moment and nodded. ''I think you're headed for trouble, Rosemary.''

''Trouble?''

''You will be unless you...'' Pip leaned to press her mouth near her friend's ear. ''Are you gonna marry him? Has he asked you again?''

Rosemary sat bolt upright. ''Marry Tanner? No. And no.'' She shifted on the keg and pursed her lips. ''Well, he hasn't exactly asked. He's just mentioned it.''

"Mentioned it? Like, when are you going to marry me? Or let's go to town and find the preacher."

Rosemary laughed aloud. "Neither, really. He's just made reference to it. As if maybe he didn't really want to before, but now he does."

Pip ran long fingers through her tousled curls. "Now he does. Does what?" She stood expectantly, her face flooded with a bright red stain, her mouth opening and then closing, as if the words she thought to speak were better left unsaid.

"Want to marry me, of course," Rosemary said softly. "What else did you think I meant?"

"Well, the other. You know, what men usually want from women. Except he probably figures the only way he'll get that is to put a ring on your finger."

Rosemary closed her eyes. "I can't believe you said that. I'm sure he hasn't thought of...that. In connection with me, I mean." Her eyelids flew upward and she glanced around once more. "We're not alone in that house, you know. Mama Pearl moved in. She didn't want folks talking about me."

"Well, Mama Pearl or not, folks are talking, Rosemary. In fact, I heard from Dex Sawyer that the men at the Golden Slipper Saloon are laying odds on when Gabe Tanner will march down the aisle."

"Well, not in the next few minutes, he's not," Rosemary said sharply. "For that matter, we haven't really discussed it, not since the first day I went out there." The memory of Tanner's words assaulted her mind as she settled back on the keg.

Things are different now... I don't know how many

*more nights I can hear you movin' around in the next
room and not want to be in there with you.... They
can consider us a couple if they want to.*

A couple. And then he'd kissed her, his lips hard
at first, until, for just a moment...

Pip's hand slapped the counter, and Rosemary
jumped. "I asked you, how much coffee?" Pip repeated.

"Oh...five pounds should do."

The door opened, a tinkling bell announcing a customer and Pip turned to the front of the store. "You
want to look around, Mrs. Frombert? I'll just be a few
more minutes."

"Maybe I'll visit with Rosemary while I wait,"
Geraldine Frombert said, marching toward the counter
as if she had a mission to accomplish.

"Pull up a keg and sit down," Rosemary told her,
forcing a grin as she took note of the militant stance
of the banker's wife.

"I won't be here long enough for a lengthy chat."
Geraldine pulled off her gloves and searched through
her reticule, her fingers waving a page torn from a
ledger book as they emerged. "I knew my list was
here somewhere."

"If you're in a hurry, Pip can tend to that first,"
Rosemary suggested. "My dinner is in the oven and
Mama Pearl has things under control."

Geraldine's mouth looked like she'd just eaten a
peck of green apples, Rosemary thought, covering her
smile with one hand.

"What keeps you busy these days, Rosemary?"

"Just the usual, ma'am. I gather the eggs and churn butter and help cook and clean."

"Humph…I hear you're staying in the very house that man lives in."

Rosemary tilted her head, wondering if she had misheard the insinuation. "Where else would I stay, Mrs. Frombert?"

"Well, I always say, it's not wise to tempt the devil. A single woman living with a bachelor provides temptation, and certainly offends the sensibilities of decent folk."

Rosemary stood quickly, her stained cheeks burning at the insult. "Could you have Scotty carry out my sugar and flour, Pip? I can get most of the rest in my basket."

Her hands transferred the tea and coffee, along with several smaller items, to the basket she had carried from the ranch. She turned toward the door, then snatched up the pail of lard, allowing it to swing from her other hand. Like a scalding wave, the temptation to swing the heavy bucket at Geraldine filled her almost to overflowing.

But she denied it, and, drawing in a deep breath, stifled the urge to retaliate in so violent a manner. "I'm sure Mr. Tanner would not appreciate being called a devil, ma'am. He's a gentleman, as are the men who work for him."

Geraldine sniffed loudly. "I'm sure," she said, even as her lifted eyebrows denied the words she spoke. "You should have found work here in town, Rosemary. Your papa would be most distraught to know what you're doing."

That was enough. The lard pail hit the floor and the basket fell beside it. "He'd be even more distraught to know that the people he called his friends for so many years have turned their tongues to wagging over my circumstances, ma'am. And not one of them offered me work. My father was a kind man. He always had a decent word to say about folks."

Rosemary bent to pick up her purchases, and her parting words were clear and distinct. "Apparently, his sermons didn't rub off on you."

Her hands trembled as she held the reins, waiting until Pip's brother loaded her purchases beside her. With a nod, and a smile that was hard to come by, she acknowledged his help and backed the mare from place, turning the buggy toward home.

The alleyway drew her attention, where a circle of children gathered near the side wall of the bank. Without intent, her hands drew up on the reins. An almost viable scent of fear swept toward her, as if a darkness pervaded the seemingly innocent gathering.

She brought her mare to a halt and slid from the high seat, holding the reins in her hand. "Is something wrong?" she asked quietly, not allowing her voice to carry beyond the group.

A small girl looked up, wariness cloaking her movement. "We're just talkin' to Scat, ma'am."

"Scat?" Rosemary felt her heartbeat increase, as a sense of peril enveloped her. "Scat, come here."

Her words carried a note of command, she was pleased to hear, and she looked about, wondering that no other passerby had halted here. So potent was the urgency of the children, she could almost feel it surging in the air.

The curtain of legs parted and Scat Pender came into view, seated on the ground, leaning on the side wall of the bank. He turned his head away and she moved toward the scene. "Will you hold my horse?" she asked the largest of the boys.

He nodded, and Rosemary relinquished the reins into his keeping, walking slowly to where Scat curled, seeking to hide his face from her. His clothing was torn and dusty, his cap pulled low.

"Scat? What's wrong?"

"Go on, all of you," he growled, waving a hand at the assembled children. They looked at Rosemary quickly, then as if willing to relinquish control, drifted away.

She squatted beside the boy, one hand touching his shoulder. "Scat? Are you hurt? Can I help?"

"I'm all right. At least, I will be. I got in a fight is all."

Her indrawn breath brought his head around. "Don't get all worried, ma'am. I'll be fine."

Rosemary shook her head, heartsick at the sight of battered flesh and an eye that was bruised and swollen. "Who did this to you?" For surely another child had not wrought this kind of damage on Scat Pender. No small fist had opened the wound that still oozed blood at the corner of his mouth.

His chin lifted stubbornly. "I said I'd be all right, ma'am. You don't understand."

"You're right there, Scat. I don't." And then the terrible vision of an angry man assailed her mind. *My pa's got a bottle, ma'am, and he don't care where I am.*

He was a drunkard, the man who provided for this boy in a slipshod manner that barely allowed for food enough to keep body and soul together.

"Where's your father?" she asked quietly.

"He's got nuthin' to do with this," Scat answered, his jaw jutting forward.

"Will you come home with me?"

As if he caught a glimpse of heaven, Scat's single useful eye opened wide and he winced as if its partner had attempted to do the same. "Ma'am..." He swallowed and turned his head away. "I can't do that."

"Certainly you can," she assured him. "Mr. Tanner will find work for you at his ranch, I'm sure."

"No, ma'am. I have to take care of my little sister."

His sister? Surely not. Rosemary scanned her memory. He'd only spoken of his father, not a word of a girl child in the household. And no mother, of that she was certain.

"We can bring her along, Scat. I know it will be all right."

"If I don't do what my pa says..." He halted, biting at his lip as if he had said too much. "I can't do it, ma'am. I hafta take care of Anna."

He hoisted himself to his feet, and his eye closed as if he hurt in a dozen assorted places. "I gotta go, ma'am."

Rosemary reached out her hand and he eyed it longingly. "I'll be fine. Truly, I will."

With limping steps, he made his way from her and

she watched, her heart heavy, holding back tears that begged to be shed. Behind her, the mare snorted, bringing her to an awareness of the young boy who awaited her return, and she drew up her skirts, turning back to the street.

"Thank you, young man, for your help."

"That's all right," he answered, his demeanor subdued. "Old Scat's got a tough row to hoe, with his pa always lookin' for a whippin' boy. Sure am glad I don't live in his house." The boy backed away and bobbed his head in farewell.

Rosemary climbed into the buggy and took up the reins once more. There must be something she could do.

"The boy was battered. There's not another word for it, Mama Pearl."

"Some things you can't do anything about. There's men in this world who just enjoy poundin' on other human beings, and that's a fact. 'Course, the way I hear it, Nate Pender's been no use to anybody since his woman died havin' that little girl. I reckon he takes out all his grief on the boy."

"That's a pitiful excuse, and you know it." Rosemary thumped the coffeepot on the stove, wishing there was a chunk of wood or a stone she could kick across the kitchen.

"Didn't say it was a good excuse. It's just one of those things that nobody does anything about. I'm sure not about to get my head blown off, stickin' my nose in."

"Well, I just may. I'm already the talk of the town,

it seems. Might as well add Scat Pender to my list and be more than knee-deep in hot water.''

"What'd you do, girl? Or is just bein' here that's got you in a peck of trouble?'' Mama Pearl's gaze narrowed as she took Rosemary's measure. "Who said somethin' to you?'' She paused, watching as Rosemary heaved a sigh and turned away. "I reckon the question should've been, what did you say back?''

Rosemary pulled a chair from beneath the table and plopped down on it. "I went in the store…'' In moments, she had quoted Geraldine Frombert, and had given herself no quarter as she repeated her own words.

"I was rude, Mama Pearl. Downright nasty.''

Pearl cast a look of commiseration in Rosemary's direction. "Sounds to me like you had due cause, honey girl. That lady thinks too highly of herself, I always did say. She's got no right to tear you up that way.''

The sound of voices from beyond the porch caught their attention, and Rosemary stood quickly. "I don't even have the butter on the table or the bread sliced.''

"Those men'll be a while washin' up. Just plaster a smile on that face, or we'll have Tanner raisin' a fuss in here. He sees you lookin' all down in the mouth and he'll have a fit, girl.''

He had a fit anyway. Rosemary eyed him gloomily as he led her to the parlor. Surely this wasn't what Mama Pearl had had in mind when she'd told her she'd find time for her to lollygag here.

Tanner's hand was firm against her elbow, as if he

were afraid she might cut and run, and his eyes were dark with questions as he turned her to face him in the center of the big room.

"Now, let's have it, Rosemary. What happened in town? You look like somebody took all the wind out of your sails, honey."

The misery she'd held in check all the way home threatened to erupt damply at his words. Rosemary held the tears back stoutly, determined not to fall back on that well-known female trick. Her mind had set on a plan, and if she wrapped it in tears, it would not be fair play.

"Do you know Scat Pender?" she asked carefully.

"I know of his daddy. A big brute of a fella. Drinks more than he should. What about him?" Tanner released her arm and stepped back, assessing her.

"Scat's in trouble, Tanner. I saw him in town. He told me he had a fight, but I don't believe him. I think his father beat him. His face is bruised, one eye so swollen he can't see from it, and he limped as if he hurts all over."

Tanner winced inwardly, but his words were laconic. "Maybe he's a scamp. Made his pa mad."

Rosemary felt her ire rise at his curt phrasing. "No boy deserves treatment like that, no matter what he's done."

Tanner shrugged. "You may be right, but he's not the first young'un to feel a switch."

"A switch?" Her voice escalated as she repeated his choice of word. "We're talking about fists here, Tanner. The boy was beaten, not punished. There's a difference."

"What do you want me to do about it, Rosemary?"

She turned from him and strode to the window, and he watched her back, admiring the squaring of her shoulders, the tilt of her head as she chose the words she would speak. He'd asked the questions purposely, set her up with his curt attitude, knowing she was fit to burst with indignation.

He'd looked for a wedge to use on his behalf, and now, unless he missed his guess, Rosemary Gibson was about to put herself squarely in his debt. That a child had suffered to make it so was out of his control, but damn, he'd be a fool not to take advantage of the situation.

She turned to him, and he hid his elation behind a frown. Her eyes traced the lines of his face, as if she sought reassurance there, and he folded his arms across his chest to better set the mood he chose to present.

"I want you to think about taking Scat on here," she said firmly.

"Here? You want me to hire on a boy? I doubt he could pull his weight, Rosemary, even if I had a place for him."

"He's strong," she said, stepping toward him a few inches, as if her persistence might sway him. "He's a good boy. I can tell, Tanner. I've always been a good judge of character."

His brow lifted at that. "Really? How do you see me, Miss Gibson?"

She lifted her head, the better to meet his gaze. "As a gentleman...mostly. You're fair," she continued quickly. "And you're kind."

"All that?"

Her nod was immediate and firm. "I think you're the sort of influence Scat Pender needs. He's just a boy, and he's been mistreated." She shivered, an involuntary movement, and her eyes held a wealth of sadness. "He wouldn't come with me today because he said he had to take care of his little sister."

"His little sister. And what do you propose to do with her when you cart Scat Pender out here to live?"

Rosemary's eyes filled with tears, tears he suspected had been close to the surface for hours. She was tender, this woman who faced him. Brave enough to face him down, but softly feminine.

And an advocate for a boy who had no idea what a champion he had.

"I'd need to bring her along. I'd say she needs a woman to take care of her.

"Have you seen her?" Rosemary's eyes were wistful now.

Tanner shook his head. "No, just caught a glimpse of the boy once in a while. Word has it he snatched a bottle of whiskey from the saloon one night last month."

Rosemary stilled, as if her breathing halted. "That's what he meant, I'll warrant, when he said he had to do what his pa said." Indignation rose to wipe out the traces of sadness in her gaze. "That man has Scat stealing his hootch for him."

"We don't know that," Tanner said quickly, though his own good sense assured him it was probably true.

"Maybe you don't, but I'd be willing to stake a

bundle on it. Why else would Scat take a bottle from Jason Stillwell's place?''

''You know Jason?'' This was a new development, one he thought worthwhile exploring.

The blush that traveled from her throat to her cheeks was becoming, he thought. Her eyes slid from contact with his, focusing instead over his left shoulder.

''I've met him.''

''Recently?''

She cleared her throat. It wasn't in Rosemary to be devious, he decided, even as she hesitated. ''I asked him for a job. That's how I met Scat the first time.''

''A job! Doing what?'' The thought of Rosemary in a saloon was not to be countenanced.

She shot him a look of disdain. ''You don't need to shout at me. I applied for the position as his accountant.''

Tanner shook his head in disbelief. ''You walked right in the saloon and applied for a job?''

''No, of course not. I went to the back door after dark.''

''After dark. You were roaming around town after dark?''

''Must you keep repeating everything I say? Yes, after dark. It seemed smarter than marching in the front door in broad daylight. Then, when I came out, Scat Pender walked me home.''

''Well, for that reason alone, I owe him.'' His big hands grasped her shoulders. ''You need someone to look after you, Rosemary Gibson.'' With a swift movement, he tugged her into his embrace, and chuckled beneath his breath as she fell against his chest.

Her eyes were wide and startled, blue and brilliant, shining with a trace of the tears she had valiantly attempted to hold at bay. Her mouth formed a whispering O, and he was drawn to it, his tongue tempted to touch the tiny bow of her top lip.

Denying the urge, he settled for a more circumspect caress, his lips forming themselves to hers, savoring the plush texture, the warmth of her flesh. She'd given him what he needed. Asking him to take Scat on at the ranch had allowed him to gain the upper hand, but pushing her past the limits of gentility was not a wise move, he decided.

"Tanner?" Her whisper was anxious. "I don't think you should be kissing me so often."

Damn, he could count on one hand the times he'd stolen a taste of those lips. Not nearly enough. "You don't know what 'often' is, sweetheart," he murmured. "I'm plannin' on doin' a lot of this in the future."

"You are?"

She sounded worried, confused perhaps, and that was exactly what he had in mind.

"Tanner, will you do something for me?"

Here it comes. "What, sweetheart? What do you want?"

"I want you to bring those children here. Surely there's room for them, and certainly they'd have a better life with us...with you."

"This is kinda skirtin' around the edge of the law, Rosemary. They're legally Nate Pender's children."

"Certainly there must be some law that prohibits what that man does." Her voice trembled with the words and Tanner cut to the finish.

"I'll look into it tomorrow, honey. I'll go see the sheriff and find out what can be done."

"Thank you. I wanted so badly to do something, but…" She bit at her lip, and his finger nudged at the spot.

"Bad habit, sweetheart." His gaze slid from the temptation of her mouth to mesh with the liquid blue of her eyes. "I'll take care of it, as best I can. But first, I want a promise from you."

Surprise chased the apprehension from her face. "What sort of promise?"

"I want to marry you, Rosemary. If I bring those two youngsters here, I want your promise to marry me."

She backed from him, and he let her go. This was a decision she had to make without coercion on his part. It was enough that he held a royal flush. Once she realized that, the going would be easy. She'd have no choice if she was as intent on bringing the Pender children here as he suspected.

"I don't know if I can do that." A dubious scowl puckered her forehead.

"Sure you can. You've had plenty of time to be thinkin' about it. I asked you, a long time ago."

"A few weeks is not a long time," she answered primly.

"It seems like a long time to me," he muttered.

And longer by the minute, now that he had her in a bargaining position.

"Well, it's up to you, sweetheart. I'm not gonna try and talk you into it. I made my offer, laid all my cards on the table. What do you say?"

Chapter Nine

Tanner's eyes bored into her, demanding an answer. His features had hardened, his jaw was taut, his mouth a thin line, as if he teetered on the edge of anger. And yet Rosemary felt no threat from him. Except for the threat he offered to her whole way of life.

Marriage to Gabe Tanner would involve crossing a line, one she'd not been prepared to face. Life in a parsonage was a far cry from marriage to Tanner. Even in her unenlightened state, she was aware of that.

He watched her, his gaze allowing her no quarter, even as she sought in vain for some small softening in the stern lines of his face. As if he had thrown down a gauntlet and awaited her response, he stood before her.

She dampened her dry lips, cleared her throat and clenched her fingers into tight fists. The air was heavy with his demand, his words alive in her head. The man wanted to marry her, and she was smart enough to understand the depths of that commitment, should she nod her head.

The welfare of Scat Pender and the unknown Anna were at stake. She'd never before faced such a decision. And now, to face a lifetime with Tanner in order to protect two children seemed a bit overwhelming.

"You're not being fair," she whispered. "You ask too much."

His brow furrowed just a bit as he considered her words. "You think so? You're askin' me to take on two children, honey. That's a pretty big job you're expectin' me to do. You know, I've got it nice and easy here. I come and go as I please. Aside from my ranch and the people who depend on me for a living, I'm scot-free.

"And now you want me to open up my house to a couple of orphans and face their daddy, who may be hauntin' my doorstep with a shotgun? I'd say you're the one who's doin' a heap of askin'."

She backed away a step, her legs coming in contact with the sofa. "I don't know what you expect of me, Tanner."

One corner of his mouth twitched, and his eyes narrowed even more as his gaze swept the full length of her. "Oh, I'd say you do."

The response of her body was immediate, a shiver of anticipation snaking down her spine. Parts of her that had received only the necessary attention for all of her life began to assume an importance that embarrassed her beyond measure.

"Tanner, don't look at me that way," she whispered.

"You might's well get used to it," he murmured, sliding his hands deeply into the pockets of his trousers.

"If I don't marry you? What then?" she asked.

"Then we go on as before. You take care of this place and I..." He rocked on his heels. "Well, for sure I don't have to find room for two young'uns in my house, do I?"

"You really mean it? You're not willing to help Scat?"

Tanner stilled, like a predator watching his prey. No longer did he wear the beginnings of a smile. His hands slid from their berth, only his thumbs hitched on the edges of his pockets, fingers widespread on his hips. His expression offered her no hope. No hint of pity touched those dark eyes.

In silence, she read his reply. Spelled out in the stark lines of his outthrust jaw, the thinned lips and veiled gaze was a denial of her plea. Could she commit her life to this silent stranger? Could she face him within the boundaries of that room containing his bed and belongings?

For all her innocence, there was no doubt in her mind what Tanner would expect of a bride.

"I can't let them...I can't live with myself if I don't at least try to help them, Tanner." The words were firm, even as her mouth trembled at their passing.

A flicker of his eyelashes acknowledged her reply, and he nodded. "We have a deal?"

Her hesitation was brief. "Bring them here. See the

sheriff and find out what you can do legally for their protection.''

''You'll give me what I want?''

He made no pretense of love. Those stark words offered her no softness, no assurance of tenderness at his hand. Only the memory of the man she had come to know over the past weeks allowed her any hope of some vestige of happiness.

He had brought to life within her a desire for his touch. She had accepted his kisses, enjoyed his companionship, come to respect him as an employer and maybe even a friend.

Could she give him what he would ask of her as his wife?

She nodded. ''I'll marry you. Once the children are under this roof, I'll become your wife.''

''You'll move your things into my room.''

It was not a question, but a statement of fact, and she acknowledged it as such, nodding her head, sensing the waters of fate cascading over her.

''There are four bedrooms upstairs, Tanner. One for each of the children and a third for Mama Pearl. So far as I can see, that leaves one. I don't think I have any choice.''

His mouth curved slowly, his grin feral, as if his mind raced ahead to that time and place. Before she could react to his movement, his hands reached for her, not nearly so gently this time. They circled her waist, scooping her against his length. His head dipped to her uplifted face, his mouth barely moving as he whispered his intent.

''I've wanted to kiss you again for the past half

hour, Rosemary. You've played hell with my good intentions, maneuverin' me around so. Now, you'll bear the brunt of my impatience.''

She felt the heat of his mouth, the power of his hands against her back as they slid to her hips, lifting her with easy strength against himself. Her arms wrapped around his neck, almost as if she must anchor herself, lest she fall. There was no chance of that.

The hands that gripped her were forceful, but not cruel. The fingertips that pressed against her flesh, even through layers of fabric, were powerful, but not harsh. And the mouth that claimed hers was hungry, but not greedy.

His lips suckled at hers, his tongue touched the tender flesh with care, and even as he sought entry beyond the barrier of her teeth, he awaited her acquiescence.

It was not to be. She drew back, just the smallest increment, fearful of the invasion, and he responded immediately. His mouth left hers, moving to taste the tender flesh beneath her jaw, then traveled to the sensitive spot he'd visited before, under her ear where her pulse pounded with an urgent beat.

His hands lowered her to the floor and she blushed as she recognized the intimate arrangement his fingers had assumed upon her person. Then there was no time to think, for those same hands traveled upward, one holding her firmly at the small of her back, the other pressing the underside of her breast.

She felt the immediate response, the tightening and tensing of her flesh as it puckered against the fine lawn of her chemise. His hand moved slowly, barely clasping, weighing the firm flesh it contained, and she murmured her protest against his mouth.

He lifted his head, opening his eyes to meet her gaze, and she was seared by the heat therein. His nostrils flared, twin flags of crimson outlining his cheekbones, and his jaw clenched tightly.

"Tanner?" She shrank from his handling, and he would not allow it.

"No. Stand still, honey. I won't hurt you...I promise." His hand was still, fingers curled around that part of her she had largely ignored all her life.

No longer.

His hand moved, shifting only inches, until it had captured her other breast, held it in that same urgent manner, as if he must commit its shape and size to memory.

And then his fingers shifted, brushing against the crest. Her indrawn breath brought a smile to his lips, allowing a sound to escape from his throat that could only be described as a groan.

"Please, Tanner," she whimpered, leaning forward to rest her forehead against his chest.

His hand moved from the treasure it had claimed, reluctantly, but with purpose. It tilted her chin upward, exposing the face she had thought to hide from his view.

"I won't touch you again," he said, the words slow and solemn, as if he spoke a vow. "Not until the day we marry. I figure I got just about enough to hold me over till then, honey."

It took him two days, not the single morning he had hoped, to accomplish his task. He'd gathered his forces, gaining sympathy for his cause, and brought the principals together in the sheriff's office.

And now Oscar Rhinehold faced the three people who awaited his reply. As he viewed the remains of breakfast upon his desk, he looked as if he needed another cup of strong coffee in his hand.

"You folks sure know how to ruin a fella's day, don't you?" He brushed at his moustache, dislodging crumbs and smoothing down the longer whiskers. "Seems like Scat Pender's found himself a whole bunch of protectors all of a sudden."

Tanner tipped his hat back and pressed his lips together thoughtfully. "Maybe we've been negligent for too long, Sheriff. It's real easy to ignore it, long as the boy doesn't complain. But, takin' a good look at him, I think his pa needs a good rakin' over the coals."

"You plannin' on doin' that, Tanner?"

"No, not me. I just want to bypass his authority over those young'uns. I figure you can do that."

Sheriff Rhinehold glanced at Tanner's companions. "And what do you folks have to do with it?"

Mary Tappan tapped her index finger on the edge of the sheriff's desk in her best schoolmarm manner. "That boy's been abused, Sheriff, and I didn't do anything about it. I thought it wasn't my business." She stood erect and her chin was firm. "I was wrong, dead wrong. He's worn bruises more than once, and no child deserves that treatment. Especially not a good boy like Scat Pender."

"How about you preacher? What's your stake

here?'' Oscar asked, turning to gaze to the other member of the trio.

"I went to the Pender home last night, at Mr. Tanner's urging. As the local minister, I felt it was my duty to find out why those children weren't in church school.''

"And?" the sheriff urged.

"The boy was in his underwear, Sheriff. His face was swollen, his body was bruised and he was limping badly. In the lamplight, it was difficult to make out his injuries. And then, too, his father sent him out of the room immediately I came to the door.

"But I saw enough to convince me that he'd been beaten. I'd say it is in his best interest to remove him from the home.''

"I don't usually do this sort of thing," Oscar said slowly. "I don't like interferin' in a family. Maybe old Nate had reason."

"Old Nate was drunker'n a skunk," Tanner interrupted angrily. After seeing the results of Nate Pender's latest actions, he'd almost gone over the edge. And losing his temper wasn't the answer. Not today, anyway.

"I guess you could say I broke the law, Oscar," he admitted. "I hauled those young'uns out of that house this morning. I'm takin' them home with me."

Oscar Rhinehold rose, his chair falling backward against the wall. He was only of medium height, but he stood tall as he spouted his censure. "You what? Damn! That's against the law, Tanner. That's kidnapping.''

Tanner shrugged. "I call it savin' the boy's life,

maybe." He leaned over the desk, lowering his gaze to Oscar's level. "They came without any arguing, Oscar. And Nate Pender was still too befuddled this morning to put up much of a fuss."

"I doubt I'd have argued with you, either, Mr. Tanner," James Worth said quietly. "Even at this early hour, you reminded me of your namesake, the angel Gabriel."

Tanner felt a flush stain his cheeks. That damn name his mother had given him had caused more than one fistfight during his boyhood years.

"Be that as it may, I need your help, Oscar. I'm gonna hold on to those kids until the judge comes in next week."

"I'll back you up," Oscar said after a moment. "Nate's about two steps from jail anyway. He's been skirtin' the law right along. I'll just have to remind him of it if he comes complainin' about you."

Tanner turned to James Worth. "I've got another problem, preacher. Miss Gibson and I need to get married, right quick. I finally got her convinced to tie the knot, and I don't want to give her a chance to change her mind. We'll be in later on today to see you. You gonna have time to say the words for us?"

"She's agreeable?" James Worth asked dubiously. "I thought she was only going to be your cook and work in your house for wages."

"Well, everyone in town knows I asked her to marry me, weeks ago in fact," Tanner said firmly. "It just took a while to make her see the light."

"No doubt marriage would be in her best interest. But I'll want to talk to her first," James said.

"You'd better do the deed, Mr. Worth," Mary Tappan said sharply. "If ever there was a man who needed a good woman, it's Gabe Tanner. And Rosemary Gibson's about as good as they get. I say, get on with it."

Tanner waited patiently, knowing that the cards were stacked in his favor. Rosemary would agree all down the line. He'd made sure of that.

"I didn't think we'd be married so soon." Rosemary viewed him from across the kitchen, her cheeks flushed from the heat of the oven.

"I brought the children with me, honey. And I told the preacher we'd be back in town this afternoon."

"It's almost afternoon already," Rosemary wailed. "I can't just trot off to town and get married like this." She looked down at her dress, an old one she saved for the worst chores.

"I'll bring in the tub for a bath and get it filled from the stove for you," Tanner offered.

Her brows rose as she gasped her protest. "I can't take a bath at high noon, right here in the kitchen."

She'd bathed at night, carefully covering the windows with quilts beforehand, waiting until the men were gone to town on a Saturday night and Tanner was busy in the barn. To do such a thing in the middle of the day was unheard of.

"I'll carry the tub to your room," he offered. "No, I'll carry it to my room. Anna can move her things upstairs right away. Not that she's got much. Nothin' but a flour sack full."

''Where is she?'' Rosemary's eyes scanned the porch and beyond, bending to see out the window.

''Cotton's unloadin' them now. They'll be up from the barn in a minute. I wanted to talk to you first.''

She brushed past him, pushing the screen door open and hurrying out to the porch. ''Scat?'' Her voice carried across the wide yard and from the barn door, a whistle answered her.

''Scat?'' Her feet barely touched the steps as she left the porch, her heart pumping as she searched for him.

He appeared in the barn door. From behind him, a child peered wonderingly at her surroundings. Much smaller than Scat, Anna was able to hide in his shadow. Her brother spoke to her, words Rosemary could not understand from this distance, and then they moved together toward the house.

Anna grasped her brother's hand, as if it were a lifeline and she must keep hold at all costs. Her hair was disheveled, her clothing wrinkled.

They drew nearer, and Rosemary inhaled sharply. She'd seen bruises on Scat's face before, but now they were fresh, dried blood still staining his cheek, probably from a nosebleed. He peered at her from one eye, and the other still bore swelling and yellow bruises from the last assault. Nate Pender must have abused the boy on a daily basis during the past week.

''Come in,'' Rosemary said, holding the screen door open. Anna hesitated, but Scat tugged at her.

''It's all right, Babe. Miss Rosemary's a friend.''

It was more than she could tolerate—to see such a frail, tiny child with no more evidence of loving care lavished upon her small body than did this girl. Rosemary fell to her knees and held her arms out beseechingly.

"Please, Anna. Won't you let me hug you?"

Anna's eyelashes fluttered as she looked around the room. Tanner had assumed a position near the window. Mama Pearl stood in the doorway beyond the table, a formidable foe should the occasion warrant. And perhaps to the child, Rosemary represented the lesser of several evils.

For whatever reason, she stepped forward, allowing herself to be touched, first by Rosemary's hands grasping hers. With care, Rosemary drew her closer, until Anna was within the circle of her arms. She held her gently, carefully, as if she were a doll made of fine porcelain, dressed in silk and lace. One hand slid to cup the tiny chin and Rosemary lifted Anna's head until their eyes could meet.

Aware that she was being judged, that the child held her verdict in abeyance, Rosemary waited patiently. The round, dark eyes rested on Rosemary's hair, and one small hand lifted to touch a wispy wave that dipped low against her cheek. The child sucked in a deep breath and spoke words that came nigh unto breaking the woman's heart.

"Can you make me smell like you? You must be made outta flowers."

"Mr. Tanner is about to fill a bathtub right now," Rosemary said softly. "He must have known you would be needing to wash up a little."

Scat carried two flour sacks, one not nearly as full as the other, and he designated the smaller one with a nod. "This here's her stuff, Miss Rosemary. The dress is her good one, and I just scrubbed it out in cold water. Pa didn't want to waste good money on soap."

"We'll figure something out, Scat," she told him, reaching one hand to touch his fingers. "I'm sure you did the best you could for your sister."

His grin was shy, and even through the bruised lid, she noted a twinkle in his eye. "I'll bet you can do better, ma'am."

Tanner cleared his throat and Rosemary met his gaze.

Sure enough, he'd turned into a mind reader in the last few minutes, he decided. Those big blue eyes of hers were filled with the thanks she dared not speak aloud.

"How 'bout if you take that child upstairs, and I'll bring the first bucket of water?" he asked, answering Rosemary's unspoken words with a smile.

"I'll carry up my small washpan full," Mama Pearl volunteered. "Won't take much more than that for a first good wash anyway."

Half an hour later, Rosemary found herself in agreement with Mama Pearl's plan. She'd scrubbed Anna's hair and lathered her from top to bottom, then rinsed her in clean water. Another double load of water from the reservoir provided a set down bath, as Mama Pearl said. Anna had lolled back in the tub, moving her body in luxuriant pleasure as the warm water did its job.

The largest towel Rosemary could find among Tanner's supply wrapped the child from stem to stern, another draped over her head. She sat atop the wash-stand as Rosemary dried the long, tangled locks, which had turned from muddy-brown to honey-gold once the layers of dirt had been dislodged from place.

"I never had so nice a bath," Anna said, as if she confided a secret to Rosemary's hearing. "I always had to wash in a bitty little pan at home." She held out her hand, allowing the towel to fall from her shoulder, and admired the cleanliness of her palm.

"My hands look better this way, don't they?"

From the doorway, Tanner watched, as he had done for the past few moments. This glimpse of Rosemary was a new vision, one he enjoyed almost as much as that of two days past, when he had kissed her in the parlor. When he had tempted himself with her nearness and almost gone beyond the edge of decency.

"You look beautiful, punkin," he said quietly, smiling as two feminine faces turned his way.

"She has beautiful hair, Tanner," Rosemary told him, lifting a tress she had been drying.

"I see," he said. And he did. For the first time, he looked beyond the prim preacher's daughter he'd brought to his home, beyond the small, spunky woman she'd revealed herself to be. Saw past even the passionate woman she showed promise of becoming, into the loving creature who would tend his own children with the same care she offered this tiny mite.

Rosemary Gibson had somehow gained entry to the most private place within him, which had for years repelled advances from any direction. His need for her raged. That had not changed, only been held in check until his ring circled her finger. But beyond the passion that drew him into her orbit, he saw a loving, generous woman who would accept him as a flawed male creature, and whose tenderness could perhaps heal his soul.

"Tanner?" Rosemary watched him, her brow lifted. "Did you hear me?"

He shook his head. "I was thinking, honey."

"You need to close the door, so we can get Anna dressed."

He nodded, willing to be apart from these females for a time. There was a boy to look after, and he suspected it would be his duty to do just that thing.

It was not to be. The yard rang with laughter as Tanner left the porch. The horse tank held a frolicking boy, Scat ducking beneath the water, still clothed but considerably cleaner. Cotton stood several feet away, his own clothing liberally doused with water.

"Thought we'd just get him cleaned up by layers, boss," Cotton offered. "He says his other set of clothes needs washing, so we stuck them in the water, too."

"I never ever hardly been wet all over before," Scat said with a grin. "Only a couple of times when my pa was drunk and I went down to the creek after dark. That wasn't near so much fun as this."

"Well, now we need to figure out how to get him dried out," Tanner said, unable to hide the satisfaction he felt at the boy's pleasure.

"Aw, an hour helpin' out with the new colts oughta take care of that, Tanner. The sun's hotter'n hades, and he'd dry right quick."

"All right. Just get him something to eat. He can

have a plate on the porch. I think I picked him up before breakfast.''

Scat's mouth turned down. ''That's all right. I don't generally eat much in the morning anyway, Mr. Tanner.''

''Tanner'll do, son. And from now on, you'll eat breakfast every day. It's a rule here.''

''Yessir, that's fine,'' Scat was quick to reply. ''I like eatin' real well.''

Just probably never found much to call a meal, Tanner decided, noting the slim frame as Scat stood up and began climbing from the horse tank. His feet were callused and tan. Apparently shoes were not included in his sparse wardrobe. He'd take care of that problem tomorrow, Tanner decided. Along with some new shirts and pants and something to put on the delicate little girl inside his house.

''Sir?''

Tanner turned back at the boy's beckoning.

''Is Anna all right? I mean, I don't want her to be worried that I'm not there with her.''

Tanner shook his head. ''She's in good hands, Scat. Miss Rosemary has her. They're fixin' her hair, I think.''

Scat brightened. ''She'll like that. I found a comb one time and I run it through ever once in a while, and get the tangles out for her.''

The laughter coming from his kitchen was more melodious, but reminiscent of that in the yard, Tanner thought as he stepped up on the porch. Through the screen, he watched as Rosemary held Anna on her lap, waiting quietly as the child ate her way through a plate of food.

She wore another dress, much like the first, faded and wrinkled, but with an air of semicleanliness about it. Her laughter was soft, not nearly so exuberant as that of the two women who watched her, and he listened with a depth of satisfaction he had not thought to feel.

Taking these children had fulfilled a need. That of righting a wrong. His own father had neglected him in many ways, but always there had been food to eat and clothing to wear.

Nate Pender had given his children nothing but a roof over their heads, and that probably was flawed, if the dampness within that shack was anything to go by. Where Scat managed to find the clothing the two of them wore was a question Tanner steered clear of.

Perhaps his gratification stemmed from the look in Scat's eye as he'd welcomed Tanner into the shack this morning. For the unspoken thanksgiving he'd felt radiating from the boy as he and his sister found a spot on the wagon bed, where hay had been spread for their comfort.

"I'm taking you home with me, Scat," Tanner had said, *offering no choice to the child.*

And without hesitation, that dark head had nodded. "Yessir, that's fine."

Now, as he reflected on his wealth of emotions, Tanner considered the task well-done. That Rosemary would fulfill her part of this bargain was a known factor. She would stand before James Worth and speak the vows today, before the sun set.

She would climb into his bed and give herself into his keeping, of that he had no doubt. And at that thought, he found a persistent throbbing coming to life once more.

"Tanner? Is Scat coming in to eat?" Rosemary asked from inside the kitchen.

"Fix him a plate. He'll eat on the porch." He turned his back on the open door, aware that the gruffness of his tone left silence in its wake.

He'd explain later. Maybe.

Chapter Ten

A full pail of warm water waited by the washstand, and a bar of French-milled soap had been placed by the china basin, ready for her use. Rosemary picked it up, lifting it to her nose as she sniffed at the delicate fragrance.

Lilac, she decided, and thought of the child who was even now sleeping in the next room. Who had wanted to smell like flowers. She'd accomplished that aim, and if Rosemary had done nothing else in her lifetime, she'd granted that desire.

Her golden hair gleaming, her clean face aglow, Anna had presented herself to Scat at the supper table. He'd allowed her to preen, burying his nose in her hair as she asked, complimented her lavishly, and then offered his thanks to Rosemary with halting words that brought tears to her eyes.

All this because of Tanner. Rosemary unwrapped the bar of soap slowly. He'd purchased the soap for her, probably on a whim. For those few short moments when he'd left her on the buggy seat, to pick up supplies, he'd said. Then, with only a small parcel in his hand, he had returned to her.

The ceremony had been short, with Pip leaving the store only long enough to arrive breathlessly at the parsonage for the few brief moments it took to turn Rosemary Gibson into Gabe Tanner's wife. The goodbyes were a flurry of wishes, waving hands and curious eyes upon them as the buggy traveled at a smart pace down the street.

Rosemary lathered a cloth with the fragrant soap and drew it over her face and neck, then down her arms and beneath them. Dressed only in her chemise, she felt pressed for time. Tanner had headed for the barn to tend last-minute chores, he'd said.

It was Rosemary's opinion that he'd simply offered her a few moments alone to prepare for her wedding night. It would take far longer than the time allotted her, she feared. In her whole experience of living, nothing she'd ever heard about or known about first-hand had prepared her for this.

Mama Pearl had patted her reassuringly just moments ago. "Tanner'll be good to you, girl. You just watch and see. He took a real shine to you right off, and his eyes light up just like Christmas candles when you come in sight."

She rinsed the soap from her skin and dried the dampness with the soft towel Mama Pearl had left for her. There hadn't been much in those few words the woman had said that would settle the questions befuddling her mind.

She looked into the mirror, scanning the image she presented. Tanner liked her hair, he'd already told her that. His hand had been on her bosom, and his gaze had touched her there with approval. She watched as a rosy hue traveled from that forbidden area to color her cheeks. She'd lived with her body for almost thirty years, and only now had it become so important.

From below, she heard voices, faint, yet unmistakable, as Tanner and Mama Pearl spoke in the kitchen. Then there were footsteps on the uncarpeted stairs, and Rosemary broke from her stance before the mirror to snatch her nightgown from the bed. She was sliding it over her head when the doorknob turned, shoving her arms into the sleeves as Tanner entered the room.

He halted inside the doorway, watching her, his gaze intent on her trembling fingers as she worked at the buttons. Then he stepped inside, closing the door behind him. Her fingers had never taken so long to perform such a mundane task. She fumbled with the final small mother-of-pearl button, and only then realized that her chemise was still in place beneath the cotton gown.

Tanner's mouth twitched and his smile appeared, tender and perhaps apologetic, she thought.

"I should have given you a few more minutes, I guess. I didn't mean to make you hurry."

"That's all right. I was done washing up." She nodded at the washstand. "Thank you for the soap. Lilac is one of my favorite scents."

"I like apple blossom, too," he said, approaching her slowly. "I just thought you might like to try something different." His hand rose to brush a strand of hair from her cheek, and then he scooped the heavy length from the back of her gown, where the fabric had captured it.

He tangled his fingers in it. "I haven't seen it down, hangin' loose, since that first day." Both hands were buried now in the heavy tresses that cascaded almost to her waist. He held up double handfuls, allowing it to flow through outspread fingers. "It's prettier than I remembered, Rosie."

She grimaced at the name he'd taunted her with one other time. "You're teasing me again, Tanner."

He shook his head. "No. You're like a rose in bloom, honey. Still just beginning to blossom."

Her laughter trembled in the words she spoke. "You sound like a poet."

"You make me wish... I just don't have enough of the right words to say to you, honey. Guess I'll have to just show you how I feel."

He looked around the room and grinned. "Mama Pearl wanted to make sure I found you all right, didn't she?" Candles glowed from the dresser, the washstand and the table beside the bed. It was a shameful waste, she supposed, but Mama Pearl had insisted, taking the lamp with her as she left the room.

Now she considered the task of snuffing them out. Maybe she'd better wait until Tanner undressed. That thought was not comforting, she decided, bending to blow out the nearest flickering flame, on the table beside her.

"I'll get the rest," Tanner said. "Go on, get in bed."

She risked a glance in his direction, then turned

back the covers, slipping between fragrant sheets. The window drew her eye and she watched as a cloud made its way across the face of the moon.

Tanner moved softly for such a big man, blowing out the remaining candles, then crossing to the bed. His clothing rustled loudly in the silence, and she heard the faint puff of his breath as he tugged at his boots. His weight depressed the mattress, and she turned her head as he slid in beside her.

The moon was almost as revealing as had been the candle glow, and she wished for a moment for the return of the cloud. Maybe even a whole skyful of them.

"You're worried about this, aren't you?" His voice was low, barely above a whisper.

"I don't know what to do." The admission came hard.

Tanner rolled to his side, rising on his elbow. "You don't have to do anything, honey. At least, nothing you don't want to do."

"I'm not sure how I got here," she whispered. "I mean, I know how, I just don't know…"

"Shh…" he said, touching her lips with his index finger. "It's all right." He leaned over her, moving that finger to trace the curl of her ear, brushing her hair behind it, the better to free it to his touch.

"I want to kiss you. That all right with you?" As if he awaited her permission, he hovered over her, his face in shadow.

She nodded, barely completing the gesture before his mouth touched hers, a tender, careful movement of his lips that promised pleasure. Her breath caught as his mouth opened a bit and his teeth touched, then closed gently over her bottom lip, worrying it, then releasing it with a flick of his tongue.

"You didn't kiss me that way before." The pressure of his teeth had brought to life a tingling sensation that traveled to her breasts, and she fought the urge to press her hands to their fullness. Instead, her fists gathered up the sheet beneath her and she clung to it fiercely.

"Didn't I?" His mouth touched hers again. "Maybe I didn't want to scare you off before I got my ring on your finger." His lips left hers, leaving a trail of kisses behind as they explored the planes and curves of her face. Her temple received adulation, and she felt the beat of her heart, there where his tongue touched the smooth skin at her hairline.

"You taste like…" He paused as if to consider her flavor. "Maybe like sweet cream," he drawled, one finger idly moving against her throat. She shivered as his tongue laved the spot his fingertip had marked, hesitating there for only a moment, then moving on, spreading a path of caresses that left heated dampness in their wake.

His gaze matched that warmth as he lifted to admire her in the moon's glow. "You're a beautiful woman, Mrs. Tanner," he announced, his voice rumbling against her skin as he bent once more, his mouth moving at the base of her throat. From there it was only inches to where her heart beat in double-quick rhythm, and she yearned bravely for his lips to travel to that place.

He'd said she was beautiful, and she shook her

head at his words. His chuckle was immediate. "You don't stand a chance of winning this argument, honey. I know a beautiful woman when I see one."

It was a wonder, his assessment of her. Of dowdy, nondescript Rosemary Gibson, who had never been considered a raving beauty, even at her best. Yet, in the past moments, she'd been described as such by a man who could have married any woman he chose among the eligible ladies in town.

His mouth bit at the buttons she had so carefully worked into place and she sensed the request he would make, even as he voiced it.

"I want to undo all these pretty little things, honey. Are you gonna give me a hard time about it?"

His fingers were agile, already making short work of the task, and she smothered her protest. Gabe Tanner didn't seem likely to take no for an answer tonight.

The buttons undone, he lifted to better see what his machinations had revealed. "I'll be damned. You've got your clothes on under this thing, Rosie."

"I heard you coming, and I didn't have time to take off my chemise," she whispered, thankful that the dim light prevented him from seeing the blush she knew was well in place.

"Hmm…" His hand was warm, brushing aside the placket on her gown, fingers against the pale skin revealed above the neckline of her chemise. His head bent, and his mouth pressed against the skin he'd touched with his fingertips. Skin that was inches closer to the rapid pounding of her heart.

''You must've used your new bar of soap here,'' he murmured. ''You smell good.''

''I did.'' Breathlessly, she inhaled his scent, so different from her own. An elusive aroma, one she'd only caught a trace of in the parlor as he touched her through the fabric of her dress.

''You gonna fuss if I take off your gown?''

It was the voice of temptation, Tanner at his best, leading her down the path he had set. She blinked at the intense look of concentration he bore, and shook her head, unable to deny him. Rising over her, he hesitated only a moment, then suited action to words as he lifted her to her knees on the mattress.

''Tanner!'' Her horrified whisper sounded loud in her ears, and then was lost as the voluminous fabric of her nightgown was pulled over her head. She'd not expected so rapid a loss of her modesty, and her fingers snatched for purchase as the chemise rose. The attempt was futile.

Only her arms and hands remained to protect her body from his sight, and she crossed them over her breasts quickly. He flung her clothing to the floor, and the sound that emerged from his throat was a denial of her purely feminine gesture. Smoothing the hair from her face, he allowed it to drape over her arms, then gently loosened her grip, until her only covering was that which he allowed.

''You said you weren't gonna fuss at me,'' he murmured. She was without concealment, save the dark swathe of waving hair that fell to offer a modest covering. From the window, the moon cast its light, garbing them both with a silvery glow, lending a magical cast to ordinary flesh and blood.

"You look like a princess from a storybook." Tanner knelt before her, bare inches away. She shivered, needful of his hands to ease the aching thrust of her breasts, yet wishing fervently for full darkness to envelop her with its protective embrace.

But it was not to be. His hands brushed aside the length of hair and then gripped her shoulders as he looked his fill. "Ahh, Rosemary. I may wrap you up in cotton batting and hide you away."

As if he worshiped the woman before him, Tanner's gaze followed the path his hands traveled. Palms and fingers shaped to match the curves of her body as he discovered anew, and without the impediment of clothing, the slope of her breasts. His hands formed her, scooping inward to mold the slender line of her waist, then resting finally on the lush width of her hips.

He towered over her, his strength apparent as his palms slid behind her, pressing urgently against the fullness of her bottom, drawing her across the mattress until their bodies formed a union of sorts.

There were no barriers here, she realized, only the flesh and bones of man and woman, face-to-face in a position of intimacy that was strangely right and perfect.

Words came to her mind, a sonnet that had spoken to her of the mystery of male and female, and she allowed the phrases expression. "'My beloved is fair...let him kiss me with the kisses of his mouth...'"

She'd read it more than once, yet never understood the meaning Solomon brought to life with the poetry of the love song he'd written. "'Rise up my love, my fair one...'"

"Say that again," Tanner whispered.

Unaware that she had spoken aloud, Rosemary hesitated, then did as he asked.

"That's from the Bible, isn't it?"

"Yes. The Song of Solomon to his beloved."

He nodded. "Do you know any more of it?"

Her whisper trembled as she gave voice to the words that came to mind. "'...his right hand doth embrace me...his banner over me is love.'"

With great care, his hands gentle against her skin, he moved to enclose the fullness of her breasts. "He touched her the way I'm touching you, Rosemary."

She shivered as callused fingers brought new life to the tender, virgin breasts he held in his hands, possessing them, lifting, weighing and brushing against suddenly sensitive bits of flesh.

She could barely contain the gasp of pleasure that quavered, aching for release, as she uttered her wonder in wispy phrases. "I never knew before...I didn't think...that this was what it meant."

"This is just a part of it, sweetheart." His tone held a measure of awe as he bent to kiss her. His arms encircled her, and within his embrace she was shifted to rest against her pillow. He was an immense shadow over her for a moment as he lowered his masculine length into place, hesitating but a moment.

She opened to him, her arms embracing him, and with a groan of anticipation, he settled against her, their bodies blending, smooth skin brushing against hair-roughened flesh. As if such a joining had been ordained, Rosemary's heart lifted in exultation.

His scent was dark and enticing, rising from heated flesh, and he handled her with care. She allowed it, reveling in the sensations he brought into being, awed by the heated response he drew from her. Her arms, hands and shoulders received attention she would have not thought proper, and then he moved beyond them, exploring where no other's touch had trespassed.

He wooed her gently, his lips offering kisses that left her breathless and yearning, his fingers agile and knowing, bringing to life a heated longing she was unable to contain.

Low in her belly, where her woman's parts lay shielded, where she knew she would one day carry his child, a steady, urgent cadence came into being. She shifted her hips and her knees lifted. He murmured approval of her movements, a low, satisfied sound, as his hands sought and gained even more access to those places she'd thought of as private and personal, places he seemed bent on claiming.

Dampness made the path easily traveled and his fingers sought out forbidden areas she'd only now begun to be aware of. Deep within her, muscles clenched in an unfamiliar, throbbing rhythm, and she moved restlessly, seeking with untutored knowledge that which would fulfill the heated urgency of her loins.

Soft moans escaped her lips, and she lifted her hand to still the sounds she could not contain. It was too much; she was too aware of each increment of flesh he explored, and above it all were the murmuring whispers he poured out upon her. Words that spoke of her beauty and the joy she brought him.

His hands slid beneath her, lifting her. And then, as if he reached toward a precipice, his breathing became harsh, and his body poised above her. Ceasing to breathe, knowing she must savor this moment for all time, Rosemary allowed him the entrance he demanded. She cried out, painfully aware of the penetration of his flesh, wincing as her body stretched to contain him. Yet, slowly, inexorably, he possessed her, filling her, claiming the right to give her his seed.

His mouth captured hers, lips caressing, containing her cries, tenderly easing her beyond the first pangs of discomfort. And somehow she had known that there would be that pain to contend with. Yet, it was but the threshold to a union of body and spirit such as she had never imagined.

He was gentle, careful with her delicate flesh, even as it rent at his bidding, murmuring words of comfort as her tears marked the moment in which she became his wife. And then the pain was dissolving in a surge of desire as he moved within her.

She stifled sounds of delight, whispering his name, riding the storm of his passion as his manhood answered the need she could not voice.

With a growl that shook his powerful frame he surged against her, within her, his arms circling to clasp her tightly to himself. Filled with wonderment, she was aware only of growing pleasure that filled her to overflowing.

"Tanner!" Smothered against his shoulder, her cry was broken, and anew, the tears ran from beneath closed eyelids. He rose to hover over her, and in the moonlight she watched as his lips drew back, his head tilting upward. His body was taut, rigid above her as he thrust deeply within that part of her he had claimed as his own.

And whispered her name.

Chairs were hauled in from the dining room as Scat and Anna were settled at the breakfast table. Tipper sat between them, his long arms stretching to provide them with more food than they could eat. Anna scooted close to the youthful cowhand, watching him with adoring eyes as he coaxed her to try a portion from every bowl and platter on the table. Tanner watched his bride, his hands clenched next to his plate as she moved the length of the table, pouring coffee from the big pot. It seemed she was ignoring him this morning, and he found it an irritation he could not hide.

"How about savin' a little of that for me, Rosemary?" he asked harshly as she fit carefully between Cotton and Bootie, filling their cups to the brim.

Her startled glance meshed with his, and, as if she had sustained a blow, she blanched and backed from the table. Mama Pearl cast him a look of warning and he shoved his chair back. Damned if he'd watch his wife of less than a day tend to everybody else but him.

Then she was next to him, and her skirts brushed his trouser leg. A faint drift of lilac soap enveloped him like a memory that teased unmercifully. He looked up at her, aware that his brow was creased, that his mouth was thin and drawn tightly against his teeth.

She met his gaze again, her eyes puzzled, a trace of pain turning her mouth down, and suddenly he felt a pang of remorse. Shame that he had brought sadness to the gentle woman who only sought to serve those men who depended on her for their daily repasts.

"Rosemary?" His hand lifted from the tabletop and rested against her waist, edging to encircle that narrow span.

Her tongue touched her lip and his eyes were drawn to the gesture. It was swollen, he realized with abrupt awareness, from his mouth suckling, biting and feasting on the lush surface of those mobile lips throughout the night hours.

"Want to take a trip to town?" he asked quietly. "We need to find clothes for Scat and Anna."

"Will they be all right here?" she asked. "Nate won't…"

He shook his head. "I don't think so. Mama Pearl will keep Anna close, and Cotton will put Scat to work in the barn."

Her face brightened at that and she lifted the pot, pouring his cup full. "I'll be ready by the time you finish eating."

"I want you to eat, too," he insisted. His hand squeezed and he watched as a slow flush rose from her throat.

"I'm sorry to be…" He could not finish the apology, not with six men sitting at attention, each of them probably wondering at the circumstances that had led to the sudden changes in this household.

"We heard you went to see the preacher yesterday afternoon, boss." Cotton, the bravest of the lot dropped caution by the wayside and spoke aloud the thought that had been on every man's mind this morning.

"You surprised? Everybody for miles around knows I've been after Rosemary for weeks. Finally got her to agree, and I figured there's no time like the present."

Tipper grinned widely. "Well, hot da…" He paused, the phrase half uttered, and brushed the back of his hand over his mouth. "Congratulations, Miss Rosemary," he managed. "Does this mean you're not gonna quit the job? You'll be here from now on?"

Rosemary smiled, relieved that the news was out in the open. "I don't intend to go anywhere, Tipper. This is my home. And Tanner is my husband."

There, she'd said the words aloud, and Tanner considered them for a moment. He was a husband. Gabe Tanner, perennial bachelor, was a married man. He'd take a heap of guff, that was for sure, beginning this morning when his buggy rolled into town.

His glance encompassed the woman by his side and the frown he'd worn vanished. The attention she'd paid to the cowhands surrounding his table seemed of little import now. That they were privileged to be near this small, sturdy creature who tended them with cheerful generosity was a minor detail.

When he closed the back door tonight, blew out the lamp over the kitchen table and headed for his bedroom at the top of the stairs, Rosemary would be waiting there for *him*. The curse of jealousy, passed down through the years by a man who had abused and degraded his wife, would stop here.

Rosemary was not Greta Tanner, not the woman who had pulled up stakes and headed for the big city, rather than face down the domineering man who'd held her captive in this house. From beside him, Rosemary looked down. The blue eyes that turned in his direction held warmth for all within this room, but only for him did she smile in so sweet a manner as she did now.

"Are you ready?" He stepped inside the bedroom and closed the door behind him.

Rosemary stood before the mirror, twisting her hair into a long curving lock, forming it to the back of her head as he watched. Ivory pins held it in place and she brushed back the wispy tresses that waved around her face.

"I like it better down," he said, tilting his head to one side.

She met his gaze in the mirror. "What did I do to make you angry at the breakfast table?"

He looked down at the floor, edging the rug into place with his toe. "You didn't do anything," he muttered. "It was me, honey."

"Well, whatever caused it, I need to know, Tanner. You were angry, and I felt abused." She turned to face him. "It might not have hurt so badly, but after last night…"

"I didn't want anyone else to smell the soap I gave

you," he said gruffly. "Those men just eat it up when you come close."

She tilted her head to one side and allowed the smile that begged exposure to curve her lips. "I can't believe you said that, Gabe Tanner. Shall I rinse off the scent when I get up in the morning? Or should I have Mama Pearl pour the coffee?"

He shook his head, abashed. "No, there's no reason to do any of that, honey. I was just thinkin' about my pa for a minute, about how I hated what he did to my mother. And then I did pret' near the same thing to you."

She crossed the room and stood before him. "I'm your wife, Gabriel. I'm not sure how it all came about, but you turned me into Mrs. Tanner last night. It was the most beautiful thing that's ever happened to me, and it's making me blush to say it. But I want you to know that there isn't another man alive who means one red cent to me."

Gabriel. She'd called him by that hated name. He turned it over in his mind. Somehow it didn't sound nearly so bad when Rosemary's voice spoke the syllables.

"Honey, don't call me that in front of anybody else. If you want to say it when we're alone, it's all right, but..."

"Gabriel?" A puzzled frown creased her brow. "You don't like the name?"

He shook his head.

"All right."

"All right? You're not gonna argue with me?"

"No, Tanner. I pick my fights. This isn't worth

making a fuss over. Just remember, I get to win the next time we disagree."

She waited for him to open the door, checking her buttons and straightening the cuffs of her dress. "I couldn't find my hat. I must have left it downstairs."

"We need to talk about that, honey," he drawled, allowing her to step from the room before him.

"Where is it?" She turned to look at him as she placed her foot on the top step.

"I bought you a new one," he said cheerfully.

"There wasn't anything wrong with the old one. It had a lot of wear left."

"Not any more." He followed her down the flight of stairs, noting the stiffening of her back, the harsh sound her shoes made on each step.

Stepping into the dining room, he reached inside the buffet, drawing forth a pale straw bonnet, crested with a circlet of flowers around its crown.

"I like this one better, Rosemary. Try it on."

"It's awfully bright, isn't it?"

He tilted his head to one side. "I reckon I'd call it cheerful."

"I'll save it for Sunday church," she decided. "Put it aside and fetch my black straw."

"Can't do that, sweetheart." He held out the new bonnet, his jaw firmly set, as if he begged an argument from her.

"What did you do with my black straw?" Her tone was ominous as she set her toe to tapping on the bare floor, one hand propped on her hip.

"Burned it. I stuck it in the woodstove and used it for firewood."

"I don't believe you," she said, emphasizing each word.

He shrugged. "I guess you better believe it, Rosemary. It's God's truth. That poor old hat was so battered and beaten to a pulp, it wasn't worth another wearing."

She eyed him for a moment, her mouth twitching as if she couldn't decide whether to smile or grumble at him again. Then, one hand reached for the straw bonnet he held, its flowered brim looking incongruous in his big hands.

She tied it in place, tilted it a bit, brushing at the brim with her fingertips. "What do you think?"

His grin was wide, his mouth generous as he bent to touch his lips to hers. Reluctantly, he released her, aware that the day would be long.

"I think you look like a bride, Mrs. Tanner. Let's go to town."

Chapter Eleven

"Tanner!" From every side, it seemed, voices lifted to call his name, and hands lifted to greet the couple who rode into town. Rosemary sat erect, shunning the protective arm Tanner had eased behind her shoulders. Her easy smile had become a painful grimace by the time the buggy reached the general store, and she slid from the seat quickly.

"You want me to go in with you?" Tanner leaned in her direction and she shook her head at his offer.

"No, you go on and see to your business. Just pick me up here in half an hour." That would surely be long enough to satisfy the curiosity of the womenfolk who regularly gathered here each weekday morning.

She was met by a chorus of greetings, her entry into the store announced by the overhanging bell that rang with each swing of the door. Pip cast her a commiserating glance, looking down from her ladder.

"Didn't you steal a march on all of us?" Bernice Comstock said joyously. "Don't think you'll get away without a wedding shower. The preacher's wife is already making plans."

From beside the rack of crockery and cookware, Dex Sawyer shot her a look of amusement. Surely he wouldn't approach her, Rosemary thought, hastily turning from his gaze. But it was too much to hope for.

From behind her, Dex's well-modulated tones spoke his words of congratulations and surprise. "You've set the whole town on its ear, Miss Rosemary. May I offer my best wishes?"

She ducked her head, unwilling to meet the scrutiny of this man who had come close to making an offer of sorts himself.

"Thank you, Mr. Sawyer. Calling attention to myself was never my intention. I'd hoped for my wedding to be simple and the celebration private."

"I'm sure it was," he said, amusement curling each word as if he sought to be let back into her good graces.

"Ignore him, Rosemary. He's just being snippy because he burned up his only kettle yesterday and has to pay out hard cold cash for another." Pip had climbed down from her ladder, approaching quietly. Her arm circled Rosemary's waist and she embraced her quickly, whispering in her ear.

"You'll be old news by next week. Just keep smiling."

"Well, I certainly hope so." Rosemary drew in a deep breath. "Now, to get down to business. I need all kinds of things for the children, Pip. Tanner traced their feet on a piece of paper, and they need under-wear and at least three changes of clothing each.''

Pip sniffed and sighed, wiping her eyes with the corner of her apron. ''They won't know how to act, will they? I doubt either of them has had new kicks in their entire lives. Let alone something to wear that didn't come out of the missionary barrel.''

Rosemary's mouth twisted in silent response, thinking of herself as a young girl digging in that self-same barrel for some decent clothes. Resolve stiffened her spine.

''I might just find myself a new outfit this morning, too, while I'm at it. I'm tired of frumpy hand-me-downs from folks who buy new and ready-made.'' Her head tilted, jaw clenching firmly as Pip grinned her agreement.

''About time, I'd say, Miss Gibson. Your pa was always so willing to give to everyone else, he forgot that his daughter could use a little pick-me-up once in a while.''

Bernice Comstock approached, carrying a bolt of chambray. ''I heard that Tanner took those poor Pender children home.'' She leaned closer, and her voice softened. ''Mr. Comstock said that Nate Pender got roaring drunk last night, too, and threatened to ride out and take them back.''

Rosemary's eyes widened as she exchanged glances with Pip. ''We haven't seen hide nor hair of him.''

''Don't worry, the sheriff slung him in a cell to sleep it off. You ought to be forewarned, though. He's been known to be a nasty drunk in his time.''

A chill traced its way down Rosemary's spine. "I've seen the results of his meanness, Mrs. Comstock. Poor Scat is a mass of bruises." She turned back to Pip. "I need to see some dresses for Anna, first."

"She's not very big is she?" Pip asked, pulling out a large glass container, brim full with checked and striped garments. She lifted an armful to the countertop. "Take a look at these. They're all of a size, should fit most five-or-six-year-olds. With a pinafore over the top, they'll fit her, even if they're cut wide."

Rosemary's fingers touched the closely woven fabric, admiring the pink checks that would bring out the color in Anna's face. "I'll take this one," she said, lifting the dress high to better admire the puffed sleeves and full skirt. "And a blue stripe, I think. Then I want something in lawn, very soft, for Sunday. Oh, and a plain pinafore for everyday, and a ruffled one for Sundays."

She smiled as she considered her choices, then leaned over the counter, speaking softly. "Tanner said he'd go to church with me, and take the children."

Pip's brow lifted. "You mean it? Tanner's going to make an appearance in church?"

Rosemary nodded. "That's what he said on the way to town. He said to find decent shoes for both children." Rosemary rummaged in her reticule, coming up with the piece of brown paper that bore the tracings of Scat's and Anna's feet.

"Boots for Scat and black shoes for Anna, I think."

"Seems like Tanner's investing a pile of money in

two children who aren't even his own," Geraldine Frombert observed.

Rosemary bristled. "Tanner's a good man. He's not worried about a return from his investment, Mrs. Frombert."

Pip stepped up with a pile of overalls across her arm, speaking hastily. "Here, Rosemary. Take a look at these for size. Scat's not big around, but he looked to me like he was shootin' up, last time I saw him."

"Yes, all right." Rosemary held up a pair of overalls, discarded them as too short and picked up the next. "I want two shirts for everyday and one for Sunday for him, too, Pip."

"Don't forget socks and underwear," Dex Sawyer reminded her from the end of the counter where he stood with his choice of the kettles on display. "I declare, Mrs. Tanner, you ought to find yourself a new dress, too. I'll warrant you'd look nice in a pink check like the one you picked out for the little girl."

Pip leaned across the counter. "We've already agreed on the new dress part, Mr. Sawyer. And he's right, Rosemary. Pink would be a good color on you."

As if she succumbed to the joint coaching, Rosemary nodded slowly. "Maybe a stripe would be better though." She looked up at Pip. "You don't think it would be too frivolous, a woman my age wearing pink?"

"I'll bet Tanner would like it," Pip whispered. "I doubt he thinks you're too old to look pretty. He sure pondered over that new bonnet you're wearing."

The pile of clothing grew with the additions Dex

had mentioned, and Pip was busily sorting through the rack of ladies fashions when the door opened with a bang. The bell rang loudly and Rosemary sensed, even before his voice called to her, that the newest customer was Tanner.

"You all set here?" he asked, his boots sounding harshly against the wooden floor. "We need to head back to the ranch, honey. Sheriff said Nate Pender left his cell this morning muttering about Scat and Anna. I won't be surprised if he shows up."

"I'd have thought Oscar would have better sense than to let Nate loose, after the show he put on last night at the Golden Slipper," Dex remarked. He leveled a warning look at Tanner. "He said some pretty nasty things about you, and about Miss Rosemary here. I'd keep an eye out."

Tanner nodded. "I meant to give you money, Rosemary," he said, reaching into his pocket. "Figure it up, Pip."

Pip made a bundle of the clothing, wrapping it in brown paper tied with several lengths of twine. She accepted Tanner's money and doled out his change, then caught at Rosemary's arm. "I put in a dress for you, too."

"I hadn't decided for sure," Rosemary whispered.

"Well, I decided for you." Pip waved a farewell as Rosemary hurried to the door, where Tanner waited with a definite lack of patience.

The ride home was accomplished rapidly, the mare keeping up a good pace. "I'd thought to enjoy this trip," Tanner said. "It looks like we're going to have to keep a sharp eye out for Nate. I want you to keep the gun loaded behind the kitchen door.''

"I've never fired a gun," she said, her gaze caught by the somber cast of Tanner's features.

He turned toward her. "You can learn soon enough. Mama Pearl can hit a rabbit at a hundred yards. I'd lay odds she could scalp Nate Pender, one hair at a time, if she'd a mind to."

"You're frightening me," Rosemary said. "I didn't think this far ahead. Why do you suppose he's so set on getting those children back? He doesn't even like them."

"Sheriff Rhinehold told me that Jason cut off Nate's supply of booze at the saloon last night. Told him it was cash on the barrelhead from now on."

"He's not much on working for a living, is he?"

Tanner shook his head. "No, and now that things are out in the open, he'll be hard put to find odd jobs."

"I wish he'd leave town," Rosemary said wistfully. "I didn't think I'd ever have children of my own." She reached for him, her fingers finding purchase on his forearm. "I can love Scat and Anna enough to make up for losing their mother. Don't you think?"

He shifted the reins to his left hand, his right arm circling her waist. He drew her closer, and she dropped her hand to clasp his thigh. Hard, muscular and heavy, the muscles clenched beneath her fingers, and she felt a moment's pause as she considered the intimacy of her touch.

"You could do most anything you set out to. Look

what you've done to me.'' He sent her a grin, and she ducked her head. "I mean it, Rosie. You've got me sayin' grace at the table, and those men of mine think you're the best thing that's ever happened to me. You've even got Tipper writin' to his ma every week.''

"She was so pleased that he's been going to church. Don't forget, you said you'd go with us this Sunday,'' she reminded him.

"Yeah, I did, didn't I?'' His gaze was on the road ahead. "My mother used to take me every week.''

Rosemary was silent, her fingers moving against the rough denim of his trousers.

"I used to wonder where she went, when she left here. She just walked down the road one day, and I never saw her again. My pa held on to me and told me I was too big to cry. Guess I was. Must've been thirteen, maybe fourteen.''

"I can't imagine a mother leaving her son behind.''

"Well, I learned young not to depend on anybody else. I've never seen a woman yet could be trusted when the chips are down,'' he said, his voice rough, his face a mask. He removed his arm from behind her and snapped the reins over the back of his mare. "We're almost there. Hope we beat Nate Pender to the punch.''

It was a vain hope. Nate had been and gone, and only by sheer good luck had he escaped in one piece.

"Couldn't get a good shot,'' Mama Pearl grumbled. "What with Anna cryin' in the kitchen behind me, and Cotton raisin' the roof out by the spring-house, things were in a fair way to bein' disagreeable all the way around. Nate rode up, ugly as sin, all whiskery and lookin' like he just crawled out of a pigpen, and first off, Scat ran howlin' from the barn, lookin' for his sister.''

"He didn't get hurt?'' Rosemary asked, as Mama Pearl drew breath.

The brightly colored turban tipped Rosemary's way, and Mama Pearl laughed aloud. "Naw, that boy can run like greased lightning. Ol' Cotton snatched him and shoved him in the springhouse, and grabbed up an ax from the woodpile.''

"See, sweetheart. I told you you were gettin' gray hair for nothin','' Tanner said, grinning widely.

"Anyway, Nate slid offa his horse and came toward the porch, and when he saw me aimin' the gun at him he hid behind his horse.'' Mama Pearl made a disgusted face. "Biggest coward in six counties, I swear. Then, what with Cotton and Scat out beyond him and Anna behind me, I didn't get to pull a trigger.''

"Probably the sight of you with a rifle in your hand was enough to send him on his way,'' Tanner surmised.

"I 'spect he was lookin' to see the preacher's daughter here, and thought he could snatch his young'uns and run.''

"He was probably still about half-lit and didn't know what the hell he was doin','' Tanner said, shaking his head.

"Do you think he'll let us be?'' Rosemary asked hopefully.

"Maybe.'' Tanner allowed.

Mama Pearl looked doubtful. "I'm keepin' this gun handy, no matter what. And this baby's stayin' close by." Anna sat at the table, a piece of bread in one hand, a glass of milk in front of her, wide-eyed and listening.

"Scat takes care of me," she announced. "He never lets Pa hurt me."

Rosemary's heart twinged with sorrow at the child's words. That Scat had been the whipping boy was a given. Only time would tell what scars their life with Nate Pender would leave on these two.

"I hate to tell you folks this, but Nate has a right to his children. There's no law against whippin' your own child, and unless Nate gets in trouble some other way, you're pret' near obliged to give him back his young'uns." Sheriff Rhinehold stood on the porch, hat in hand and spoke to Rosemary through the screen.

"Tanner around?" he asked, his big hands smoothing the edge of his hat brim before he replaced it on his head.

Rosemary nodded. "He's out beyond the barn."

"You alone in there?" Oscar asked, peering past her into the shadowy kitchen.

"No, Mama Pearl's in the dining room, and Anna's upstairs."

"Well, nobody's told Nate that the judge ruled against you folks, and I doubt anyone's gonna run right out and give him the news. But you want to be ready if he shows up."

"I don't think I can just hand him these children,"

Rosemary said, sensing a loss of strength in her legs as she considered what might happen.

"Just wait and see," Oscar advised. He turned from her, heading toward the barn and the large corral behind where Tanner worked with his colts.

"I won't go with him." Scat appeared at the end of the porch, his face dark with anger, brows drawn low. "No matter what any judge has to say, Anna and me ain't gonna live with Pa any more. I'll just pack up our stuff, and we'll head west."

Rosemary's heart went out to the boy, so brave and so alone in the world. So young to be the champion of another, at an age when he should still be able to depend on adults for protection and love.

"I won't let anything happen to you, Scat," she promised.

Scat sat on the edge of the porch, his legs swinging. "You won't be able to do much about it, Miss Rosemary, if Pa finds out what the judge said."

"Let's wait and see what Tanner says before you make any plans to leave us."

Scat looked up, his expression bleak as he nodded briefly, then bent his head once more. It was more than Rosemary could bear, to see the boy in such despair, yet determined to protect his sister any way he could.

She opened the screen door and stepped onto the porch. "Can I sit by you?"

His shoulders shrugged, and accepting that small sign as agreement, Rosemary smoothed her skirts and sat on the edge of the porch, swinging her legs in rhythm with the boy beside her. With a tentative gesture, she enclosed his shoulders in a loose embrace, unwilling to encroach, and then realized that she feared for naught.

With a soft cry, Scat turned to look at her, making no attempt to hide the tears that gathered in his eyes.

"I'm scared, Miss Rosemary. If it was just me, I'd be gone already. But I don't know if I can take care of Anna, all by myself. I wish I was bigger, so I could get a job."

"Oh, Scat." There were no words to express the compassion that burgeoned within Rosemary's breast. She bent her head to touch his, placing a kiss against the tanned forehead. "I wish things were different for you. Can't you trust Tanner to know what to do?"

He shook his head. "Tanner can't help if he's in jail, and that's what'll happen if he don't do like the judge says, I'll betcha."

"Please don't run, not now," Rosemary begged.

The boy hesitated, then tilting his head to better meet her gaze, he nodded. "All right. I'll stay for now, but if Pa shows up and tries to take us back, I'll run, and take Anna with me, Miss Rosemary."

"For now, just stick close to Tanner or Cotton, all right?" she asked. "I'll keep Anna with me."

The boy nodded and slid from the porch, then turned back as his booted feet hit the ground. "Ma'am, I didn't thank you for the clothes and the new boots. They're kinda crampin' my toes, but Tanner says I'll get used to it."

He stuck one foot forward, eyeing it judiciously. "I never had boots before. They're right pretty, ain't they?"

Rosemary nodded, finding speech difficult when her throat was so thick with emotion. She watched as the boy trudged toward the barn, then scooted backward and rose to her feet.

"That boy's got too much to bear for a young'un," Mama Pearl said from the doorway. "Come on in here, girl, see what I did to the dining room. This'll cheer you up."

Rosemary followed agreeably, grateful for the words that had interrupted her fretting. Pa had said more than once that it was a sin to keep on worrying once a body'd put their problems in God's hands. And every angel behind those golden gates must know that Rosemary had done a heap of delivering up Scat and Anna into heaven's care.

"Oh, my!" Her exclamation of delight was spontaneous as she stood within the wide doorway of the dining room. Mama Pearl had stripped the dust covers from the furniture, opened wide the draperies and pried up the windows, allowing a breeze to blow through the room.

The furniture was made of oak, carved and embellished, and fit for the finest house in town, Rosemary thought. She walked past the long table, her fingertips coasting across the tops of five chairs on either side, and one on each end. The circuit complete, she turned to the long sideboard, tracing the deeply cut design on the edge, bending to peer at herself in the oval mirror inset within the tall back. A pink-cheeked hoyden was captured there, with dark hair and blue eyes that held a trace of sadness.

"I look like something the cat dragged in," she

said, her smile rueful as she turned to Mama Pearl. She gazed at the chandelier, globes and chimneys gleaming in the sunlight that cascaded through the windows.

"It's beautiful." Even to her own ears, her murmur was wistful. "I've never seen another like it. Not even the one in the parlor."

"Old Walt Tanner fixed this room up for his woman, hopin' to keep her here with fancy furniture and colored lights." Mama Pearl sniffed as if a particularly virulent scent had passed her way. "He'd oughta known that treatin' a woman right makes more sense than spendin' money."

"He wasn't kind?" Rosemary asked, glancing at the doorway, lest someone overhear. Speaking unkindly of the dead and departed was not her usual behavior, yet she felt an urgency to know more of Tanner's family.

"Kind!" Mama Pearl almost shouted the word. "The old man was about as far from kind as any man ever was. Thought because he bought her fancy things, she'd be happy. Then one fine day when that drummer came by and told her she'd look mighty good in one of the big houses in Shreveport, what with her bein' so pretty and fine-figured, she started in thinkin' that she might as well take a hike."

"Tanner said she walked down the road and never looked back."

"Sure enough. 'Course, I always did think that fancy drummer fella figured out how to snatch her up. He was one fine lookin' man, he was." Mama Pearl nodded her head, smacking her lips as if tasting a particularly savory treat.

"You act like you didn't blame her. She left her son behind," Rosemary protested.

"She knew he was gettin' to the place where he'd take hold and get his hand in the runnin' of things here. Walt Tanner just buried himself behind that desk in there and let Tanner do it."

Rosemary shook her head. "I couldn't do that, just walk out that way."

"No, I don't 'spose you could, honey. But then, you got a different upbringin' than Greta Tanner. And you got a man that treats you right. Greta wore bruises more than once around here. There wasn't any love to give in Walt. Between 'em they sure made a mess of things."

Rosemary listened with a growing sense of sorrow, recalling the words Tanner had spoken last week on the way home from town. He'd learned young not to depend on anybody else. And he'd learned early on not to trust a woman.

She had her work cut out for her.

"They're gonna be raisin' the roof for the new schoolhouse next week, Saturday," Tipper said. He held the big bowl of potatoes in one hand and spooned out an enormous portion to his plate. He'd come in late, after hauling a load from the sawmill. Now he recounted the news from town.

"Really? They have enough money?" Rosemary asked.

"They didn't come lookin' for any from me," Tanner said with a glance at Rosemary.

Tipper snorted loudly. "I got stuck payin' mine, first of August. They must have somebody does nuthin' but check up on bachelors in this town. Ever since that crazy tax got passed last year, I feel like the ladies are keepin' an eye on every fella in town."

"Yeah, I've been afraid to show my face since last week." Bootie spoke around a mouthful of food, but his words were so sour, Rosemary didn't have the heart to correct his manners.

"How do they collect the money?" she asked.

Tanner's voice was dominant as three different men began explanations. "They gave bachelors a year to find a wife. That year was up on August first. If a man can't prove he's asked a woman to marry him during the past year, he pays, and pays through the nose."

He watched as Rosemary assimilated his answer. The moment she lifted her gaze to meet his, he was sorry he'd been so blunt and unfeeling in his choice of wordage.

"If I'd truly turned you down, you'd still have been exempt, wouldn't you?"

"I was tired of bein' a bachelor, Rosemary." His words were met with laughter as one, then another of the men disputed his claim.

"He'd never have got married if you hadn't come along, ma'am," Cotton said stoutly. "Tanner was about the least likely candidate for marriage as any man I ever knew."

"Then I suppose he was fortunate that I arrived on

the scene, wasn't he?'' she answered, ducking her head as she shuffled the food around on her plate. ''I'm sure he's pleased as punch to be an old married man.''

The voices stilled, and the men began eating at a swifter pace, cutting an occasional glance at Tanner, then back at Rosemary, quizzical expressions marring their usually good-natured faces. Tanner thought every one of them looked like he'd stepped atop an anthill and was trying to figure out how to make an escape.

One by one, they excused themselves, the manners Rosemary had coached them in coming to the forefront as they begged her leave to exit the kitchen.

She nodded at each in turn, as if she were the schoolmarm and the grown men around her lads in a schoolroom. Tanner felt his way cautiously as the last of the men closed the door behind himself.

''I've snapped your garter someway or another,'' he said, leaning back in his chair. ''And I'll be damned if I know how.''

''As you so elegantly put it, Mr. Tanner, my garter is not snapped. I'm just very pleased that marrying me bore at least one benefit to you. I hope the money you saved was a tidy sum.''

''Yeah,'' he drawled. ''As a matter of fact it was, me bein' a landowner.'' She was irritating him now, with her chin set like a bulldog and that nose up in the air.

''Well, just think! If I'd turned you down, you'd have been saved the burden of having a wife underfoot, not to mention the two children I've foisted on you.''

Tanner cocked his head. She was on a roll now, madder'n a wet hen. He might as well go all the way and set her skirts on fire with his final salvo.

''Well, the fact is, Miss Rosemary, I got a free cook and housekeeper out of this deal, not to mention some other benefits I won't name right now. And I'm not complainin' about any of them.''

He'd never seen her move so fast, on her feet and on the run. He bolted from his chair and grasped her arm as she would have escaped the room. His arms encircled her and his mouth met hers with a degree of desire he hadn't expected to find in this meshing of lips. He was about half set to blow, and about halfway to being as aroused as a man could get.

Even the mumbling sounds coming from Rosemary's throat as he slaked his immediate hunger in the sweetness of her mouth were not enough to deter his passion. Yet, whether he liked it or not, he had an angry woman to deal with.

He gave her room to breathe, but his lips brushed the skin of her cheek and throat as he spoke. ''Hush, sweetheart. I'm sorry. I shouldn't have pushed you quite that far, and I don't blame you one stinkin' bit for bein' mad at me.''

''Well, that's mighty big of you, Gabe Tanner. If I'd known that a firm refusal would have been to your benefit, I'd certainly have done things differently.''

His hold gentled, his hands moving in a caressing fashion over her back. ''Would you, now? And where would you be, Rosie?''

Her eyes fell from his gaze and she shook her head. "That's the sad part. I don't know what I'd have done."

"Well, to tell the truth, I'm glad you came here, and I'm even happier that you married me, honey." He held her away and looked her up and down. "You've managed to crawl under my hide like no one else in this world ever has. I've got a powerful yen for you, Mrs. Tanner."

From beyond the pantry door, Mama Pearl's woeful tones could be heard as she clattered crocks and pans in a harsh medley of sound. "Are y'all about done fightin' out there? I got work to do."

Tanner laughed aloud. "Come on out, Mama Pearl. We're just havin' a little discussion, but I reckon it's about settled."

Rosemary stepped back from his hold and smoothed back her hair. Somehow, he'd managed to undo her best efforts, and dark waves hung on either side of her face.

"I like it that way, sweetheart," he told her softly, his fingers tugging at the pins that bound her hair in place at her nape. He'd succeeded in pulling out four or five before she stomped her foot in exasperation. But it was too late, and the carefully twisted and wound length fell from place.

"Now I've got to redo it," she muttered, holding out her hand for the return of the dark bone pins he held.

He leaned to whisper in her ear. "Come on upstairs with me and I'll help you."

Her look of disdain was priceless, he thought, as she shook her head firmly.

"I don't think that's a good idea. I can do it right here."

He sighed, an exaggerated sound that almost made her smile. Her lips twitched, her eyes twinkled, and he was satisfied. He deposited the pins in her outstretched hand and closed her fingers over them.

The sun couldn't set fast enough to suit him, he decided.

It had been a long week since his wedding night.

Chapter Twelve

They'd gone to bed in the dark for the past week, Rosemary swathed in her long, white gown. Her halting explanation of a woman's monthly problem had been most embarrassing for her, and Gabe had tried his best to be understanding. Not an easy task for a new bridegroom.

Tonight looked to be a different situation altogether. He'd managed to talk her into one, lone candle. And that one was as far from the bed as she could get it. She'd placed it on the washstand, behind the privacy screen, and then cast him a sidelong glance when he folded the screen against the wall.

It seemed that Rosemary would be an obedient wife, but only as far as her modesty would allow. He'd thought she was over the first hurdle already, but there she sat on the bedside, already garbed in her white nightgown, as if she were mulling over her next move.

It would be flat on the mattress, if he had anything to say about it, Tanner decided. Stripped to the barest essentials, in order to spare her dignity, he watched her. If he played it right, he could be beneath the sheet before his drawers hit the floor. Thumbs at the waistband, he slid from the garment.

Rosemary looked over her shoulder, caught off balance as the mattress shifted with his weight. Her eyes took in the broad width of his chest, seeming to focus on the dark triangle of hair in its center. She shot a quick glance at the length of him, and he fought the chuckle that threatened to emerge.

He could see the wheels turning in that head of hers, wondering what he wore on his bottom, and wary of finding out. One hand lifted to coax her beneath the sheet, and she placed icy fingers against his palm.

"You're cold, Rosie. Come on over here and let me get you warm." Though how she could possibly need warming on such a beautiful summer night was a poser. Her fingers trembled and he tightened his grip.

She was scared. Well, maybe not scared, but sure enough she had a case of nerves. He'd hoped... Well, no matter.

Rosemary turned, sliding her feet next to his, placing her head in the precise center of her pillow. The sheet was drawn up tightly beneath her chin and Tanner exhaled loudly.

"What? What is it?" she asked quickly, turning to him with a cautious air.

"I don't want you to be worryin' about what's gonna happen tonight," Tanner said quietly. "I

thought we'd gotten that out of the way last week."
And tonight he'd hoped to be home free.

"I'm not worried," she denied, her gaze touching
his, then slanting off to one side. "I really don't like
the room so light."

And he'd been wishing for a lantern right over the
bed.

"You think I'm being foolish, don't you?" Her
forehead was furrowed with the tension she'd managed to build up, and he ached to dispense with every
speck of it.

He rose on one elbow, and his index finger touched
the creases and worked at erasing them. "Naw, I
think you're a lot of things. Pretty…"

Her lips pursed and an impatient sound rumbled in
her throat. The tip of her tongue slipped between rosy
lips and moistened the flesh it touched. He watched
it in rapt admiration.

"You think I'm pretty?" Her blue eyes were less
wary now it seemed, warming to his cause.

"Damn right. And a lot of other things. I mean,
pretty's fine, but there's a heap of pretty women in
Texas. I'd rather have honest and capable and loving,
any day of the week."

"Rather than pretty?" She sounded doubtful at that
and scanned him with a scornful look. "Men like
pretty. Not that I really think I am…pretty, I mean."

His hand admired her skin, brushing against the
firm flesh of her forehead as he noted the disappearance of her frown lines. Her cheek was soft, her ear
nicely furled. And then there was the soft curve of
her throat, just beneath her jawline. He touched the

fragile skin, felt the pulsing of her heart beneath his fingertips, then bent to place his mouth there, where the beat trembled beneath his lips.

"I think you're the prettiest thing I've ever seen, Miss Rosemary." He lifted his head to find her eyes rounding in surprise. "I've seen pretty at its finest, like skittish mares, and newborn fillies and the sun rising in the east."

He ducked his head, feeling a bit foolish, as if his words had exposed him to ridicule, then decided to brazen it out. "Anyway, you're the best of the lot, honey. You've got a shine on you like a new penny, and your hair makes me want to wrap myself up in it."

"Like a new penny?" Her mouth trembled, then twitched, then turned up at the corners. Her eyes crinkled and pure mischief lit their depths. "Now, maybe a whole bushel of new pennies would be pretty, Mr. Tanner. Just one isn't worth a whole lot."

Damn, if she wasn't teasing him. He grinned his response. "Trust me, Rosie. You're worth a whole lot." He gathered her in his arms and rocked her against himself. "You're not afraid, are you." It was a statement of fact, he realized. The wary look was gone, replaced by amusement, and he was more than pleased with the knowledge.

She lifted her arm and twined it around his neck. "I was a little bit worried, at first...tonight I mean."

"Oh?" He tilted his head back and watched as her cheeks bloomed. "How's that?"

"I kept thinking about last time, and wondering if

I was too forward. And if I was what you expected. And I almost asked Mama Pearl about…''

"No, don't do that," he said quickly. "You want to know anything, you ask me." The thought of Mama Pearl giving him one of her gimlet stares was not to be imagined. The woman would skin him alive if she thought for one minute he'd done damage to her lone chick.

"I couldn't bring myself to ask her, anyway," Rosemary admitted.

"Ask me, then." He bent lower, his mouth sweeping the width of hers, tasting the peppermint tooth powder she'd used.

"I just wanted to know if I did what I was supposed to, if it was what you expected. Last time, I mean."

"And how the dickens was Mama Pearl supposed to know the answer to that one?" he asked, hardly able to contain his amusement.

"That's why I didn't ask her."

"Well, I can set your mind at ease, pretty lady." His fingers eased the sheet lower until the buttons on her gown were all exposed, lined up neatly from throat to waist.

"You were just fine. Better than fine. You were…" He hesitated, at a loss for words that would tell her what she needed to know.

"I told you that you were beautiful, didn't I?"

Her head nodded, the movement slight, as if she urged him to continue.

"Well, you were. Not pretty, like you are now, but beautiful, like the stained-glass window at church.

And, to tell you the truth, I don't know which is better. But beautiful is the way a bride should be, Rosie. All fresh and new and…'' He hesitated. "Innocent. You were innocent.''

"And now? I'm not any more, am I?''

His grin was wide. "Yeah, you are. Just not so much as before. But now, you know kinda what to expect, and I can tell you're not worried about my touching you, and your eyes are shiny and you're… Damn, you're pretty as a picture.''

Not worried about him touching her. Her breasts already yearned for his big, warm hands to enclose them, peaking and rubbing against the fabric of her gown as she shifted against the mattress. And he was thinking she was hesitant.

If he'd blown out the candle, she'd have been more willing to pull the yards of nightgown over her head. As it was, her courage was flagging at the thought.

"Rosie…'' He bent to kiss her again and she welcomed his caress, her mouth softening beneath his, her lips allowing him entry.

She didn't even mind his calling her Rosie. It rolled off his tongue so softly, the whispering sound of it beckoning her. Even in the midst of his kisses, she was conscious of long fingers working at her buttons, then brushing over the crests of her breasts, pausing to lift and enclose them within broad palms.

Anticipation had drawn her into knots all evening, her remembrance of her wedding night an acute entity, nudging her with bits and pieces, until her flesh pulsed with the memory of pleasure such as she'd never dreamed of.

Tanner had turned the page she'd thought never to read. He'd changed her life beyond her wildest imaginings. He'd exposed the part of her that had long yearned for the secrets of marriage, the joys of knowing one man and one woman could seek and find happiness together.

All that had seemed beyond her reach. Before Tanner.

So, mixed with her yearning for nightfall to envelop them with its aura of temptation had been lingering thoughts. Thoughts that brought hesitation to her movements as she'd prepared for bed. She'd had a long week to consider it. Perhaps she'd been too forward, too willing. Maybe she'd not been reticent enough, as befitting a new bride.

Her doubts had almost pushed her into confiding in Mama Pearl. Now she was glad she hadn't.

She'd been nervous before, thinking about the candle glowing against the wall in the far corner of the room. Now, its glow was reflected in Tanner's eyes, and she was swept up in the storm of his loving, his mouth and hands warm against her skin.

He was strong, and she reveled in it, allowing him to sweep her gown from her. Her hands fluttered for a moment, needing to provide cover, but his captured them, keeping them hostage. Held at her sides, her palms turned to match his, her fingers lacing with longer, stronger partners. And then, she waited.

Knowing what was to come made it even more exciting, she decided. Being aware of the power of his manhood brought her body to fever pitch, as she considered his broad shoulders and the long length of his body lowering to cover hers.

He spoke but broken phrases, seeming to need no reply, and it was just as well, for she'd lost all ability to speak. So taken with the sensation of her own bare skin against his, her legs twining against longer, firmer flesh, with muscles hard and powerful beneath her hands, she gave herself up to the bliss of womanhood.

For that was surely the only word she could think of that described the joy he brought to her. Bliss. From the entry of his powerful arousal into her tender flesh, to the final whispering cries she uttered against his shoulder, she was transported to a world inhabited only by the two of them.

"...a husband and wife shall cleave together...and the two shall become one flesh."

The phrases swept through her mind, each syllable singing with majestic sweetness. Solomon hadn't spoken them, as wise as he was, for these words had been ordained from the dawn of creation, from the beginning of the world.

And tonight, Gabriel Tanner had unveiled their mystery.

Saturday dawned clear, the rising sun illuminating a bustling hullabaloo that centered around Tanner's barnyard. His men awaited breakfast, their faces shining with early-morning ablutions, tools lined up on the wagon bed and chores completed.

Their sounds of merriment carried across the yard to the kitchen, and Rosemary stood in the doorway, her smile widening as she heard their laughter vibrate in the air. The breeze carried just a touch of chill on its wings and she shivered, wrapping her arms around herself.

"You cold?" Tanner spoke from behind her and she shook her head, rubbing her hands together.

"No, just caught a draft. It feels almost like fall coming on, doesn't it?"

"Smells that way, too," he agreed, his body forming to curve around her back. His chest was warm against her shoulders and she leaned her head back, delighting in the ease he offered. There was no holding back with Tanner, whether someone watched or not. When he touched her, like now, his arms around her waist, his fingers clasping her own, it was with tender care.

"Will there be a big crowd at the schoolhouse?" she asked.

He nodded, and she felt the movement against her hair. "I expect so. Most everyone has their hay cut. Crops are pretty well in. Not much goin' on except for butchering."

"When will you do that?" she asked, wrinkling her nose at the thought.

"In a couple of weeks. We'll want to cut up a couple of pigs to fill the smokehouse for the winter. Don't usually butcher beef ahead of time, just as we need it."

"Do I need to do anything?" Perhaps her tone gave her away, for he laughed and rocked her back and forth.

"Naw, you can just grind up some shoulder meat

to cook up for oat sausage. Mama Pearl will know what to do. Just pay attention to her and you'll be all right.''

Her sigh was heartfelt. ''I'm not much of a ranch wife, am I?''

His fingers tightened for a moment. ''You suit me just fine, Mrs. Tanner.''

''You want to ring that bell?'' Mama Pearl's call came from the pantry and Rosemary turned to watch as the woman placed syrup and jam on the table.

''You ring it, Tanner,'' Rosemary said quickly. ''I need to lend a hand.''

He nodded and stepped out onto the porch. In moments, the kitchen rang with laughter as the men found their places around the table. Scat scooted onto a long bench and was the subject of much poking and prodding as he took a share of teasing. Anna sat quietly on a chair beside Rosemary's chosen seat and listened, wide-eyed, as the men prepared to eat.

Tanner stood, and the noise dwindled, ceasing as he cleared his throat. The blessing he spoke was familiar now to Rosemary, and she hugged her delight close as his deep voice intoned the words. His chair scraped the floor noisily as he took his seat, and the voices raised once more.

Anna leaned close, her hand almost shielding her soft lips. ''Who was he talkin' to, Miss Rosemary? He always does that, ever time we eat, but I can't never tell who he's sayin' those words to.''

Rosemary closed her eyes. Surely the child had heard of… But, apparently not. She bent to whisper in Anna's ear. ''He's asking a blessing on our food, sweetheart. We're thankful we have such wonderful meals, and he was thanking God.''

''I heard my pa talk to God sometimes. When he got mad, he hollered *'God'* a lot.''

Rosemary cringed within. ''I don't think it was the same thing at all, Anna. After a while, we'll talk about it, and I'll see if I can explain it to you.''

''You ever been to a wall raisin', Miss Rosemary?'' Tipper asked, catching her attention.

She glanced up, smiling at his eager expression. ''No, I can't say that I have.''

Bootie raised his fork. ''You'll have to cheer for us, ma'am. We'll be on the team buildin' the west wall of the schoolhouse.''

Tanner broke in. ''The men choose teams to see who can have a wall ready to go up first. This oughta be easier than buildin' a barn. It's pretty close to the same thing, only smaller.''

''Is there a prize for the winners?'' Rosemary asked.

Cotton chuckled. ''Yeah. All the ladies get to dance with us. Ain't enough ladies to go around, Miss Rosemary. So the winners get first pick when the fiddles get to goin' good.''

''I didn't know there was a dearth of womenfolk around here,'' Rosemary said.

''Well,'' Cotton drawled, ''I sure enough had a hard time lookin' for one that wasn't already taken or not about to be agreeable when I was lookin' for a likely prospect last month.''

''I suspect that's why the Bachelor Tax raked in

enough cash for the new school," Tipper said glumly. "Cost a pretty penny to stay single for another year."

"Maybe they'll repeal it, now that the schoolhouse is pretty near paid for," Bootie said hopefully.

"Too late for you, boss," Tipper said with a sidelong glance. He lifted a heavily laden fork to his mouth. "Not that I hear you complainin'."

Cotton cleared his throat. "You better stuff your mouth with food, boy. Them words comin' out of it are gonna get you into trouble if you don't watch out."

Tanner's brows lowered as he considered the young ranch hand. "You think I got something to complain about, son?"

Tipper chewed hard, his head moving rapidly back and forth. "No sir, I surely don't. I was just joshin' you, boss."

Tanner's eyes swept the length of the table, touching upon each man in turn, pausing as he reached Scat. "How about you, boy? Anything to say?"

Scat's chin rose defiantly. "I'd say anybody married to Miss Rosemary's a pretty lucky fella...sir."

Tanner nodded solemnly. "I'd say we're agreed on that." His gaze narrowed as he focused on Rosemary, and she felt scalded by his scrutiny, her face burning as the attention of seven men was turned in her direction.

She rose hastily. "You all need to mind your own business and eat your breakfast. I'm clearing the table in five minutes." Her head was high as she turned aside.

How he reached her so quickly was a mystery, but

surely those were Tanner's hands on her waist as he whispered in her ear. "You're red as a beet, honey." His mouth nuzzled against her cheek. "Warm, too."

She stiffened and shook her head, aware of his chuckle as his big body shielded her from the men at the table. She was sheltered there, her hands clutching the edge of the counter for dear life, her eyes filling with hot tears. Behind her, chairs scraped the floor, voices faded as the screen door opened and closed, and boots clumped their way across the porch.

Only the soft murmurs of Mama Pearl as she spoke to Anna remained, and then as the child's laughter rose, catching her attention, Rosemary leaned her head back against Tanner's shoulder.

"Was it worth it? Marrying me? Did you save enough to make it worthwhile, putting up with all I brought with me?"

His arms enclosed her and his voice rumbled against her ear. "Oh, yes. You're worth it, and more." He turned her in his arms and tipped her chin up, forcing her to meet him. "I paid the tax anyway, sweetheart. The men don't need to know, but I wanted the schoolhouse built, and they were some short. So I stopped by the mayor's office and gave them enough to finish buying the windows and flooring."

She blinked back her tears, and he thought she had never been so lovely. Her eyes damp, her cheeks flushed, and wispy curls coming loose from her hastily assembled braid; she was the very essence of beauty to him. Her forehead creased and her mouth puckered as if she considered some great mystery, and he laughed aloud.

"Why?" she asked. "Why pay the tax and marry me, too? If you were going to spend the money on the schoolhouse anyway, you needn't have…"

He touched her lips with his index finger. "Maybe I felt differently about the whole thing, once I had you here. Maybe, just maybe, I didn't want you to think for the rest of our lives that I only married you to save myself some money."

She blinked, and a tear slid down her cheek. He brushed it away with his fingertip and touched the corner of her mouth. "Will you smile for me, sweetheart?"

Her lips trembled and he could not resist their appeal. His head tilted, his mouth meshing with hers, and she sighed, the soft sound bringing to his mind a memory from early morning. Just so had she breathed out his name as the first birdsong of a new day had pierced the silence within their bedroom.

"Gabriel." She'd been wrapped in his arms, warmed by his loving, and her whisper had brought him a rare kind of happiness he'd thought never to attain. Now, he lifted his head to look down at her, her lips damp from his kiss. Her eyelids fluttered, half-open and hazy with desire he had brought to life, and deep within, he felt the rush of pure delight once more.

"I don't know the right words to say, Rosie," he whispered. "I never believed much in love between a man and woman, not till now. I never said that word out loud before, but I'm sayin' it now."

"Do you love me?" she asked, her words hopeful, yet restrained. "Don't say it if you're not sure." She bit her lip and he shook his head, one finger pressing against her mouth.

"You only do that when you're confused, honey," he told her softly. "And there's nothin' to be worried about this morning. Maybe I'll never know for certain, but I guess I'm sure as I can be, Rosie. I married you because I wanted to, not because I had to. I took these kids into our home because it was the right thing to do, not to get you in my bed."

She smiled, blinking back fresh tears, and lifted on her tiptoes to bless him with her lips, touching his mouth in numerous small tributes, as if she could not spend more than the space of a second in one spot. Her hands clutched at his hair, pulling his head down, tilting it one way and then the other, as her mouth spread its bounty across his cheeks and chin, up to his forehead, from one temple to the other.

"I love you, Gabriel Tanner," she whispered, her breath sweet in his mouth, her body pressed firmly against his own. He held her in an iron grip, lifting her with ease, and her arms slid to circle his neck, pulling herself even closer, until her face was buried in the crease of shoulder and neck, and her warm breath sobbed out the words close to his ear.

"I love you…I love you…" A sigh so deep it must have been born within the depths of her soul vibrated against his throat, and she relaxed there, shivering with an emotion he recognized.

The urge to pick her up and carry her to their bed, where the covers still held the scent of their early-morning loving was so enormous, so immense, he trembled as he denied its temptation. This day would be long.

"Rosemary?" He lowered her to the floor and held her steady. "We should be leaving."

From the doorway, the brightly colored turban atop Mama Pearl's head caught his eye, and he met her level gaze.

"You two about done with your monkey-doodlin' around?" she asked. "We need to clean up this mess and get our dinner packed up, Miss Rosemary."

"Yes, of course." Rosemary's legs assumed their normal strength as she levered herself away from him, and Tanner suffered the loss. Her cheeks bloomed with color, and the look she cast in his direction was pleading.

"You go on now," she said firmly, allowing just a trace of humor to tinge her words. "Unless you want to wash up these dishes."

"No, ma'am, not me," he said emphatically, backing from her. "I've got a wagon to finish loading and a boy out there bound and determined to climb rafters today. I'm not sure which is gonna be the hardest to tend to."

He left the kitchen in half a dozen long strides, crossed the porch in less, and was down the steps before the screen door slammed behind him. The fullness in his groin was lessening, his mind churning with the day's events to come, and he grinned to himself.

The woman was a handful, sure enough. But she was his handful, and not cut from the same cloth as others he'd come across. She'd be faithful and true, and he'd be willing to bet she'd be around for the long haul. The vision of his mother was rapidly fading, the image of her trudging down the lane becoming a dim memory that caused only a moment's pain.

He'd determined years ago not to be like his pa, tied to a whiskey bottle. And Rosemary brought hope near to blooming. She was a far cry from the woman who had walked away when things got tough.

The sun was up in full force as the wagon lurched into motion, his biggest draft horses pulling it down the lane. Cotton held the reins, and all around it were ranch hands, mounted on gleaming horses, with a clean shirt tied to each saddle, in preparation for the dance later on.

Rosemary drove the buggy, Anna beside her, Mama Pearl squeezing the child from the other side. Tanner brought up the rear, watchful as Scat rode beside the buggy, the better to keep an eye on his sister.

It promised to be a beautiful day.

Chapter Thirteen

The west wall was up first, held in place with two-by-fours, ten men cheering their own efforts. Rosemary clapped until her hands were red and her face was tired from smiling. Such fun had never come her way in her entire life.

The town had turned out in great style—even the hotel owner, Samuel Westcott, had arrived with a load of chairs and tables to set up under the trees. Baskets of food filled long plank tables, with sawhorses holding the heavy load. The sun was high in the sky as womenfolk began emptying the food onto the oil-cloth-covered, makeshift tables, and their voices rang in merriment as they prepared the meal for the menfolk first.

Scat was given the task of pumping water as the men washed up, their faces red from exposure to the sun's rays, their hands and arms covered with saw-dust. Two little girls manned brooms and swept saw-dust-laden trousers as the men lined up to wash, and there was a general hubbub as the younger men chose partners to share their plates of food.

Rosemary had never seen so many people in one place, and all of one accord. The four walls were up and nailed in place, ready for the rafters. Tanner stood before her, hands propped on his hips and grinning to beat the band.

"We won the contest," he boasted. "I get first pick for the dance later on."

"Who you choosing?" she asked, tilting her head as she mocked his stance.

"You'll find out, Mrs. Tanner." He motioned, jutting his chin toward the shelter of tall oak trees where the tables and chair were rapidly filling. "Come on, I put a blanket on the ground for us."

"I don't have a plate," she said. "I'll wait till all the men get served."

"I filled mine up enough for both of us," he told her.

"Go on, honey," Bernice Comstock said from beside her. "Isn't every day a good-looking man makes an offer like that."

With a quick glance of thanks, Rosemary escaped her post, and followed in Tanner's footsteps. She looked around quickly for Anna and Scat, and found them lining up behind the last of the menfolk at the tables.

"They're fine," Tanner said, following the direction of her gaze. "They're havin' the time of their lives."

"I know." Rosemary settled on the quilt and

reached for the plate of food. Tanner gave it over and stretched out beside her.

"I'm a tired man in need of nourishment," he complained, leaning on one elbow and slinging his hat to the corner of the quilt.

"This is delicious," Rosemary said, savoring a tender bite of pot roast.

"Looks good," Tanner observed, leaning closer.

She speared a bite and offered it. He accepted, allowing his mouth to hold the tines of the fork, then licked the center of his upper lip. "Fork tastes like my wife was there first," he murmured softly.

She smiled and offered another bite, green beans heaped high, with bits of ham throughout. The next was for herself, and then she chose a chicken leg and handed it to him. "Chew on that for a while. It's all yours—I didn't even nibble."

His strong white teeth bit down and he chewed with vigor, then looked up to where Scat was making his way toward the shelter of the trees.

"Scat! Come on over here, will you?"

The boy nodded, carefully balancing his plate in one hand, a tall glass of lemonade in the other. "Yessir," he said cheerfully. "What you need?"

"I'll settle for that glass of lemonade you're totin', son." Tanner held out his hand, a grin well in place.

"Sure, I'll get another for myself," Scat said easily. "Sure is a good time, ain't it, sir?" He leaned forward to offer the glass and his smile was brilliant. The worry lines were long gone from his youthful face, and Rosemary said a silent prayer of thanksgiving for their disappearance.

"Keep an eye on Anna, son," Tanner said. "And enjoy yourself."

With a quick wave, Scat was gone, heading for the table where huge buckets of lemonade were being served. Tanner drank deeply of the cool drink and offered the glass to Rosemary. "Want a swallow?"

She peered within. "That's about all you left me."

His grin revealed no shame. "I figure you can fill our plate the second time around when we get that cleaned up and bring back a jugful on your way."

"Who waited on you last year at this time?" she asked smartly. "Seems like you're getting kinda bossy."

He gave the chicken bone a final look and tossed it onto the plate. "I need to keep up my strength, ma'am. And just in case you didn't know, nobody ever waited on me before. Not like you do, honey." His gaze roamed her slender form, hesitating momentarily on the line of her bosom, then up to where her mouth twitched in amusement.

"I fear you're taking advantage of me, Mr. Tanner." Her fork scooped up the last bit of potato salad and she held it aloft. "Bet you thought you'd get the last bite, didn't you?" With an easy motion, she slid it into her mouth and licked the tines clean.

"You have got that down pat, sweetheart," he murmured. "I do like the way you slide that..."

"Stop!" She tossed the fork down on the quilt and was on her feet before the words could leave his mouth. "I'll get you some more food."

His gaze warmed her back as she walked away, and then as she reached the table and looked back, he lay flat on the quilt and covered his face with his hat. Warmth spread throughout her being as she watched him relax, hands beneath his head, one knee bent.

Beyond the trees a thicker grove formed hiding places and several of the children began a game of hide-and-seek, their voices raising over the general commotion as they played their game. Anna ran into a thicket and Rosemary watched as the child designated as 'it' began to search.

With a squeal of delight, Anna raced to the tree earmarked as 'home' and shrieked her triumph. That the girl had even known how to play the game was a surprise to Rosemary, and she watched in delight as, one by one, the children ran from their hiding places.

Another game ensued, and again the child ran toward the same thicket, this time going farther into the grove, until she was out of sight. In moments, the group had gathered around the home tree again, and Rosemary watched for Anna to appear.

Around the picnic tables, men and women milled about, filling their plates and eating, seeking out friends and looking for a place to sit. Rosemary felt like an island, desolate for a moment as she watched the children start up another round of hiding, as she realized that Anna was missing from the group.

The plate Rosemary was holding found a resting spot on the table as she set out toward the swiftly scattering children.

"...eighteen, nineteen, twenty. Here I come, ready or not!" shouted a reed-thin young boy. He opened his eyes, grinned widely at Rosemary as she approached, and then ran helter-skelter into the wooded area.

"One, two, three on Joseph!" he called, racing back toward the tree, the hapless boy who'd been found hot on his trail.

Rosemary walked on into the wooded area, past the thicket where Anna had hidden only moments before. "Anna?" she called softly, not willing to disturb the child's play, yet sensing that all was not well.

She stepped into the edge of a darker copse, pushing aside bushes as she went, calling for the girl, her voice louder as she went deeper into the underbrush. Then, from ahead, beyond a small knoll, she heard Anna's voice answering.

"Miss Rosemary!" There was a shrill quality about the calling of her name that set Rosemary's heart pounding at a faster pace. And then the cry was repeated, this time with a trace of panic and a sob accenting the syllables. "Miss Rosemarr...ry!"

Her dress was hampered by a branch snagging it, and Rosemary glanced down to find herself tangled in a briar patch, the thorns snatching at her skirt, tearing it in several places. But even the sharp stinging of nettles against her flesh did not dissuade her, and she plunged ahead.

"Anna?" Her voice was breathless, but it obviously carried to where the girl was, for in the next moment, Rosemary heard the small voice reply.

"I'm here, ma'am." In a small hollow just over the crest of the knoll, Anna stood beside her father, who held her arm in a tight grip.

"Thought that'd get you here, missy," Nate Pender sneered. He turned to Rosemary, releasing Anna for a moment, and she fell to the ground, crying.

"Run, Anna," Rosemary said quickly, ready to do battle for the child. With hardly a backward glance, Anna scurried from her father's side and ran past Rosemary.

"You're the one I wanted to talk to, anyway," Nate said slyly. "You got a choice, smart lady." He filled his chest with air and lifted his chin in an arrogant gesture. "You can either see to it I get my supply of likker from the saloon, or I'm gonna find a way to hurt those kids of mine, real bad. I might even get them back, by hook or by crook, and you'll never lay eyes on them."

She looked at him, a spectacle of fallen man if she'd ever seen one, and shook her head sadly. "You don't want those children. We both know that. You're a miserable man, Mr. Pender, and you don't deserve Scat and Anna."

"Mebbe, mebbe not, but I'll take 'em, iffen you don't do as I say," he threatened, puffing out his chest, sneering the words.

Rosemary trembled, her hands clenching tightly, and then her vision focused on the man who pranced before her, looking· like nothing more than a banty rooster. He strutted around the clearing, and Rosemary laughed aloud, her words taunting. "You're about as worthless a creature as God ever created, Nate Pender."

He stopped dead in front of her, breathing hard. "Don't you laugh at me, young woman. The last gal that got smart with me lost three teeth for her efforts.'' His nostrils flaring, his teeth bared, he considered her through narrowed eyes, scanning her from the crown of her head to the hem of her dress.

"Might be you need a lesson in manners, girlie,'' he snarled. His hands reached for her and she stepped back, losing her balance as he grasped her arm. She fell hard, then lost her breath as Nate landed atop her.

Coughing, gasping for air, she fought him off, kicking and scratching, punching wherever her fists could land a blow. Her vision dimmed as she struggled, aware only that the weight of this man was crushing her against the hard ground, that his hands were harsh against her arms, his body too heavy to be pushed aside.

Her chin tilted back and her lungs filled with air. She shrieked aloud, some small part of her mind aware that Tanner called her name.

As if he, too, heard and recognized the sound, Nate's head lifted high and he jumped up, looking down at Rosemary as if he'd been scalded by her touch. "Damn woman. You got yourself into this, with your smart mouth and busybody ways.''

The vibration of pounding feet and a great thrashing about in the undergrowth announced the arrival of Tanner. Nate's eyes widened and he turned to run, in his haste stumbling over an exposed root. Beneath the overhanging branches of the willow tree, Gabe appeared, and with one lunge was at Nate's throat.

His hands were powerful, his face twisted in rage, and Nate hung in his grasp. Rosemary cried out, fearful of the results of Gabe's anger. Should death be the result of this fiasco, she would consider the blame to be her own. Horror lent strength to her words and she called out to him.

"Stop, stop, Tanner!"

"In just a damn minute, Rosemary," he grunted. His fist buried itself in Nate's belly, and the man went down like a felled tree. It was not enough for Tanner. Picking up the howling man by his belt, he slammed another fist into his jaw, then tossed him aside, his lips drawn back in a snarl that gave utterance to words Rosemary had never heard him speak.

"Gabriel!" She called his name, frightened for the emotion that held him in its grip, not for herself, but for Nate Pender, who even now looked petrified.

"You touch my wife again, Pender, lay one finger on her, even look like you're gonna speak to her, and you're a dead man. You hear me?" He dragged the hapless Nate up by his shirt and held him at arm's length. "As God is my witness, I'll see you—"

"Gabe!" Rosemary shouted. "Enough!"

Gabe dropped the man, and turned to her, seemingly unaware of Nate's retreat on hands and knees, his mouth bleeding, curses flowing like water from his mouth.

Tanner knelt beside Rosemary. "Are you hurt?" His hands swept her body, his fingers catching in the torn places on her clothes, where thorns had done their work, and he glared at her.

"Did Pender try to tear your clothes off? Did he hurt you?"

She shook her head. "I got caught in the brambles. He only fell on top of me, and I couldn't push him off.'' Her grip was strong, her eyes pleading for comfort, and Tanner answered her need. He lifted her into his arms, sitting with her on the grass, kissing her, soothing her, his touch gentle but thorough as he examined the scratches on her arms and legs.

"I got all tangled up in the brier patch,'' she whispered, wincing as he touched a deep scrape on her calf.

"What were you doin' out here by yourself?'' he asked, his voice rough, his anger bleeding over to her. "You're just damn lucky I heard Anna carrying on, or I wouldn't have come after you.''

"I couldn't see Anna, and I set out to find her. I didn't want her lost in the woods, and then I found that Nate must have carried her off. He must have known I was watching and took a chance on getting me alone.''

"What did he say? Did he try to...'' As if he could not put voice to the words that filled his mind, he hesitated, and Rosemary shook her head quickly.

"No, nothing like that. He threatened me, but not that way.''

"I wonder why he didn't just take Anna and run?'' Tanner's hands softened as he pulled her dress down into place, covering her legs.

"He doesn't really want Anna. He wants me to furnish him with booze. I think he's desperate. Geraldine told me the other day that no one in town will talk to him and he can't find work.'' Rosemary's hands twisted in her lap. "I aggravated him, Tanner. A lot of this was my fault. I laughed at him.''

At Tanner's sharp look and exclamation of denial,

she nodded firmly. "He looked like a banty and I was so upset and nervous that I started to laugh and it made him mad."

Tanner rocked her in his arms. "If you don't take the cake, sweetheart." He looked down at her, silently considering her. "Well, I think he'll stay away for a while. In fact, I'd be willing to bet he's gonna hide out somewhere, once the sheriff hears about this. He won't want to be seen."

The walk back to the picnic was long. Tanner avoided the brier patch, and took Rosemary to a spot on the creek bank where he washed her scratches with his bandanna and a piece of her petticoat. Her face clean, and her hair once more braided and brushed free of leaves, she felt presentable enough to rejoin the townsfolk.

The picnic was about wound up, the baskets being packed and put beneath the trees to stay cool. The men had returned to the school building and were swarming over the walls, securing them firmly, several of them forming the rafters to place atop the structure.

Tanner salvaged a glass of lemonade for Rosemary from the final bucket and brought it to her where she waited on the quilt. "I want you to stay here, honey. I'm gonna talk to the sheriff and then work on the building. I need to keep an eye on Scat."

"Is Anna all right?" she asked, looking around for the girl.

"Mama Pearl has her. She's all washed up and ready to take a nap." Tanner squatted beside Rosemary, one hand brushing her cheek. "Will you talk to the sheriff after a while? I don't want to make a big fuss and ruin the day for everyone. But, don't think for a minute that Pender will get away with what he's done.''

''I'm fine,'' Rosemary said, forcing a smile. ''I'll talk to the sheriff, and I'll sit here and watch. You go on ahead.''

She leaned back against the tree and examined the part of her dress that was visible. Half a dozen tears were apparent, and she rued their presence. Without a doubt, she would forgo the dance later on. And she'd looked forward to it all week. The thought of dancing in a dress that had suffered such damage was beyond imagination, and she traced the mutilated fabric with her fingers, wishing for a magic needle with which to sew each strand into place.

She twisted her mouth in a rueful grimace. From the corner of her eye, she caught sight of a swaying skirt and a pair of black calf slippers heading her way, and she prepared herself to be cheerful.

''Hi, Rosemary.'' It was Pip, and Rosemary's facade of gaiety went by the wayside.

''Come sit with me,'' she said, patting the quilt invitingly.

Pip needed no further invitation, stretching out her feet before her and leaning back with a sigh. ''I've been running all day, what with folks forgetting things and sending me back to the store.''

Pip's eyes widened as she leaned closer. ''What on earth happened to your dress? It looks like you took a pair of scissors to it.''

"No," Rosemary said glumly. "I got into a patch of brambles and tore it up."

"You need to watch where you're going…or was someone chasing you?" Her words were teasing as she whispered them close to Rosemary's ear.

"No, actually I was looking for Anna, and…"

Pip sat upright, a stunned expression replacing her grin. "I didn't know she'd come up missing. Did you find her all right?" Her hands fluttered, then fell to her lap. "How silly. Of course you did, or everyone would be out looking."

She nudged Rosemary's hands aside and investigated the torn dress, then tilted her head up and offered a suggestion. "Why don't we go down to the store and—don't shake your head at me. I've already made so many trips today that one more won't make a bit of difference."

"Actually…" Rosemary looked around. "I've been waiting for someone I need to talk to."

Pip rose quickly, then bent to tug at her friend's hand. "Come on, we'll be gone and back in no time."

If the sheriff was in sight, Rosemary surely couldn't see him, and she followed Pip's urging with a spontaneous smile and shrug of agreement.

"All right. I really looked forward to dancing, and I told Tanner I wouldn't dare be seen like this." She glanced to where Mama Pearl sat amid a circle of quilts, each holding one or more sleeping child, then nodded again.

"If we hurry, we won't even be missed."

"You must have worked magic, Rosie. I'd swear that dress was blue this morning." Tanner swung her at the edge of the dance floor, careful not to run into another couple. The newly laid floor of the schoolhouse held more dancers than it could comfortably accommodate, but no one seemed to mind the squeeze.

"You'll get the bill the next time Pip sees you."

"I don't mind," he said, holding her against himself as he dodged an exuberant pair, who were intent on circling the floor at full tilt. His voice dropped as he spoke against her ear. "Did you talk to the sheriff?"

She nodded. "I saw him on the way back from town. The sheriff said he doubted we'd hear much more from Nate Pender, and I hope he's right."

"Did he ask you to file charges against Nate?"

Rosemary nodded. "He said to come into the office and he'd make it official. I don't want the children to be any more upset than they are, Tanner. I talked to Anna and told her that her pa was probably not coming back. I only hope I'm right. At any rate, she's about forgotten the whole thing. I wonder if she doesn't think she dreamed it all, spending half the afternoon asleep."

"Well, if that little girl can put it out of her mind, I'll eat my hat," Tanner said, his deep voice a growl. He touched Rosemary's forehead with his lips and she looked up to meet his penetrating gaze.

"Nate Pender is a lowlife, if ever there was one, and you can't depend on him to act like the folks you knew back in your parsonage days."

The music ended, and Cotton approached with a

wide smile and hand outstretched. "Do I get to dance with the bride?"

Rosemary placed her palm in his and curtseyed in a genteel gesture. "I'd be delighted, sir."

Tanner frowned. "Bring her back to me, Cotton. And no fancy footwork, you hear?"

"Sure, boss." Cotton's eyebrows wiggled as he stood back and viewed Rosemary's splendor. "New dress, huh, boss lady? You're sure mighty purty tonight."

A final wiggle of his brows brought a half smile to Tanner's lips and Rosemary blew him a kiss as the ranchhand led her into a sweeping circle.

The festivities wound down once the punch bowl emptied for the last time. One by one, folks headed for the door, men carrying children slung over their shoulders, women taking empty lemonade containers home, and finally, the fiddle player with his instrument tucked beneath his arm. A lone young man remained, busily sweeping the new floor, sawdust flying in front of his broom.

"You ready to head out?" Tanner asked, catching Rosemary midyawn. "Where's Mama Pearl and Anna? I didn't see them leave. Or Scat, for that matter."

"They've been gone almost an hour. Mama Pearl took the buggy and Anna home. She said it was time for her chile to go to bed. Scat went too, along with a couple of the ranch hands." Rosemary looked out into the night beyond the schoolhouse doorway. "She really loves that little girl, Tanner."

"So do you, honey. In fact, you make it look

easy." He swept the new door back and forth as if he tested its hinges. His hand on the latch, he turned to her. "She's a lucky one, sure enough. Some kids never have even one person who cares about them that way."

"Like you?" She placed her hand over his. "Surely, your mother loved you. Maybe she couldn't help what she did."

Tanner's fingers moved from beneath hers, and his look was a warning. "I don't want to talk about my mother. I've just about put her from my mind these days. But I'll say this. She taught me one thing, and she did that well. I learned not to depend on anyone else for love.

"If I get it free and up front, that's fine, but I don't think I'll ever be able to take it for granted."

Her throat was full, her whisper strained. "I told you this morning that I love you, Gabriel, and I guess I thought you felt the same." She raised her hand as if to still a reply. "You don't have to return my feelings. The love is still yours."

He led her out of the building, into the night, his hand holding hers in an iron grip as they walked toward his horse, tethered in the field next to the school.

"Give me time, Rosemary. I'm doin' the best I can. Just don't expect too much from me." He pulled the stake with a mighty tug and rapped it sharply against the ground, freeing it from excess dirt. He tucked it neatly behind his saddle.

"We'll have to ride double, Rosemary. Looks like the wagon's long gone. Cotton must've figured I could handle gettin' you home without his help."

Rosemary nodded tentatively. "I don't know if I can reach the stirrup."

"You don't have to." Reins in one hand, Tanner was in the saddle, his movement so smooth Rosemary blinked in surprise. "Turn around," he said, and she obeyed, her back to the stallion.

Tanner reached to her, bending low from the saddle. He lifted her, fingers tight around her waist, and for a moment she was airborne. Then, as if he were an old hand at the game, he settled her in the saddle, her bottom tucked neatly against his groin, the horse shifting as her skirts flew.

Rosemary reached to tug them down, and Tanner's chuckle vibrated in the night air. "Nobody's gonna see your pretty legs but me, Rosie."

She thought to argue, but his voice was softer, his good humor somewhat restored—and for that reason alone she would allow her calves to be exposed to the world in general.

From the far side of the schoolhouse a voice called out. "Everyone set to ride?"

A light inside the building flickered and died, and the door was pulled shut with a resounding thud. "All set here," the young sweeper's voice called out.

"Good night for a ride," Tanner said, the pressure of his knees seeming to set the horse into a quick trot. "Relax against me, honey," he told Rosemary. "You won't bounce that way if you let me take your weight."

She did as he asked, leaning against his chest, her head tucked against his shoulder. One big hand touched her leg, fingers widespread, easing her skirt from place. She drew in a startled breath, and from behind her Tanner's words were slow and seductive.

"I told you to lean back and let me take your weight. First thing you do is get all upset."

"Tanner!" The single word was a warning, and he relented, allowing her skirt to fall back into place.

He bent to nibble at her ear, then the tender skin beneath it. "Reckon I can wait," he murmured, sliding that recalcitrant hand around her middle, edging it beneath her breast, and allowing her to feel the pressure of each finger.

"Tanner?" She repeated the warning, and was answered by the sound of satisfaction he growled in her ear.

"Just enough to hold me over, till we get home."

Chapter Fourteen

Even bright sunlight couldn't make Tanner feel better this morning. He tilted his hat lower over his eyes, darkening his view of the green pasture.

He'd been downright ornery last night, talking to Rosemary the way he had. Damn, the woman could poke and pry until she made all his sore spots come splashing to the surface. He'd tried, truly tried to be what she wanted, but pain kept leaking through, tainting his disposition some days until he almost hated himself for the words that escaped his lips.

She'd been quiet last night, as if her feelings were hurt, even though she'd allowed his hand freedom to cuddle and caress, and he'd tried to make things better once they got home.

Maybe there were things that even a good night of loving couldn't put right.

Tanner led the colt out of the corral and into the pasture, releasing the braided rope halter and allowing the youngster to kick his heels and run free. He'd spent over an hour working with this one lone colt.

An hour he should have spent washing up and putting his Sunday-go-to-meeting clothes on.

Instead he'd brushed and cared for the yearling, then worked him at the end of a lead rope until they were both sweating up a storm. A quick rubdown had solved the colt's problem. He looked to be a likely prospect to stand at stud, along with his daddy, the big stallion who had sired him.

Tanner felt the sun hot against his back, drying the damp spot on his shirt where his perspiration had soaked the fabric. The braided rope ran through his fingers as he watched the cavorting yearlings, racing back and forth past the more sedate mares, with weanlings close by. The smaller, newest members of the group kicked up their heels, imitating the half-grown yearlings, and Tanner leaned against the rail to watch.

"Sure is a nice-lookin' bunch, ain't they?" Cotton joined him, and Tanner glanced at the older man.

"Tipper get the buggy ready for Rosemary yet?"

"Ain't you takin' her to church?" Cotton asked, eyes intent on the panorama before them.

"Not time enough to get cleaned up. She's probably ready to leave."

Cotton's gaze slid over Tanner. "You got a good reason to be upsettin' that girl this morning, boss?"

"She's not upset." He felt his jaw clench.

"Who's takin' her to church?" Cotton pressed on, and Tanner had to admire his bravery. The man was about as close as he'd ever be to a good cussing out.

"Whose business is it?" The words came out in a gruff, drawled sequence of syllables that should have been a warning.

Cotton was oblivious to danger. "You don't want to do like your daddy did. You got a good woman, and she's tryin' hard to make herself into a good wife for you, boy."

"Leave my pa out of it," Tanner said, grinding out the words. "Rosemary's fine. I've seen to it she got to church ever since she got here, even hauled her there myself last Sunday. Tipper can do the honors this morning."

"Tanner." As if speaking her name had conjured up the woman herself, Rosemary spoke from behind him, and Tanner's shoulders tensed. He supposed he owed her more than one apology, but offering it in front of Cotton was not what he had in mind.

"Yeah?" He turned to face her, acknowledging her presence.

She was subdued this morning, wearing one of her dark dresses, as if in mourning. Her blue eyes held not a glint of humor or a trace of affection. They examined him with a sort of wary speculation.

"I need to be workin' on that harness, gettin' it ready for tomorrow," Cotton mumbled, nodding at Rosemary as he headed for the back door of the barn.

Tanner stuck his hands on his hips, his legs apart, as if he readied for a battle. "I thought you'd be gone by now," he told her.

She was silent, her expression almost sorrowful as she considered him. "I'm leaving now. I thought you might like to tell me goodbye."

His hands itched to reach for her, his body longing for her warmth. She was all that was kind and good and loving, and she expected the same qualities in her husband.

Her chin tilted up, her eyes glazing with a film of tears, and he could bear the separation no longer. With two long strides, he was in front of her. With one agile movement he'd gathered her in his arms, and scooped her from the ground. Their bodies so close they might have been in the very act of loving, she clung, her arms somehow circling his neck, her face buried in his shoulder.

"Damn, I'm sorry, Rosie. I'm all out of sorts this morning, and takin' it out on you. I should've gotten cleaned up and taken you to church."

Her voice was muffled against his shirt, but he heard the tears that vibrated each word. "I don't even know for sure what I did to make you angry with me, Gabriel. I thought you were pleased with me when you went to sleep. And then this morning, you got up like a bear with a sore tooth."

He didn't even try to smother the chuckle her observation brought to mind. "You about got that right, honey. And I should have been in one dandy mood after you were so sweet to me."

He shook his head, eyes closed as he considered his actions. "Hell, I don't know why I get so miserable. Cotton's doin' most of the lookin'-after with Scat, and Mama Pearl's taken over the fussin' with Anna. And I'm standin' around feelin' like I ought to be the one that's playin' the part."

He lowered Rosemary to the ground and brushed at her dress, where the dust from his shirt had clung. "I told you they could stay here, but I guess I wasn't thinkin' about what you'd expect of me. Or the danger to you with Nate runnin' around causin' trouble.''

His hand paused as it dusted off the bodice of her dress. ''I'm not good at this, Rosemary.''

''No one expects you to be their father, Gabriel. You've taken them in and given them a home. That's all I asked of you.''

''Maybe so, but I think you were hopin' for more.''

Her smile was sad, her lips twitching as if she held back tears. ''I try not to expect too much of you.''

A sense of shame, so overwhelming he shuddered at its weight, swept over him. ''Come on, let me put on a clean shirt and change my boots. I'll take you to church. We'll see how fast that little mare can haul a buggy.''

''Are you sure?'' Her voice was hopeful, and she scampered to keep up as his long strides led her through the barn and out the other side into the yard.

''I'm sure.'' At the horse trough, he shed his shirt and bent low to splash the water over his body.

''I'll get a shirt for you,'' Rosemary said, almost running as she left his side. He watched, water dripping into his eyes as she climbed the steps and went through the back door into the house.

Sure as hell didn't take much to make her happy. And at that thought, the wave of shame rolled over his soul with redoubled strength. Maybe going to church was exactly what he needed this morning. The hate that had propelled him for almost twenty years was eating him alive, and the thought of it spilling over onto the woman he'd married was not to be tolerated.

* * *

He'd mended his fences. That alone was cause for celebration, as far as Tanner was concerned. The day had gone well, riding to church, arriving just as the bell pealed its last note. They'd lined up in the family pew, looking like they belonged there, he'd decided.

Except for bedtime, when Rosemary had spent over an hour settling Anna into her bed, soothing her fears and finally waiting until the child's eyes closed in slumber. On tiptoe, she'd left the child's room and lifted a finger to her lips as Tanner met her in the hallway.

"She's asleep, finally." Her eyes rolled expressively as Rosemary uttered the weary statement.

"She's gonna wear you out," Tanner'd told her, struggling for a smile. Rosemary looked like she'd been pulled through a wringer, he decided. And he'd been planning all day for a warm settlement of their differences once he got her into bed.

Now even that had gone by the wayside. He stood by the bed, watching as Rosemary's chest rose and fell in an easy rhythm. She was asleep—sound asleep, in fact. She'd pulled her nightgown over her head, easing from her underwear beneath its folds, then climbed into the big bed.

In just as long as it took him to check the doors downstairs and shed his own clothing, she'd managed to fall asleep. Locking his house was something he'd rarely done in the past, but with Nate Pender on the loose, it seemed like a good idea. And Rosemary had dozed off while he raced down the stairs and back up to their bedroom.

He blew on the fat candle, his breath a mighty puff, spewing his ire upon the flame. Sliding into his bed, he propped his hands behind his head, then turned to view Rosemary's profile.

She slept like a baby, her hand curled loosely next to her face. He couldn't resist touching her, not to rouse her, but simply to feel the texture of her skin beneath his fingertips. His hand lifted and fell, and he was only too aware that his intent was purely selfish.

He was hoping she'd awake, turn to him and offer herself to his arms. Yearning, as if he'd been denied her touch for a long time. And yet it was not so. He was tempted, his hands moving beneath his head, and he pressed downward upon them, lest they betray his need.

Such foolishness. He'd lived for thirty-four years without Rosemary in his bed. Now, after two weeks of her presence beside him, he was acting as if she'd gotten under his skin.

She rolled toward him, mumbling beneath her breath, and he called her name, softly, hopefully.

"Rosemary? Honey?"

A muffled sound was his reply, and then she settled against her pillow, and a soft snore escaped from her mouth. "Well, hell's bells! Come here, honey," he whispered, reaching for her and turning her to her other side. His arms enclosed her and she shifted, backing into his warmth, her bottom nestling against him.

It was worth it, the discomfort she brought with her a small price to pay for the satisfaction of holding her throughout the night's hours, Tanner decided. He closed his eyes, and focused on the work he faced on the morrow, determined to ignore the thrumming of his manhood.

"Scat!" The shriek from the next room assailed his senses, and even before its echo had died, the call was repeated.

"Scat! Miss Rosemary!" Accompanied by loud sobs, Anna's voice rang anew.

His grip on Rosemary was broken by her swift movements as she fled his arms. "I'm coming, Anna," she called, her voice husky with sleep. She reached for her robe, staggering as she headed for the door.

From the hallway, Tanner heard voices blending, then the sobbing of the small girl as Rosemary entered her room. Scat's slim form stood in the doorway and Tanner sat up in bed. "She's havin' a nightmare, I think," the boy said quietly. "I figured Miss Rosemary could do better than me."

"Yeah, well you better get back to bed," Tanner told him, quelling his first instinct to offer company to the boy. It was enough that Rosemary would probably stay the night in the next room. He'd be damned if he'd spend his sleeping hours trying to solve the problems of the world.

Breakfast was a quiet affair, with Rosemary looking like something the cat dragged in and wouldn't eat. Even her hair had suffered the effects of the night, he noted, pulled back in a long tail she'd tied with a piece of yarn. She was moving slowly this morning, tending to her chores, but without the usual smiles and greetings.

As if they sensed the wary peace between the boss and his lady, the men kept silent, addressing neither Tanner nor his bride. They ate quickly, then left the house, taking Scat with them. The boy turned at the door to cast a long glance at his sister.

Rosemary waved him on. "She's fine, Scat. We're going to bake cookies this morning." Her arm draped in a protective gesture across the small girl's shoulders, and Scat nodded in agreement.

Tanner pushed his cup to the edge of the table, then watched as Mama Pearl brought the coffeepot from the stove.

"Sure haven't noticed the sunshine today, have you, Tanner?" she asked, pouring his cup to the brim.

"What's that supposed to mean?" he asked, scooting his cup across the table, ignoring the wave that slopped over one side, then the other.

"Looks like you're sittin' under a thundercloud," the older woman told him.

"There's no clouds inside the house," Anna announced. "You're just funnin' him, ain't you, Mama Pearl?" She grinned at Tanner, and he was hard put to ignore her words.

"I guess it depends on how you look at it," he said after a moment, lifting his cup to sip the dark brew. It tasted bitter, and he deposited the cup with a thud on the oilcloth. His chair scraped the floor as he pushed back, and with a fluid motion, he took his hat from the hook and headed for the door.

"Tanner?" Rosemary's tone was hesitant, and he closed his eyes against her appeal.

"Yeah?" His back to her, he waited before the screen door.

He heard an indrawn breath, and it scraped at his resolve. Looking over his shoulder, he allowed his gaze to swallow her whole, taking in the uncertainty in her eyes, the pale cast of her skin and the uptilted chin that spoke of a courage she drew from her depths.

Her eyes dropped from his and she shook her head. "Nothing. I'll talk to you later."

His nod unseen by the woman at the table, he turned back to the door.

"Goodbye, Tanner," Anna called cheerfully, oblivious to the mood he'd set.

He waved a hand in reply, unable to totally ignore the child, then stomped down the steps to the yard, a deep sense of guilt his companion.

"Child, that is one ornery man," Mama Pearl said with judicious force. The oatmeal kettle bore the brunt of her ire as she scrubbed at it in the sink, and her mutters of aggravation filled the air.

"Are we really gonna make cookies?" Anna asked.

Rosemary was forced to oblige. She'd made the offer impetuously, grasping at a task she was certain the child would enjoy, unwilling to allow her to be caught up in the disaster that had developed overnight.

No, it had been coming on for several days, she realized, now that she thought about it. Tanner had been cast into the midst of family life, when all he'd bargained for was a new bride.

She'd sensed his mood last night, when she'd awakened to Anna's cry, and even as she'd rolled from bed, realized that sleep had come upon her with the weight of a shroud. She'd hoped for a quick resolution to Anna's fears, but the child had clung to her, and it was not in Rosemary's heart to put her aside.

The sound of Tanner's boots on the stairs this morning had sounded as an alarm in her head, and she'd hurried to the kitchen, barely put together, still buttoning her dress as she followed him down moments later. It was too late to catch him. He'd headed for the barn, and she was left to make the biscuits while Mama Pearl cast long looks in her direction.

Now, with a weariness she could barely suppress, she set to measuring baking powder into the flour, then mixing it with sugar and eggs in the bread pan. She cut a chunk of butter and scooped it into the mixture. A splash of vanilla, some nutmeg and a dash of milk were the final touches, and she set to working the blend with a large spoon.

"You don't want to forget the salt," Mama Pearl said mildly. "Here, Anna, come get her a dab."

The little girl hurried to obey and walked carefully back to Rosemary with her hand curved to hold the white grains. She lifted her hand, emptying it in the bowl, then climbed back on her chair to watch. "I never made cookies before," she told Rosemary softly. "But once Scat brung me one from the store."

Rosemary halted the movement of her spoon.

"Your pa didn't ever get you any cookies?" Such a thing could hardly be believed.

A snort from Mama Pearl and a renewed attack on the dishes in the sink was enough to bring a smile to Rosemary's lips. "That's prob'ly the least of what that child's been missin' all her life."

"Well, today you can eat all the cookies you want," Rosemary promised, feeling renewed strength as she thought of the hateful man who had neglected his children for so long. "You just watch while I work this dough a little, and then you can help me roll it out and we'll cut out some to put in the oven."

The glow in Anna's blue eyes was enough to make the whole project worthwhile, Rosemary decided a half hour later, when the first pan came out of the oven door. With a towel around her waist and a glass of milk at hand, the child watched with anticipation as Rosemary placed two lopsided specimens on a plate.

"Are they both for me?" Anna's eyes widened at the sight of such abundance, and Rosemary nodded. If Tanner wanted to pout, he could just go ahead and step on his lower lip, for all she cared. Tending to a needy child, whether it meant spending the night away from her husband, or baking cookies when she was bone weary, was more important than catering to an ornery man.

"I'm sorry."

"No, I'm the one…"

As one voice, their words blended in the dark, and Rosemary turned to be enveloped in Tanner's arms.

She'd ignored him all day, and then felt guilt at her actions. He was being childish, but then, perhaps he had a point.

At any rate, she determined to make it up to him, no matter what bad dreams roused Anna tonight. She'd sat beside the child for fifteen minutes, then tucked her in with a firm admonition to think only good thoughts. The old doll she'd found in her trunk had been a balm to the child's fears, and within moments her eyes had closed, even as her arms clutched the well-worn relic from Rosemary's childhood.

Now she turned without hesitation to Tanner's embrace, aware that her own words had been spoken in tandem with his apology. His mouth sought hers and she tilted her head back, welcoming him gladly.

"Cotton told me to set things right with you, honey. He told me I was… Well, you don't want to hear what he said."

"Worse than a bear with a toothache?" she asked with a giggle.

"Yeah, worse'n that," Tanner agreed. "I wasn't fit for man or beast to be around, all the livelong day." He held her tightly, as if he must ensure that she could not escape his touch.

"I wish…" Rosemary kissed him with the luxury of knowing that her kisses were welcome, that her every advance was met wholeheartedly.

"You wish what?"

"I wish we could own the pair of them," Rosemary said quietly. "I wish Nate had no claim."

Tanner was silent for a moment, and then he shrugged. "I reckon when the judge finds out that

Nate put bruises on you the other day, he'll change his mind.''

"And how will that go over with you?" She held her breath, closing her eyes as she awaited his reply.

"I guess it'll be fine. It's just takin' some gettin' used to. I told you, honey, this is a new field for me to be workin' in. I'm not sure I know the right things to do, and I sure as hell don't like it when you're so worn-out tendin' a couple of young'uns, while their pa runs the countryside.''

"I hardly even see Scat," she said, smiling at his words.

His grunt was either accord or a sound of disagreement, and right now she didn't care which. She lifted to one elbow, then scooted until her forearms were crossed on his chest. His face was in shadow, but she caught the white gleam of his teeth for a moment, and decided he had grinned at her.

"Do we have to talk about them now?" she asked, one finger moving to blaze a trail through the thick mat of hair on his chest.

He shifted, his arms circling her and tugging her into place on top of his big body. She laughed quietly at his maneuvers, finally coming to rest with her knees on either side of his hips. Her gown had ridden up and she felt the warmth of his skin on her legs. She wiggled as a bulge of fabric prevented her from comfort.

"Let's just get rid of this thing," Tanner murmured, his hands whisking the gown over her head, then tugging it from between their bodies.

Rosemary was open to him, and more than vulnerable to the prodding length of his arousal. She savored the feeling of power her position provided, and with a determined movement, she lifted her lower body and captured that firm object, holding it between her legs. Then she eased downward until their flesh rubbed together in a slow rhythm.

"You wanta do that again?" he asked her, his voice a deep rumble in his chest.

"Do this?" she asked innocently, repeating the movement.

The rumble became a groan and his head tilted back. "Yeah. One more time, Rosie."

She obeyed, enormously aware of the twitching captive between her thighs. A pleasurable warmth enveloped her female parts, and an answering quiver within her depths sent a message she could not ignore.

Tanner had wooed her well over the past nights. Readying itself for his taking, her entire being became softer, more malleable against his firm strength, her soft hidden depths heating and swelling in anticipation of his loving. She rose again, lifting herself until that firm member she held captive came close to reluctant freedom. Then, with a soft, shivering chuckle, she parted her legs, tilting her lower body carefully, until she contained the prize she'd handled with such delicate, teasing solicitude.

Tanner's groan was audible, and Rosemary hushed it with her fingers, shivering as his tongue traced the edges of each one. His hands slid down to cup her bottom, lifting her until she was well and truly pierced with his full length. He held her thus, as if he must gain his breath before allowing her to move.

She was full, her flesh twitching as she accepted him, her eyes closing as she absorbed the part of him that claimed her so thoroughly.

And then his hands moved to clutch her hips, lifting her in small increments, until she feared to lose the prize she had claimed. It was not to be, for he lowered her again, his words guttural and broken.

"Rosie…ah, Rosie. Sweet…merciful…heaven… above," he whispered, the words spaced as if he must draw breath between each syllable.

She brushed her face against his shoulder, her mouth seeking the lobe of his ear. "I love you, Gabriel." Her whisper breathed his name, and she gloried in the right she had claimed to call him thus.

"Gabriel…"

Chapter Fifteen

"Miss Rosemary?" The calling of her name broke the spell she'd managed to weave as she worked the butter churn, her eyes closed, her mind dwelling on things her father might have called carnal.

"Rosemary?" Those male tones were nearer, and Rosemary's eyes opened wide, blinking at the sunlight that streamed through the kitchen door. She scooted her chair back, allowing her dress to fall in place.

"Yes? I'm coming," she answered, hastening to the door. There, hat in hand, golden hair gleaming in the sunshine, Dex Sawyer awaited her. His horse tied to the hitching rail, he'd only come as far as the porch steps.

The man doubted his welcome, that much was obvious. And well he might, since she'd failed to acknowledge his apology in any concrete fashion. Her conscience nudged her and she opened the door wide.

"Come in, Mr. Sawyer. I was churning and had my mind on other things."

He accepted her invitation, his smile indicating relief. "You're sure Tanner won't mind if I come in the house?" he asked, standing before her just inside the kitchen.

Rosemary shrugged. "Why should he? Mama Pearl is here, and Anna," she added as the child scampered into the kitchen. "Sit down, Mr. Sawyer."

Dex accepted a chair, sitting at attention, and held his hat against his knee. "This isn't a social visit, ma'am. There's bound to be trouble, and I thought you and Tanner should know of it."

The warmth of Anna's small body against her thigh was a reminder of the child's presence, and Rosemary's intuition was put on alert. "Why don't you go on upstairs with Mama Pearl?" she suggested, leaning to speak quietly to the girl.

Anna hesitated, plainly taken with the handsome stranger, her head tipped to one side as she surveyed his dapper appearance. And Dex was truly decked out, Rosemary decided. New trousers, sharply creased, shiny boots and the obviously new Stetson headgear proclaimed him a gentleman, a fact even Anna was not oblivious to.

"Do I hafta?" she asked, smiling at the visitor.

Rosemary shot Dex a look of amusement. "I fear you've made a conquest, Mr. Sawyer." She turned Anna with one hand on her shoulder and headed her to the doorway. "Upstairs, Anna. You may come back down before Mr. Sawyer leaves."

Her fingers wiggled a farewell as the child headed through the doorway, and Rosemary turned back to

Dex. "Is there a problem with Nate Pender? I'd hoped he was long gone."

"He was at the back door of the saloon last night, looking for the empties from the bar, so he could drain them out. When that didn't work, he said he'd come haul away trash and sweep the place out. Laura Lee told him to leave, and he was giving her some guff when I happened into the kitchen.

"The man's a danger, Miss Rosemary. I don't like the way he's talking, blaming you and Tanner for his troubles. Everyone in town knows those kids are better off where they are, here with you, but old Nate's got a short nose, thinking that he's lost his rights."

"He doesn't give two hoots about Scat and Anna," Rosemary said harshly. She sat down in her chair, moving the churn from its place. "Is he making threats?"

Dex leaned closer. "He got to rambling, feeling sorry for himself, once I got him out to the alley. What he said made me think he might come after them, saying that there were folks who'd pay good money for a couple of young'uns.

"That little girl's a beauty, Rosemary, and Scat's of an age when a man could almost get a good day's work out of him. There are those who would deal in children's lives that way. We both know that."

Rosemary felt bile rise in her throat. "No, I didn't, Mr. Sawyer. I suppose I've been sheltered all my life, but such a thing has never occurred to me."

Dex rose from his chair. "I come from a big city, ma'am, and there are things that go on in this world that make me sick. Grown men and women can ruin their lives if they please, but when it comes to a helpless child, my anger comes to the forefront.''

''Do you think...'' She hesitated to speak the words, dreading to voice aloud her fears for the children she'd chosen to shelter.

Dex nodded, answering her unspoken question. ''Yeah, I think, all right. You need to watch every minute, Miss Rosemary. I don't know if his whiskey supply is down to nothing, or what, but from the looks of him last night, he's in tough shape. He had the tremors pretty bad, and his eyes were wild. Scared the bejabbers out of Laura Lee. And she doesn't scare easy.''

Rosemary looked out the door. If only Tanner were in sight. And yet, would he only be upset that once more their lives were to be in a state of chaos because of her actions? She rose from her chair, considering her choices. ''I'll tell Tanner as soon as I can when he comes in,'' she said.

''You want me to go hunt him up?'' Dex asked.

''No, I'll take care of it.'' She walked to the door and he followed, stepping onto the porch.

''Tell Anna I'll see her another time.''

Rosemary touched his coat sleeve, brushing the superfine fabric with her fingers. ''Thank you for coming. I'll give Anna your message. She was quite taken with you, you know.''

His smile erased the grim lines from his face as Dex covered her hand with his own. ''I still wish you'd have come to cook for me, Miss Rosemary. I might have had a bride of my own by now.''

''You need to look elsewhere, Mr. Sawyer. There's

a fine young lady in town who'd be perfect for you.''
Her cheeks flushed as Rosemary spoke, and she bit
at her tongue. Pip would kill her if she knew what
she'd suggested.

"Pip?'' Dex asked, eyebrow uplifted. "She's got
a sharp tongue on her, and not the time of day for
me.'' He donned his hat, straightening it with an
expert twitch, then patted her hand once more. "I
must head back to town, ma'am. I just wanted you to
be aware that Nate Pender is still around, and he's
not done yet.''

Rosemary claimed her hand, plunging it into her
apron pocket, and nodded. "Thank you. I'll tend to
it.''

She watched as the sleek mare broke into a quick
trot, and was treated to a flashing smile as Dex tipped
his hat. The man did have a way about him, she had
to admit.

The sun seemed immobile, held in the western sky
for an infinite moment before it slid over the horizon.
Shades of pink and blue, and all the various hues in
between cast their glow, radiating from the spot where
that red ball had disappeared. Tanner's breath escaped
in a deep sigh as his arm settled across Rosemary's
shoulder.

"Thought we'd never get done today,'' he murmured. "Poor Tipper was wantin' to head for town
tonight, and now he's dead tired. I suspect his new
girlfriend will have to wait till Saturday to see him.''

"Who is she?'' Rosemary tilted her head to peer
upward. "I didn't know he had a sweetheart.''

"I'm not sure she knows it yet," Tanner said with a chuckle. "He saw her over at the train station last week when I sent him to pick up an order I had shipped in from Shreveport. She was all alone and tryin' to tote a couple of heavy pieces of baggage, and Tipper took pity on her.

"She was headin' for the hotel, so he stuck her up on the wagon seat and dropped her off. Seems she's got work there, waitin' tables and cleanin' rooms."

"They sure weren't giving away positions when I needed one," Rosemary said, her irritation visible in the words she spoke. "In fact, Samuel Westcott made it very clear that I was wasting my time even making inquiries."

"And aren't you glad?" Tanner asked smugly. "If he'd taken you on at the hotel, you'd have missed all this." His other arm enclosed her in an embrace, tugging her tightly to his side. Bending over her, he nudged her face into position, his mouth taking possession of her lips in a kiss that smacked of satisfaction.

"You are so arrogant sometimes," she grumbled, and then her brow arched as she moved from his touch. "I might have done very well at the hotel. Just think of all the nice gentlemen I'd have met."

"You've got all the nice gentlemen you need, right here," Tanner quipped. "There's me, and Cotton, and Tipper, and—"

Her fist found his midriff, the blow fettered by her position. "Didn't know you were a mean woman, Miz Tanner," he said with a wink.

The word *mean* spurred her memory of Nate Pender, and Rosemary shrank within herself, drawing from the embrace she'd reveled in only moments before. "I fear I have no concept of that word. Not the least notion of what sort of mean things exist in this world." How could she have let Dex Sawyer's visit slip from her mind, when she'd waited all afternoon to tell Tanner, hurrying through the supper chores, seeking him out when his own were done?

Tanner let her go, his eyes losing the glint of humor they'd possessed. "What happened? What are you talkin' about?"

"Dex Sawyer was here today," Rosemary said, glancing behind her, unwilling to allow Anna within hearing distance. "He warned me about Nate, said the man was making threatening noises at the saloon. He said things about folks being willing to pay good money for…"

She could not repeat the horrid thought. The idea that a father would do such a thing was unthinkable.

"For children?" Tanner asked. He sat erect and Rosemary nodded, glancing at his set face. "That's what Dex said?"

"Yes. He told me that Nate was desperate. And that's about as desperate as a man could possibly be, I'd think." She shuddered, wrapping her arms around her middle. "Am I so naive? I've never heard of such a thing. I know about slavery, of course…but this is different, the idea that a man could sell his own child."

Tanner turned her, his big hands on her shoulders, and Rosemary obeyed his silent command, looking up into his grim expression. "Slavery included this very thing, honey. There were men who sold women who'd borne their children, and I'm sure some of those children were included in the exchange. Men have done dreadful things for years. It used to be common practice, treating daughters like pieces of property. Years back it was commonplace, exchanging a daughter for a bride price.

"The only difference here is that Nate is talkin' about a little girl, and marriage is far from what she'd be headin' for. In this time and place, folks won't stand for it."

"What can we do?" Rosemary felt helpless, immobilized by a sense of desolation so immense it seemed she might drown in its depths.

"Mostly just keep a close eye for now," Tanner said.

"Maybe I should take them from here. Maybe I could hide with them somewhere, at least until Nate gives up and goes on his way."

Tanner's fingers tightened their grip on her shoulders. "Don't even think it," he said harshly. "You belong here. If we have to, we'll turn them over to the sheriff and let him keep them safe. But you're not going to put yourself on the line again. I won't have it, Rosemary."

"It's my fault they're here," she reminded him. "I'm responsible for them."

Tanner's mouth thinned, his jaw clenched and his eyes grew dark with fierce anger. "Well, sweetheart, I'm responsible for you. You're my wife, and my first consideration is to keep you safe. If that means that those two young'uns have to be put up somewhere else for safekeeping for a while, then that's what we'll do.

"But I'm not lettin' you out of my sight," he vowed harshly. "I saw what Nate Pender did the last time he got his hands on you. It's not gonna happen again."

Her mind in turmoil, Rosemary gritted her teeth, unwilling to answer his edict. That it would be futile, she had no doubt. Tanner was on his own ground here, and his mind was made up.

"Miss Rosemary, I heard what that pretty man said to you." Her arms tight around Rosemary's neck, Anna confided her secret in a whisper.

In her new nightdress, the little girl resembled nothing so much as the angels pictured in her mother's Bible, Rosemary decided, thinking of those heavenly beings. She could only hope one of them was the guardian of this child whose innocence was threatened.

"What did you hear, Anna?" Her fingers stroked the rosy cheek, brushing a golden tress into place, even as her heart stumbled in its beating. Pray God such filth would never touch this child.

"He said my pa was gonna get money 'cause Scat can work good." The soft lips trembled, and a lone tear glittered on Anna's eyelid. "I don't want him to hurt Scat no more, Miss Rosemary. If my pa takes us away, we won't never get any more cookies, and Scat will have to do bad things."

"Oh, sweetheart!" Rosemary bent low, scooping the little girl into her arms. She rocked to and fro, crooning her wordless song of comfort against the sweet-smelling hair. "Don't you worry, I'll never let anything happen to you."

"What's she talkin' about, ma'am?" Scat stood in the doorway, his eyes dark with anxiety, his hands clenched at his sides.

Anna pushed Rosemary from her, reaching her arms out to her brother. "Oh, Scat! I heard that man say that Pa is mad at us, and he's gonna get us."

"He's not," Rosemary said quickly, glancing at the empty hallway behind the boy. "Close the door, Scat. I want to talk to you."

"Yes, ma'am." The door closed softly and Scat approached the bed, allowing his sister's fingers to bury themselves in his shirt. "Who was here today?"

"Do you know Dex Sawyer?" Rosemary asked.

The boy nodded. "He plays the piano, and one time he gave me a big hunk of roast meat for me and Anna for dinner. He told me if I needed anything I could ask him."

Rosemary blinked in surprise. It seemed that Dex Sawyer had hidden depths. "Well, he was here today, and he told me that your father is very sick."

The boy snorted. "He ain't sick. He's a drunk. He always looks bad when he's needin' whiskey."

Rosemary nodded slowly, considering the wisdom of being blunt with the boy. It seemed he had his father pegged, and he certainly had seen the seamier side of life already. A bit more enlightenment might not be out of place.

"Your father is apparently thinking of taking the

two of you away. Finding new homes for you, maybe.''

Anna tugged at Rosemary's sleeve, gaining her attention. "He said folks would pay good money for us, remember."

"He wants to *sell* us?" Scat asked, his eyes bleak as the meaning of Anna's words made an impact. "Anna's just a baby. What would anybody want with a baby?"

Rosemary closed her eyes. "Lots of folks might be happy to have a little girl like Anna in their home, Scat. You, too, for that matter." The tawdry purposes of Nate Pender were not so obvious to the boy, it seemed. And for that she was thankful.

"Well, me and Anna can be on our way, Miss Rosemary. We don't want to be causin' trouble here, and if Pa knows where we are, he'll be comin' after us. I don't think Tanner would be real happy about that."

"Let's think about it for now," Rosemary told him, removing Anna's grip from the boy's shirt. "Come on, sweetie, you need to be in bed. We'll just keep this a secret, all right? Tomorrow, we'll see what we can do."

"That means you don't open your peep, Anna, you hear?" Scat said harshly, bending over his sister.

Anna's eyes widened, growing moist with unshed tears. "I always do whatever you say, Scat. I won't say nuthin'," she murmured, shaking her head as an added embellishment.

The boy stood erect and Rosemary met his gaze. "You better come up with a good idea, Miss Rosemary," he told her grimly. "Else I'll have to figure something out, in a right hurry."

"Yes…" Rosemary nodded. "Yes, I'll come up with something. In the morning," she promised.

Mama Pearl shook her head, her voice troubled. "Tanner'd have a fit, sure enough, if you skedaddled with those young'uns." Her glance toward the doorway was quick, as if the man in question might even now be watching from the porch. "I wouldn't want to be in your boots if he caught up with you, girl."

Rosemary shrugged, her jaw tight. "He won't hurt me, and you know it. I'm not sending them to town with the sheriff, and that's for sure. If I have to, we'll find a place in the woods to hide."

Mama Pearl turned on her heel, pacing to the window and back. "Look here, girl. You're not hidin' out in no woods. I won't have it. If worse comes to worst…" Her big, brown eyes snapped a message. Rosemary was not alone in this. She had an ally.

"I haven't left yet," Rosemary said soothingly. "I just need to come up with something that will keep Scat from bundling up Anna and running off with her. He won't hear of the sheriff taking him to town. I'd be willing to stake my life on that."

"Well, if Tanner keeps as close an eye on you as I think he will, you'll be hard put to get out of his sight, and that's a fact, girl. That man's not about to turn loose of you."

"Well, I'm not about to turn loose of Scat and Anna. If Tanner can't come up with a better idea, I'll have to take things into my own hands."

Mama Pearl held up a hand in warning. "I'm gonna take a run out to my daughter's place, see if I can come up with somethin'. You just mind yourself while I'm gone. Gettin' dinner on the table oughta keep you out of mischief till I get back."

Rosemary nodded. "I've got mending to do, and I've got cinnamon rolls started today." She watched as the other woman took her apron off and hung it on a nail. Mama Pearl straightened her turban and brushed at her dress.

"I'll find me a horse not bein' used this mornin'," she said. "Reckon I can still ride astraddle, once I get up on that animal's back." She halted in the doorway, nodding her towering turban at the gun hanging in place above her head.

"I showed you how to aim that thing." At Rosemary's nod, Mama Pearl's lips drew back from her teeth in a grimace. "Don't you be afraid to pull that trigger if you have to, honey. Any man comes snoopin' around lookin' for trouble, you better be quick 'nough to give it to him."

"I can do that." And she could, Rosemary decided, watching as the older woman made her way to the barn. In a few minutes, she rode forth, ducking as she passed beneath the wide doorway. Her hand lifted in a quick wave, and then she was gone, riding across the field and into the woods.

The mending was a lost cause, Rosemary decided, after the third time she'd poked her finger and made it bleed. It was no use. Her gaze traveled across the room to where Anna was intent on dressing her new doll.

"We could make her some new things to wear," Rosemary suggested, smiling as small fingers buttoned minuscule buttons.

"She's got two dresses, Miss Rosemary," Anna observed. "That's lots. So long as one's clean for company, she's happy."

And that said a lot for the child, Rosemary decided, rising to check on the cinnamon rolls. The bread pan was full, almost to overflowing, as she lifted it from the shelf behind the stove. Her pot of chicken stew was bubbling nicely, and she stirred it to be sure it wasn't sticking to the bottom of the pan. Then she moved on to the task of making the individual rolls that would please the men of this household.

She formed them quickly, patting out the dough into a large rectangle, then sprinkling cinnamon, sugar and currants over the whole area. A bit of rich cream blended with the mixture and Rosemary rolled it quickly, slicing off thick pieces. Her agile fingers made quick work of the task, and she stood back only minutes later to admire her sheets of rolls, ready to rise a final time.

"You do that so good, ma'am," Anna said, her elbows resting on the edge of the table. She was on her chair, leaning forward to watch intently as the flour flew and Rosemary's hands completed the job. "I sure like the smell of that brown stuff you sprinkled all over the place."

Rosemary bent and dropped a quick kiss on the child's cheek. "So do I, sweetie. My mama always put cinnamon in her cookies. Nutmeg, too, now that I remember it." She thought wistfully for a moment of the woman who'd given her life. Anna had missed such memories.

The table was laden with cooling cinnamon rolls when Mama Pearl rode back across the field. Cotton, hands on hips, watched from the barn door as the woman rode toward him. Their voices mingled in the still air as Rosemary went to the porch, Anna on her heels.

"What they fightin' about, Miss Rosemary?" Fingers clutched at Rosemary's skirt as the child pressed against her side.

"I think Cotton's mad at Mama Pearl, ain't he?" Anna surmised. Releasing Rosemary's dress from her grip, the little girl jumped from the porch and ran to meet Mama Pearl.

"We made dinner," she cried, prancing backward as she crowed her delight. "I'm glad you came back. I missed you."

"You get yourself in that house, you hear?" Mama Pearl scolded. "You shouldn't be out here, child."

Her gaze lifted to meet Rosemary's as she neared the porch. "Ol' Cotton's mad as a wet hen, 'cause I borrowed one of the horses when he wasn't lookin'. Guess he'll just have to get glad, won't he?"

Her arm across Anna's shoulder, she hustled the girl into the house. "Come on in here, girl," she told Rosemary. "I been to my house, and my daughter's not there. She left me a message sayin' she's gone off with that fancy man of hers." Mama Pearl lowered her voice, leaning forward.

"My house is empty. It's got a good lock on the door, and canned goods on the shelves. There's big old shutters inside the windows. If you're lookin' for a place to hide for a few days, till Tanner can get Nate Pender straightened out, you can hide out there.''

"We're gonna hide?" Anna asked wonderingly.

Rosemary crouched before the child. "It has to be a secret, sweetie. I don't want Scat to take you away.''

"Scat'll take good care of me," Anna vowed, her lip protruding, her chin jutting stubbornly.

"I know. But I'd rather be with both of you," Rosemary told her.

"We got to feed these men first, before you go makin' up your mind to anything," Mama Pearl told Rosemary.

Rosemary sat down on a chair, her hands clenched tightly in her lap. "I want to do the right thing."

"You're gonna make Tanner mad. I told you that before.''

"I don't want Scat to run," Rosemary whispered. "I have to do what's right for the children. I brought them here. It's my fault their pa is so set on making trouble.''

"You just get up now, girl, and set the table and we'll have those men in and out of this kitchen in no time flat. There's time enough to decide what you're gonna do this afternoon.''

"Where'd Mama Pearl go this morning? Cotton said she took a horse and rode off while he was out back." His arm around her waist, Tanner escorted Rosemary into his office. Barely a remnant of his father's presence remained in the room. Tanner's own record book lay open on the desk, his scent hung in the air. The curtains had been pushed aside so that the window could be open to the fresh air.

Rosemary didn't need to be enveloped by his aura now, and she drew from his touch as he closed the door behind them. "Why don't you ask her?"

His eyes glittered with frustration as he gripped her shoulders. "Between the two of you..." He halted, bending to look directly into Rosemary's eyes.

"I won't have it, honey. Sheriff Rhinehold told me he's comin' out here with two men later on today, and they're gonna escort Scat and Anna to town. Once this is settled, once Nate Pender is out of the picture, the two of them can come back, if that's what you want."

"If that's what *I* want? Are you willing to adopt them?" She'd harbored the fear of his refusal for days, and she held her breath as Tanner's head shook in a negative reply.

"Hell, I don't know," he muttered. "I don't know what kind of a man it'll take to be a father to that boy. I sure don't have the know-how." His jaw tensed, drawing the skin tightly over his cheek. "I'm not even sure I know how to..."

"How to love him?" Rosemary asked in a near whisper.

Tanner's head drooped. "Yeah, I guess that's it." He searched for words, and his lips tightened, drawing into a thin line. "Look, Rosemary. You know how it is. My pa was a drunk. My mother ran off and left me. Nobody ever taught me how it's supposed to be in a family.''

His voice dropped to a near whisper. ''Hell, I don't know what love's supposed to feel like.''

Her heart twinged within her breast and she stifled the urge to wrap her arms around his neck. ''Well, I do,'' she said with vigor, gritting her teeth against her overwhelming need for this man. ''I love them both, and I don't want the sheriff to take them.''

''Maybe you need to love them enough to let them go,'' Tanner said sharply. ''The sheriff can see to it they're safe in town.''

''And we can't?''

''Yeah, I suppose we can hole up and wait for Nate to show his hand. Or else we can get the kids out of here and go out lookin' for the man. I can't be two places at once, Rosemary. I want you safe, and that isn't gonna happen until Nate Pender is put away.''

''How can that be done?''

''He made threats against the two of them. If Dex Sawyer is willing to swear to what he heard, I expect the judge will find some way to jail Nate.''

''For how long? How long do we have to keep looking over our shoulder, waiting for him to show up?''

Tanner shook his head. ''I don't have all the answers, honey. But the sheriff's sure that if the young'uns are in town, Nate will…''

''You're talking about making them bait in a trap, aren't you?'' Rosemary backed from his grip and walked to the window, looking with unseeing eyes into the fields beyond the house. "I thought better of you, Tanner."

"I'm thinking of you," he said stubbornly. "Nate will leave you alone, once he knows the kids aren't here. There's men in town enough to keep them safe. Once Nate makes a move, he's done for."

Chapter Sixteen

"Where are we goin'?" Anna's tone was petulant, probably, Rosemary thought, because she'd been hauled out of bed and stuffed into her clothing before dawn.

"Never mind, sweetie," Rosemary said softly. "You just be still now, and come along." The child obediently trudged along at her side, and Rosemary wished she were not already so burdened with a valise. There was no way on earth she could carry the girl with the strength of one arm.

As if God had given her a golden opportunity, the sheriff had not been able to come out to the ranch to pick up Scat and Anna. And so, for another night at least, they had slept under Tanner's roof. The promise of an early morning visit from Sheriff Rhinehold had awakened Rosemary in the dark of night, and she'd spent a sleepless hour considering her choices.

There weren't many. One, she could acquiesce to Tanner's plan and watch Anna and Scat ride off to town, bait in a trap not to her liking.

Two, she could finagle some way of removing them from the immediate danger. To that end, she trotted several plans through her mind. The most likely, after a silent debate with herself, was to go to Mama Pearl's cabin.

Tanner was no dummy. He'd find them there, but perhaps not until he'd recognized that Oscar Rhinehold's plotting led only to danger. The thought of Nate's hands on Anna sent a chill to Rosemary's depths. It could not happen.

It had been a restless night, with Rosemary awake more than she was asleep. It was before dawn when the sound of the big barn door closing carried on the still air. In moments she'd heard Tanner's name called from beneath the bedroom window.

"Tanner!" In an urgent half whisper, Cotton repeated the summons, and beside her, Tanner rolled to the edge of the mattress and sat up.

She'd heard him mumble, felt the mattress shift as he rose and walked to the window, then listened intently as Cotton told him of a mare down with colic.

She couldn't have planned it better. That the mare was in danger was a worry, but for now, it would be Tanner's worry. She'd heard his muffled oath as he stumbled across the floor, and watched through her lashes as he tugged his boots on.

The fact that he'd closed the door with care, easing it shut so as not to disturb her sleep sent a pang of remorse through her. But not enough to deter her from her task.

She'd slid from the bed as his boots touched the

stairs and within seconds was rousing Scat from slumber.

"Scat! We have to move quickly. Get dressed and take along clean clothes. I'll get Anna."

Bless his heart, the boy had not opened his mouth, only tossed back the sheet and darted about the room, doing as she had directed.

Anna was grumpy, rubbing at her eyes and clutching her doll with one arm. "Where we goin', Miss Rosemary? Why do I hafta get up in the dark?"

"Hush, now, sweetie. Just come along." With trembling fingers, Rosemary dressed the girl, slid her shoes in place and then snatched up a clean dress and underwear.

She stuffed them in her valise, along with a change of clothing for herself. The morning star was shining brightly as they slipped from the back door and set out across the field. Behind them, footprints in the dew left a trail, and Rosemary could only hope for sunshine to dry the tracks before Tanner set out to follow. A horse and wagon would have made it easier, but with Tanner in the barn, she had no chance.

From the edge of the woods, she looked back, relieved to see lantern light flickering through the barn window. What had caused the ruckus was certainly a sign from heaven that her prayers had been heard and answered, as far as she was concerned. Yet, the thought of Tanner laboring to save his mare nudged at her conscience as she made her way through the trees. Leaving this way was probably underhanded, but it sure beat the dickens out of Scat running off with his little sister.

* * *

"I surely don't know where they are," Mama Pearl said with staunch enthusiasm. "I called 'em, all three of 'em, and then I checked the bedrooms, and they was gone. I never heard a thing," she said, emphasizing her lie with a shake of her head.

And it was a lie. Tanner was dead certain of it. There was no way those three had fled the house without Mama Pearl's awareness of the deed. He slapped his hat on the kitchen table.

"Well, they're gone. Sun's up and I suspect the sheriff's on his way out here by now, and I got enough egg on my face to feed ten men."

"That's all you're carin' about, Tanner? Egg on your face?" The rebuke was less than subtle, and he favored Mama Pearl with a glare.

"I'll lay odds you told her where to go, didn't you?" he growled. "Where'd they head for? Your old place?"

"Don't know what you're talkin' about, boss man." Her stance was stubborn, arms tucked beneath her ample bosom. If there was a speck of guilt in her demeanor, he couldn't see it.

Tanner looked out the kitchen window. The morning sun was high in the sky. The horse he'd treated for colic was finally settled in her stall. "Damn woman could be halfway to the next county by now," he muttered. Probably not though, he decided, with two young'uns in tow, one of them no doubt dragging her feet.

"Sheriff's comin'," shouted a voice from the yard,

and with one last, exasperated glance at the woman across the room, Tanner shoved past the screen door.

"You seen any trace of Nate?" Hat pulled low over his eyes, Oscar leaned from the saddle.

Tanner's eyes clashed with the other man's. "Don't you know where he is? Thought you were keepin' him in sight."

Oscar shook his head. "Had a man watching him. Next thing I knew, Dex Sawyer was bangin' on my door, tellin' me that old Nate swiped a bottle of whiskey from behind the bar early this morning. Last anybody saw of him, he was headin' toward the woods north of here. And another thing," Oscar said, holding up a hand. "He took a horse tied in front of the general store. Old Homer Pagan's havin' a fit."

"He stole a damn horse?" Tanner shook his head in disbelief. Taking a man's horse was a sure jail sentence, if not cause for hanging.

"Yeah. Don't know what the man's thinking. Must be the whiskey makin' him act so stupid."

Tanner stomped past the lawman, heading for the barn. "I'll get my horse, Oscar. We got problems enough here to go around. Rosemary took the kids and left, early this morning. I suspect she's on her way to Mama Pearl's cabin."

Sheriff Rhinehold set his gelding in motion, keeping pace with Tanner. "Well, she better hope she don't run into Nate up there in the woods. That's the same direction he was headin'. Didn't anybody notice she was gone?"

Tanner shook his head. "I sure didn't, not till I went in for breakfast a few minutes ago. I was in the

barn with a colicky horse since before dawn. And
Mama Pearl says she didn't hear a thing.''

Oscar grunted his disbelief. ''I can't imagine that.
That old lady's got an ear to the ground twenty-four
hours a day.''

Tanner stepped into the tack room, lifted his saddle
down and reached for a bridle, then opened the stall
door where his stallion waited. ''I don't suppose
you'd like to come along.''

''I'm comin','' Oscar said. ''You just better hope
Nate don't find 'em first.''

And that was a bit of wisdom he could have done
without, Tanner decided.

''You sure you know where we're goin'? You ever
been to Pearl's cabin?'' Scat carried his own gear
along with Rosemary's valise, his feet taking two
steps to her one.

''Slow down,'' she panted, shifting Anna in her
arms. ''Of course I know where we're going. Mama
Pearl told me yesterday that her place is where the
track forks, and we go to the left.''

''Well, if there's a fork ahead of us, I sure hope
it's loaded with something to eat,'' Scat grumbled.

If she hadn't been so weary, she'd have laughed
out loud at his words. Knowing there was a supply at
the cabin, she'd barely thought of food, only to snatch
up a loaf of bread and three beef turnovers from supper last night as they left the kitchen. And at that
thought, she halted.

''Open my valise and get those beef pies, Scat,''

she told him. Conversation was stealing her breath at an amazing rate.

"Can I have one?" Anna asked, leaning back to look directly into Rosemary's face. Her arms were wrapped tightly around her protector's neck, as if she must anchor herself, and Rosemary hitched her higher again.

"Give your sister one first," Rosemary gasped, closing her eyes as she sought to catch her breath.

Scat opened the valise and retrieved the food. "Here's one for each of you."

Rosemary slid Anna to the ground, then settled herself in a grassy spot, eyeing the plump turnover. Food had never looked so good. She bit into the flaky crust and chewed slowly, savoring the flavor of meat and vegetables. "We can't be far from the fork," she said, wishing for a swallow of coffee.

"Can't even tell where the sun is," Scat grumbled through a mouthful of food. "Bet we've been walkin' for ten hours."

"Not even four, I'll warrant," Rosemary corrected him. And at a pace that would never set a record, she thought privately. Anna had been more of a deterrent to speed than she'd expected.

Scat glanced at her as if evaluating her strength. "Why don't I go on ahead and see if I can find the fork?"

"That sounds like a good idea. We'll be along in just a minute." With Scat out of sight, Rosemary would be able to find a convenient bush. She'd be willing to wager that Anna's need was as urgent as her own.

She watched as the boy picked up his load and moved down the track, and then looked around for a likely spot. Anna watched her quietly, offering no protest when Rosemary led her to a stand of low shrubs and helped her with her drawers.

"I feel better now," Anna said, tugging her dress into place after a few minutes. "I can walk for a while."

Rosemary sent her silent thanks to the heavens as she nodded agreeably. "Can you wait for me over by that big tree?" she asked Anna.

Her own need was dealt with quickly, and she approached Anna, offering her hand. The child grasped it with confidence. "I can walk a long way now. It won't be much farther though, will it?" she asked, her voice more cheerful than Rosemary felt.

In fact, if the truth be known, she was beginning to doubt the wisdom of her plan, such as it was. Only the imminent arrival of Sheriff Rhinehold had pressed her into this venture. Surely she could gain some time, and keep the children with her and away from Nate.

"Miss Rosemary!" Scat's loud whisper wheezed out her name as he ran helter-skelter toward them. He stumbled, almost falling as he reached her side, and Rosemary was stunned by the terror written on the boy's pale features. "He's up there! Pa's up ahead, sleepin' under a tree. I almost walked right up to him, Miss Rosemary."

He drew a breath, and hung his head, his narrow shoulders slumping. "He'll get us now, won't he?"

Rosemary drew him to her side, her own fears well

in place. "No, or course, not, Scat. We'll be very quiet, and get past him."

Scat looked up at her, fear leaching the color from his cheeks. "Miss Rosemary, if he comes after us, I want you to take Anna and run. Pa can't hurt me, not any more than he already has, anyhow. But I don't want him to touch Anna."

Her heart lurched within her breast as Rosemary bent to press her mouth on Scat's forehead, and it was a measure of his fear that he allowed the caress. "I won't leave you to face Nate alone, Scat. I wouldn't do that to you. I didn't bring you home with me just to let him have you again. Don't you understand that?"

"Yes, ma'am, I do. But you don't know what he's like. He's mean, Miss Rosemary." His words trembled and she felt the spasm of fear vibrating from his narrow shoulders.

"Well, we're going to walk very quietly, and carefully down the track, and when we get close to where you saw Nate, I want you to let me know. We'll be very quiet. Do you understand, Anna? No talking or whispering at all." Rosemary's low tone was firm, as she dealt out her instructions. The shivers of apprehension that roiled within her must not be apparent to these children, and she stiffened her spine as she readied them for the trek ahead.

They paced quietly, only the birds overhead breaking the silence. Within a few minutes Scat held up one hand, looking back at Rosemary over his shoulder and pointing ahead toward a towering elm tree. Beneath it, almost blending into the dried leaves and

weeds around its base, was Nate Pender, head tilted
to one side, mouth open. A bottle beside him gave
mute testimony to his condition, and Rosemary
breathed a faint sigh of relief. Perhaps he was too
drunk to be aware of their passing.

They walked quickly toward the man, then, seeking
the most silent path, they trod carefully, stepping only
where no dried leaves or twigs would give away their
passage. Anna turned her gaze upon her father, and
her eyes widened fearfully. Rosemary put a finger to
the child's lips and shook her head, the admonishment
clear.

They'd managed to get a good distance beyond the
tree, and Rosemary was about to heave a sigh of relief, when a horse meandered through the trees beside
the pathway they walked. Saddled and bridled, its
reins trailed on the ground, and it halted every few
feet, dropping its head to the ground to graze.

Anna drew in her breath sharply and clung to Rosemary's skirts. Her index finger pointed at the animal
and she whimpered. "He's a big horse."

And from the viewpoint of a small girl, Rosemary
had to agree. That the creature had no interest in the
three passers-by was obvious, but to Anna, the horse
was a threat, and there was no denying her fear. Rosemary bent to pick her up, and sheltered her against
her shoulder, where Anna buried her face.

The horse bent his attention in their direction and
a low whinny greeted them. Rosemary hurried on,
only to hear another louder and longer greeting from
the horse.

"Is he comin' to get us?" Anna whispered. "Do I hafta be afraid?"

"No, of course not," Rosemary answered. "The horse won't hurt you, honey." But your father might. Should Nate waken, and see them, they would be in for it. And that thought increased her pace as she hurried around the next bend in the track.

Behind them, a growl of anger marked Nate's awakening, and Rosemary heard the thrashing about in dry leaves as the man attempted to rise. She looked back, her heart beating almost out of her chest, Anna heavy in her arms, but saw no trace of Nate. Ahead of her, Scat motioned to a trail, partially overgrown by underbush, but a trail nonetheless, easy to follow.

They left the track and hastened through the trees. Ahead, the sun was shining, the sky appearing beyond the shelter of the woods and within minutes a small log house appeared. Tucked neatly between two trees, it looked abandoned, yet flowers grew around the doorstep.

"This is it, I'll betcha, Miss Rosemary," Scat murmured, waiting for her at the edge of the clearing. He ran ahead then, lifting the latch on the door, and opening it easily. His head poked inside and then he backed away, waving at Rosemary impatiently. "Come on. It's empty."

With her last burst of strength, she hoisted Anna higher in her arms, and followed Scat into the cabin. Her eyes scanned the interior, but closed shutters lent no light. "Close the door, Scat," she said quietly, fearful of Nate's impending appearance.

"Miss Rosemary," Scat said quietly. "I need to go

get help. If Tanner don't come help us, I don't know what we'll do.''

"I need you here," Rosemary told him, the thought of the boy fleeing his father almost too frightening for words. She'd taken the responsibility for these children, and awesome as it was, she was in charge.

Scat thought otherwise, if his stance was anything to go by. He stood before her, shoulders thrown back, his jaw jutting forward. "Miss Rosemary, I don't mean to disobey you, but this is something I think Tanner would expect me to do. I'm leavin' and I want you to bar the door and look after Anna.''

The twelve-year-old child suddenly assumed the proportions of a young man, and before her very eyes, Rosemary saw the transformation take place. She could only bow to his decision, and she nodded, reluctantly, but with admiration. "Go on then," she whispered. "I'll look after your sister.''

The boy nodded and slipped through the doorway, his feet flying as he ran toward the trees. Rosemary watched no longer, but closed the heavy door and lifted the heavy bar from beside it, fitting it into the wooden braces on either side of the portal.

It was almost dark within the single room cabin, and she went to the window, cracking the shutter enough to allow a narrow finger of light across the floor. "Anna, I want you to find a chair to sit on, and I'll get the bread out for you now." Even as she spoke, she saw Nate come through the trees, staggering and gesturing with one hand, the bottle gripped in his fist.

Scat had disappeared and Rosemary heaved a sigh

of relief. Now to keep Anna occupied and unafraid until help should arrive. If Tanner ever forgave her for this mess, it would be a miracle.

"You think they're at Mama Pearl's place? I thought her daughter was livin' there." Oscar rode behind Tanner, their animals keeping a fair pace as they followed the track. It had borne prints of three persons when Tanner checked it out, fresh tracks to his eye, and he'd followed his hunch.

"No, the place is empty, and I've a hunch that old lady sent them there." He scanned the ground in front of him, even as he cast watchful glances to the wooded areas on either side. "I think Rosemary's planning to hide out from Nate till he gets tired of lookin'. I just wish she wasn't so blamed ignorant about some things."

"You don't want to let her hear you say that." Oscar answered. "I'll bet she's a hellion when she's riled."

"Well, she'll be more than riled when I get my hands on her. Nate's been makin' noises about sellin' those kids, Oscar. The man's pure evil, through and through. I hate to think about him gettin' his hands on Rosemary again."

"Anybody with a mind to buy a child ain't too high up on the totem pole either, to my way of thinking," Oscar said stoutly. "I hope he's changed his mind and used that horse he stole to head for kingdom come. I'd just as soon not have to stick him in my jail again, let alone tie a noose around his neck."

Tanner slowed the pace of his stallion, holding up

a hand to halt Oscar's progress. Ahead, he'd caught sight of a shadow near the side of the shaded trail, and he watched, allowing his eyes to blur out of focus. There, he saw it again, a splash of color amid the green underbrush. And then a figure rose from hiding and stepped onto the narrow trail.

"Scat!" The name was barely breathed when Tanner urged his horse into motion, the sheriff close behind.

"Tanner?" The boy was forlorn, his face dirty, hair disheveled, his eyes wide with fright. "Tanner, you gotta hurry. My pa's there, at Mama Pearl's cabin, and I'll bet he's givin' Miss Rosemary a hard time of it."

"Is she inside?" Tanner asked quickly. "Did she lock the door?"

Scat half nodded his head, an indecisive movement. "I sure hope so. I told her to, anyway. My pa caught sight of me, but I hid behind trees."

Tanner leaned down to give the boy a hand up, hoisting him behind the saddle. Scat grasped his waist, and Tanner felt a strange warmth as those skinny arms snaked around him and grimy hands clenched his belt.

"I'm sure glad you showed up." Scat's head bent forward, and he allowed it to rest against Tanner's back as they rode ahead. "Watch for the fork to the left. It's just ahead a ways."

"Yeah, I see it," Tanner told him after a few moments, looking back over his shoulder. "You all right, boy?" Tearstains greeted his gaze and he compressed his lips, wishing he were able to offer comfort, the way Rosemary did. So easily she could touch and soothe, easing hurts with a fleeting caress.

"Yeah, I'm fine. I just wish he was dead, Tanner. I hate my pa." Each word seemed bathed in sorrow, and Tanner nodded.

"Let's get down and walk the rest of the way. You with us, Oscar?" He slid Scat from behind him, then dismounted.

"You got your gun?" Oscar asked.

"You bet." Tanner slid his rifle from the side of his saddle, then headed through the trees to where the clearing lay, the cabin coming into sight as he stealthily made his way down the narrow path. The birds were silent, the air shimmering with heat.

A crumpled bundle on the ground stirred as Tanner reached the edge of the clearing, a horse lifting his head to sound a greeting as it wandered, grazing nearer the cabin. The man within the grimy rags lifted his head, his jaw slack, eyes glazed, as the other two men strode toward him.

"Whadda'ya want?" Nate muttered. "This here is nobody's business but mine. Don't need no sheriff. I can get my young'un back by myself. Just hafta wait 'em out." His filthy hand lifted to wipe at his mouth, and he groped for the bottle on the ground beside him.

He tipped it, his bleary eyes sad as a single drop hung suspended on the lip, then tossed it aside with an oath. His head swayed from one side to the other, and as if it were tempting him, sun glinted from the handle of the weapon he'd carried to this place.

Nate leaned precariously, almost losing his balance as he stretched out his arm for the gun. "I kin hold my own," he bragged, sneering at Oscar. "I got me a gun. You better leave me be, lawman."

"Don't pick it up, Nate. You're drunk as a skunk. You sure enough don't need a gun in your hand."

"You're not stoppin' me, sheriff," Nate blustered, hoisting himself to his feet, the weapon hanging from one fist. His head lifted, and for just a moment, Tanner saw a glimpse of evil blazing from the bloodshot eyes.

"Watch it, Oscar," he murmured, edging to one side. Better that they did not present a single target, he thought, glancing to see where Scat was positioned. And then caught his breath in a gasp of horror. The boy stood on the opposite side, his eyes intent on the dangling weapon his father held, his freckles prominent against pale cheeks.

Nate Pender swayed on his feet, his arm rising slowly, as if the gun he held were too heavy for his limited strength, his head bobbing as his gaze traveled from one target to the next. And then he swung his hand, the weapon pointing in Scat's direction.

"You could'a given your old man a hand, boy," he growled. "You never was any good," he growled. "Just like yer ma. Always givin' me sass." He lunged at the youth, and whether or not his aim was true, Tanner could not be sure. He only heard the sound of a hammer cocking as Oscar crouched to fire.

"Drop it, Pender!" Oscar called roughly. "Now."

Tanner was breathless, unable to stir as the tableau was acted out before him. Scat's lithe body spun to one side as Nate cocked the gun he held, both hands joining to perform the act. He held it before him, then turned in a clumsy movement and aimed it at Oscar, swaying in place. His finger clenched on the trigger and Tanner watched as it tightened, his own rifle swinging into firing position.

A shot rang out, and as if the air had been expelled from a high-flying balloon, Nate Pender crumpled to the ground, howling mightily. Blood flowed from his hand, and curses from his mouth.

"Well, hell's bells!" Oscar stepped forward, his gun still held ready and smoking as he approached the wounded man. "Damn fool acted like he wanted to be killed. I'd better wrap up that hand of his."

Scat's gaze was fixed on his father, his skin ashen as Oscar bent to pick up Nate's weapon. His eyes were bleak as they met Tanner's, his lips working. And then he turned, one hand lifting to cover his mouth and stumbled into the undergrowth at the edge of the clearing.

Tanner cast a longing look at the cabin. "Rosemary!" he bellowed loudly. "You all right in there?"

The door eased open and two figures stepped onto the porch, Anna half-hidden behind Rosemary's skirts. One hand lifted in a wave as Rosemary glanced past Tanner to where Scat huddled beside a bush.

Tanner turned to follow her gaze, then moved quickly to the boy's side. Scat bent low, the meager contents of his stomach already on the ground.

"Come on boy, let me help you," Tanner said quietly, bending to touch the bony spine. His other arm eased around the child's waist, and he supported Scat's weight as tremors rattled the slender frame.

"I'm sorry, Tanner. Didn't mean to be such a

baby," Scat gasped, wiping his hand over his mouth, while great gasps of air filled his lungs. "I thought I wanted him dead. Now just seein' all that blood drippin' offa his hand made me puke like some little kid."

Tanner reached quickly for his bandanna, a clean one he'd tucked into his back pocket upon arising, and pressed it into Scat's hand. "Here, clean your mouth. Blow your nose, too. And then you just listen to me, boy."

He turned Scat away from the scene of his disgrace and drew him toward a tall tree that offered shade beneath its branches. A heavy hand on the boy's shoulder urged him to the ground and Tanner joined him there.

"Let's talk for a minute," he said bluntly, then closed his eyes, wishing desperately for some sort of guidance. If Rosemary's God was out and about today, this would sure enough be a good time for Him to be looking after things.

Chapter Seventeen

"My pa used to be drunk sometimes," Tanner began, feeling his heart clench as he spoke the words.
It still had the power to hurt, he discovered, this ac-
knowledgment of his father's problem. "As a matter
of fact, there at the end, he was drunk most of the
time," he said quietly.

"He did? He was?" Scat swiped at his nose with
the back of his hand, and Tanner resisted the impulse
to use the bandanna on him. "Like my pa?"

"Yeah...almost like your pa." He lifted his head,
watching as Rosemary led Anna away from the cabin.
She glanced his way and nodded, as if she somehow
knew what he was doing was of special import.

"My pa didn't beat on me when my mother left.
He just wallowed in his whiskey bottle and left the
raisin' of me to somebody else."

Scat edged closer. "Who did the raisin'? Did you
have a new mother?"

Tanner shook his head. "No, nothin' like that. Ol'
Cotton just took over. Did a better job, I expect, than

my pa could have done. Anyway, I turned out pretty well I think, all things considered.'' He glanced at Scat's rapt expression. ''I've just had a hard time gettin' over bein' mad, ever since. It still gets me rankled now and then, and I get downright ornery.''

''Mad at your pa? Like me, you mean?'' Scat's shoulders hunched as his gaze swept to where the sheriff was loading the drunken Nate Pender onto the back of a horse. ''I doubt I'll ever...'' He shook his head. ''I feel downright ornery right now, Tanner. You think I'll ever quit feelin' this way?''

Tanner's big hand rested on the boy's shoulder. ''You will, Scat. One of these days, you'll look back...'' He paused, midthought. How could he offer hope for a light heart and a lack of rancor for the boy, when his own hatred had festered for so long within his breast?

''When did you get over hatin' your pa?'' Scat's fingers tugged at a blade of grass, his head bent as if he could no longer watch the tableau taking place before them.

Tanner cleared his throat, aware suddenly of exactly when his hatred had vanished. ''It wasn't all that hard, once I found someone who made a difference in my life, someone who made me realize that I was wasting my time on anger, and dredgin' up old feelings.''

''Who?'' Scat asked, then followed the line of Tanner's gaze to Rosemary and Anna, who were approaching. ''Miss Rosemary? You're talkin' about her?''

''I married her, didn't I?'' Tanner heard the defensive note in his voice and he glanced quickly at the boy. "A man gets married for a lot of different reasons. Sometimes because he likes a woman."

"Well, I like her, too," Scat admitted quietly. "She treats me good, like a ma would, I guess. Almost like she loves me." His glance skated over Tanner and then dropped once more to where his fingers spread wide against his pant legs. "I guess she's made a difference in my life, too, just like she did yours, Tanner."

"Well, how you feel about Rosemary and how I feel...there's a difference in the way we like her." Tanner cleared his throat, wishing he'd avoided this particular subject. "The way I feel about Rosemary..." At that moment he looked up to find her standing just feet away, her eyes intent on him, her lips parted.

"Scat!" Anna stumbled the few feet to where her brother sat and lunged at him. Her arms circled his neck and she pressed damp kisses against his cheek. "We was worried about you, but Miss Rosemary said you was smart and you could run faster than Pa."

"Did she?" His eyes were shiny with tears, but his grin delivered a message of adoration to his little sister as he settled her on his lap. "I knew she was takin' good care of you, Anna." He glanced quickly to where the sheriff was leading the stolen saddle horse with Nate swaying in the saddle from the middle of the clearing. "We'll be all right now, sissy. You and me can take care of ourselves just fine."

Anna sat upright, frowning. "We're not still leaving, are we? I like the way Miss Rosemary brushes my hair, better than how you do it. She irons my dress and everything. You're not gonna take me away from her, are you, Scat?''

His shrug was barely perceptible. "It depends.''

Tanner leaned close. "I don't think Miss Rosemary's about to turn either one of you loose, boy.'' His hand squeezed Scat's shoulder. "Neither am I.

"But for now we need to get on home. Have to figure out a way to get there, though. I'm not real fond of walkin', as it happens. But it looks like that's what we'll be doin', you and me, son. We'll let the women ride the horse.''

From the edge of the woods, Oscar signaled with an uplifted hand, and Tanner rose, heading for the lawman. "I'm takin' Nate to town now,'' Oscar said quietly. "He'll have to see the doctor and then appear before the judge. I doubt it'll go well with him. He'll be lucky if he don't get strung up. I sorta favor stickin' him in a cell for the rest of his life.''

The lawman's sigh was deep. "I sure hate to see those young'uns put through any more hassle than they've already had to put up with. I'll warrant there won't be any problem gettin' them put in your custody.''

"Not if I've got anything to say about it,'' Tanner said quickly. "Scat and Anna are goin' home with Rosemary and me. This should be the end of it for them.''

With an assenting nod, the sheriff mounted his horse and leading the animal Nate had stolen, rode from sight into the trees. Tanner turned back to the three who were watching him from under the tree.

His family. For the first time, he recognized them as such, and his heart seemed to swell.

"Gather up your stuff," he said, striding in their direction. "You got anything inside, Rosemary?"

She tilted her head to look up at him. "Where do you propose we go? Seems to me you couldn't decide what to do with us yesterday, Tanner." Her stubborn little chin was working overtime, he thought, wishing he could plant a kiss just a bit north of that jutting feature.

"Well, I got that problem all solved now. We're headin' home." The words rang with determination, and he felt a flush ridge his cheekbones as he faced her down.

"I don't know about that, Tanner. We came in a package and we're still a bundle, the three of us. Just because you showed up and sorted things out doesn't mean you can just put things to rights so easily."

"Do tell." His murmur was low and his hands itched to grasp her by the middle and hoist her over his shoulder. Were it not for the two children watching, she'd be well on her way inside the small cabin.

The sound of a harness jingling and the rattle of an approaching wagon drew him from his contemplation of the woman who defied him. With a final look of warning, he turned his attention to Mama Pearl, her turbaned head held high. She braced herself firmly on the seat as she drove the team of horses through the brush and into the clearing.

"You folks need a ride?" she asked, grinning widely. "I followed right along, Tanner, but you musta rode them horses to beat the band. No way I could keep up.''

Her gaze skittered around the clearing, pausing on the open door of her house. "Is that man inside?''

Another female ready to do battle, Tanner decided. Must be catching, this woman thing he was having to deal with. "No, Sheriff Rhinehold's takin' him to town, Mama Pearl. Nate Pender's days of causin' trouble are over.''

"We want to go home, Mama Pearl.'' Anna's words were wistful as she left her brother's side to run toward the wagon. Scat was directly behind her, reaching for her.

"Help her up there, Scat,'' Tanner told the boy. "You get aboard, too. Miss Rosemary and I will be along shortly.''

"Yessir,'' Scat said, scrambling into place.

Rosemary cut Tanner a glance of derision and headed for the wagon. "I'll ride with Mama Pearl. You can ride the horse, Mr. Tanner.''

He caught up with her in three long strides, capturing her in his long arms, his hands clasped at her waistline. "Y'all go on ahead now,'' he said firmly to Mama Pearl. The woman nodded agreeably and set the team into motion. It turned in a wide circle and in moments was heading back down the track.

Tanner bent to brush his mouth against Rosemary's cheek. "Now we're gonna talk, honey.'' She held herself rigid and, without relaxing his hold, he turned her in his arms. "Look at me, Rosie.''

"You sure like to take over, don't you, Tanner? Everything has to go your way. First, you let me know that what I have to say doesn't matter. That the children must go to town to be kept safe." She inhaled deeply, her nostrils flaring as she prepared for another attack.

"Now you're taking over again, sending the children back to the ranch and telling me what to do."

"Yeah, I guess you got that right," he said agreeably. "It's what happens when you get married to a man, sweetheart. Especially one who's tryin' to take care of you and keep you out of trouble." He leaned to drop a kiss on her parted lips, and she turned her head from the caress.

He felt strangely bereft at her rebuff. His Rosemary was not acting her usual self, and for the first time, he felt a pang of fear, as he wondered whether his recent ornery behavior had produced fruit not to his liking.

"Maybe I shouldn't have tried sending them to town, Rosemary, but I wasn't sure we could keep someone from gettin' hurt out there at the ranch. Then when I found out you'd set off walkin', you about scared the bejabbers out of me.

"And as it turns out, old Nate came damn close to gettin' his hands on all three of you." Nothing seemed to be coming out of his mouth the way he meant it. Now it sounded as though he were scolding her, and that was the last impression he wanted to make at this point.

"He was half-drunk when he got here," Rosemary said, scoffing at Tanner's fears, even as she attempted to erase the memory of her own. "I could have handled him."

Tanner nodded. "Maybe. Maybe not. But I sure don't think it was worth the risk you took." His hands tightened on her. Forget the niceties. The woman was just begging to be set to rights.

She lifted her chin and met his gaze. "What were you saying to Scat? Is he all right?"

"I talked to him about his pa and about mine, how we both had to put things behind us and go on from here."

"Did he believe you? Will he be satisfied to stay with me?"

"With us, you mean?" He felt a frown furrow his forehead, and he bent closer. She didn't budge. Defiance curled her lip, and he'd swear her teeth were clenched.

"Have you changed your mind? You said you didn't think you could love them enough to be a father to them." Her voice faltered, and her words emerged as broken pieces of sound. "If you can't love them...what if you can't ever love me? I don't think I can stand that any longer, to live with you and know that you don't really love me."

Damn, he'd really messed up. All his huffing and blowing had shattered any trust she'd ever had in his feelings. It was back to the beginning, and he'd never been much of a one when it came to soft talking.

He lifted her, his hands tight around her waist, his fingers gripping with bruising strength. Her face was level with his own when he attempted to sound aloud the words he'd only begun to realize as truth. Words that glued themselves to his tongue and refused to peel loose. Even now, as he spoke, it felt as if cotton were lining his cheeks and the roof of his mouth.

He swallowed and tried again. "Rosemary, I do love you. You don't have to believe it, but it's true anyway." There, it was coming easier now, and he drew in a deep breath, blurting out the rest. "I guess I love those kids, too. Enough to adopt them and give them my name and raise 'em the best way I can. I don't want Scat to grow up without a man to keep him straight."

He watched as slow tears formed in her blue eyes and rolled slowly down her cheeks. "If you're gonna cry every time I tell you I love you, I guess this'll be the last time, Rosie," he muttered, lowering her to the ground, wiping at her cheek with his fingertips.

"Tell me again, Gabriel, please." She turned her face up to his, closing her eyes as if she received a benediction in the sound of his words.

It wasn't nearly as difficult, he found, the second time. "I love you, Rosemary Tanner. I love the way you holler at me, and the way you snuggle with me, and mostly the way you love me back, I guess."

She was more than he could resist. He bent, snatching her up in his arms, and headed for the cabin. The door shut with the pressure of his booted foot and he carried her to the bed in the corner, lowering her to the quilt. A quick trip back to the door, where he lowered the bar in place, assured privacy, and Tanner was halfway out of his shirt by the time he returned to where Rosemary waited.

"What are you doing?" she asked, peering up at him.

"What does it look like?" His pants were undone, and he sat on the edge of the narrow bed to tug his boots from place. His underwear was the last to go, and he'd probably broken all records he decided, as he stepped out of the last of his clothing.

She lay quietly, watching him, and he sat beside her. "I'm gonna take my good old time gettin' you undressed," he murmured. "I hope you're not hungry, honey. It's gonna be a long wait till supper."

"I don't need food, Gabe Tanner. I just need you," she told him quietly. "I need to hear you say those words again, and then I need you to show me."

A bubble of anticipation swelled within him, and he felt a surge of emotion that surpassed happiness by a long shot. She was all his, this small, feisty, loving woman he'd had the good sense to marry. His hands trembled as he loosed her buttons and spread wide the dress she wore. Beneath it a sheer, lace-edged vest covered the most lushly feminine curves he'd ever set eyes on, and he bent to place reverent caresses with his mouth and tongue on the exposed flesh.

She was nicely rounded, and her scent alone brought him to arousal. He nudged the fabric lower. "Will you be cold if I take this off?"

"If I am, I'm sure you'll keep me warm." She reached for him, her arms open, her lips parted, her eyes closing as if she invited his kiss.

It was all he needed, all he would ever want—that soft, alluring lilt in her voice as teasing words enticed him. It was his best dream come true as those generous lips opened to his, and the warmth of her embrace clasped him to her.

It was as it should be, as it would always be if Tanner had his choice.

Epilogue

Nate Pender was sentenced to jail for more years than he could hope to survive. The judge pronounced his decision and then turned to a more appetizing matter, that of adoption proceedings for Scat and Anna. Within minutes, their future was secured, a fact that was affirmed weeks later when the Reverend Mr. Worth performed a naming ceremony on a Sunday morning.

The words he spoke and the sight of Scat and Anna before the altar had the whole congregation in tears before the thing was done. And before many weeks had passed it was obvious to the eyes of the townsfolk that another ceremony, one of infant baptism, would soon be at hand, as Rosemary's lush form revealed the unmistakable lines of pregnancy.

After a meeting of the town council, the Bachelor Tax was taken from the books, after less than a year of existence. Since the schoolhouse was built, and the town had realized sufficient funds to raise the teacher's salary for the next five years, it was deemed unnecessary to continue the tax that had caused such an abundance of complaint among the bachelors in the community.

Spring arrived, bringing a record crop of colts and fillies to the corrals and pastures of the Tanner ranch, and by the time the meadow flowers were blooming, the livestock on the place were supplying new inhabitants for the barns in abundance.

Early in June, another birth proved imminent, as Rosemary was taken to her bed in childbirth. Anna held her hand throughout most of her labor, Mama Pearl presiding, with a new turban to mark the occasion.

Tanner was a constant presence, ever watchful, ever near. And when the waiting was almost over, and Anna was sent to stay with Cotton and her brother, Tanner held the woman he loved in his arms. His voice was what she needed, his arms around her endowing her with strength to bring this babe forth into the world.

He knew he had never loved her more as she strained to deliver his child, and it was with a deep sense of relief, mixed with a full measure of pride, that he heard the words of triumph from the foot of the bed.

"It's a boy, a big strappin' boy, sure 'nough," Mama Pearl announced with glee, her face gleaming with perspiration as she held the child aloft. "Just you look at that young'un," she chortled. "Come take ahold, Tanner, whilst I cut the cord."

With a final touch of his lips to Rosemary's forehead, Tanner placed her against the pillows and stepped quickly to claim his child. His hands were filled with a wiggling, squalling presence that took his breath in wonder. He eyed the babe, red-faced and dark-haired, a replica of himself, if he wasn't mistaken.

"We sure got us a boy, Rosie," he said, the urge to laugh aloud with pure joy impossible to contain. He watched as Mama Pearl cut the cord, then snatched up a square of flannel, wrapping it around the infant. Slate-blue eyes held him in an unfocused gaze, and Tanner was gripped with an emotion that only multiplied his joy, bringing quick tears to his eyes.

"Let me have him." Rosemary held out her arms as Tanner approached. He bent to her, and watched as she gathered the newborn to her breast. Her hair was damp with sweat, her face still pale from the hours of labor, but there was about her a glow such as he'd never seen. A radiance that defied any standards of beauty.

"I want his name to be Adam," she said. Her gaze lifted to his and he nodded. It was a strong name, fit for their child. For this day, all would be as she desired.

And for all time, she would be his. What more could a reformed bachelor ask of life?

* * * * *

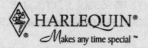

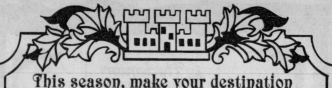